ALL THE RULES AND ROADS WERE GONE.

We were washing slowly away from land, having just undergone a disaster of epic proportions, but our social strata was still in place.

And I was at the bottom with the shellfish.

KATHY PARKS

the LIFEBOAT CLIQUE

KATHERINE TEGEN BOOKS
An Imprint of HarperCollins Publishers

Katherine Tegen Books is an imprint of HarperCollins Publishers.

The Lifeboat Clique

Library of Congress Control Number: 2015943594
ISBN 978-0-06-239398-2

Typography by Carla Weise
18 19 20 21 22   PC/LSCH   10 9 8 7 6 5 4 3 2 1
❖
First paperback edition, 2018

TO MICHAEL,
MY HUSBAND, MY LOVE

the LIFEBOAT CLIQUE

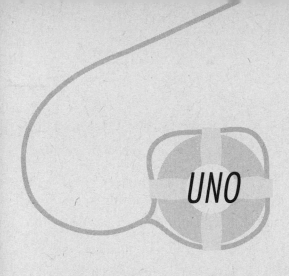

UNO

just before he drowned.

Of course, I suppose that's what happens when you're dying of thirst. It turns you into a drunk. Not a fun drunk but a dying drunk, when all the cravings come to a screeching halt except for that of plain, cool water and the brain shrinks back to the dumbest part, the part that sees horses galloping on the flat ocean and talks about crazy things and generally makes a drunken, dying ass of itself.

The problem with this theory is that Trevor Dunham talked about his Man Part even back in ordinary times, when he was slinking down our school hallway or getting

1

his lunch tray or drumming two pens on the zinc counter of chemistry lab. Apparently, that particular organ was the driving force of his life. The muse that guided his path. The wingman that helped him pick up girls. The dog that caught his Frisbees.

And yet the whole dying-of-thirst thing made him step up the crotch talk considerably. Slumped in the swivel chair in the drifting boat we'd found and thought would save us, he described his Man Part, which he'd nicknamed Ranger Todd, in minute detail. Ranger Todd had a favorite color and a favorite childhood memory. Ranger Todd told jokes. The more Trevor died, the more Ranger Todd came to life. It was hopeless and horrible and annoying.

P.S. Don't drink seawater.

I didn't know Trevor that well at all. He was the drummer in a garage band called Death Stare and had a lean surfer's body, a permanent tan, and a shock of blond hair that he kept long in front so he could flip it this way and that instead of using words. He was one of the popular kids who just ignored me, except for the time he suddenly approached my locker and demanded: "Go on, thump them. Thump my abs." And kept saying it until I did it, thumped his steel abs and thought I heard a clang somewhere.

There were five of us in the boat at that time: Trevor,

myself, and the three girls I would least like to be cooped up with after a catastrophic seismic event. Sienna Martin, soccer captain and winner of the Bitch Most Dedicated to the Craft of Bitchiness title at Avenwood High School, thought she saw an airplane and waved her arms at it. Hayley Amherst joined her, because she went along with everything, and the two of them cawed like insane pelicans at the empty sky and the plane only Sienna could see.

"Stop it. For God's sake, there ain't no helicopter," said Abigail Kenner in her I-lived-in-Texas-three-years drawl. Abigail was the person most responsible for this disaster. Not the big one—the giant wave that hit the West Coast. The smaller disaster that encompassed this gently bobbing boat and our prospects of sharing it as a coffin. She was the one who had the stupid party in a house that sat on a low bluff in Malibu.

It wasn't even her house. And I wasn't invited. But I went, anyway.

We used to be best friends. But then I killed her dream and ruined her life, at least according to Abigail, and she punted our friendship and joined the cool kids and turned everyone in school against me for something that was all her fault.

Perhaps that is why I hated her the most. Because I once loved her like a sister.

She should not, by all rights, have been popular. Straggly red hair, freckles, boyish gait, terrible dresser, affected Texas accent, horrible use of basic grammar—and yet she was. She had defied the odds and won the lottery. She was a constant reminder that it could be done—and I hadn't done it.

Back to Trevor.

We didn't quite know what to do with him or his pal Ranger Todd. We weren't much better off ourselves. We were dying, too. Dying in the worst possible way: together. An ungainly assortment of cool kids and outcast, all in one convenient boat. We were like one of those ice cream flavors that never quite work, like Grapefruit Praline.

Actually, Grapefruit Praline ice cream sounded awesome to me.

Hayley was absolutely freaking out. Crying and begging Trevor not to die. We tried to make Trevor get under the broken awning and at least get out of the sun, but he just sat there, his eyes going dull, drumming on his knees and singing a song about Ranger Todd that went something like this:

Ranger Todd, Ranger Todd
Go, boy
Go, boy

Go, boy
You're so awesome
I love you
Ranger Todd

Right up there with One Direction, I suppose, but it would have to do as a death chant. After an hour or so of this, Ranger Todd suddenly detached and fell out of the boat. At least it did in Trevor's seawater-ravaged mind. He began calling for Ranger Todd in a sad, hopeless voice. Before anyone could stop him, he dove off the boat and started swimming away. He got five or six strokes in before he sank beneath the waves.

Of all of us, he had seemed the most likely to survive. But that was the cruelty of fate, whether you were dying at sea or simply trying to get through high school. Sometimes fate kissed you. Sometimes it snubbed you. Sometimes it passed you a love note, and that note was a lie.

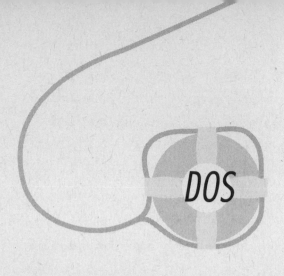

DOS

MY NAME IS DENVER REYNOLDS, ASSASSIN OF DREAMS, Killer of Friendships. Had I stayed in Wisconsin, perhaps I could have been something else. Maybe Denver Reynolds, Openly Tolerated Semiwallflower. Or Denver Reynolds, Girlfriend to Someone Fairly Cute. Or at least Denver Reynolds, Nontraitor.

I moved to LA four years ago, when I was twelve, and I hated it from the start. The myth is that LA can create you, turn you into everything you ever thought you could be. Fill you up with that kind of sparkle that makes for huge houses and adoring crowds. But the truth is, LA can turn on you if you're not on your guard.

The first time I saw a tsunami evacuation sign near Venice Beach, I thought it was a joke, or some kind of advertisement for a product whose logo would later be added to the bottom right.

"That's nothing," Abigail, who was then my best friend, told me when I breathlessly reported what I'd seen.

"Nothing? Stop me if I'm wrong, but that sign mentions the possibility that a giant wave is going to come along and drown everyone."

Abigail let out a gust of air so that her bangs fluttered, her sign that my thoughts were ridiculous and barely worth her time. "There's also the possibility that any second a goat will kick you in the face, or a tornado will suck you up and drop you down in Fresno. Or maybe an asteroid will come out of nowhere and turn you into a dark stain on a crosswalk. Back in Texas, a longhorn would just as soon stomp you as look at you. I don't care about no longhorn, and I don't care about no wave. I'm gonna be a soccer star, stomped or unstomped, wet or dry."

YEARS HAD PASSED since I'd seen that sign, and I had almost forgotten it. Other signs had taken its place. Invisible signs that sometimes rose up when I was taking a shower or walking to class. In the darkness of my bedroom, when I was trying to sleep, the signs were in helpful neon.

YOU HAD ONE FRIEND, AND SHE TURNED ON YOU.
SUCKS TO BE YOU.

LA COULD GIVE A SHIT ABOUT YOU.
SO COULD THE ELEVENTH GRADE.

YOUR STUDENT COUNCIL DOES NOT CARE
WHETHER YOU GET BETTER CAFETERIA FOOD
OR WHETHER YOU LIVE OR DIE. THEY ARE
POWER-CRAZED DITZES AND WOULD-BE ALPHA
DOUCHES AND YOU ARE ONLY WORTH YOUR
VOTE WHICH ACTUALLY MEANS NOTHING
SINCE THE ELECTION IS RIGGED.

If you noticed, the signs were getting longer and losing their punctuation. But there was no sign that said LOOK OUT FOR THE EARTHQUAKE AND THE RESULTING TSUNAMI. And I really could have used one.

The morning of the great wave started like it always did, just me trying to sleepwalk through high school. Because that is what you do. You sleepwalk. You have a role and a place and a mark on your head that designates

8

your rank. You are certain, when you walk through those doors, who will talk to you and who will not. You know if the jocks will be mean to you, if your voice will be heard in class by anyone but the teacher. You know if you are the hunter or the prey. You know if people think you're smart or funny or pretty or geeky or annoying or cool or—worst of all—if they don't think anything about you. Everyone is neatly separated, like a stamp collection.

And I was a commemorative 3-cent noncollectible with a moon scene. It would take over fifteen of us to even mail a letter.

And if I sound bitter, that's because I was. A bitter little stamp left off the envelope of life. But no matter what, I was determined to survive high school. I, Denver Reynolds, would survive.

AT LUNCHTIME, IN the cafeteria, I received my first surprise of the day. I got The Look. An unmistakable moment that led to an unmistakable night and insured that I was in the absolute wrong place at the wrong time.

I'd given up on high school. Given up on anyone trying to understand me or like me or see my value. Having lost Abigail in such a sudden and spectacular way, I had given up on trying to make new friends. I was a bird in a cage, waiting for graduation day: that window that would open as I turned my sad beak to the possibilities of the sky.

But at that moment, The Look gave me hope.

Our high school lunchroom was set out in an orderly grid. If you Google-Earthed it and zoomed in from above using the satellite setting, you would find that the students were carefully designated by tables. The geek table, the loser table, the student council table, the deeply committed Christian table, the drama table, the jock table, the rising young felon table (from which oily-looking, detention-bound shoplifters and fire starters glared balefully), and several uncategorized tables, where I sat with various other students who didn't really fit into a group and who ate their lunch fast. There were, in addition, half a dozen tables of ascending social importance that led to that hallowed table in the center of the cafeteria where the most popular kids sat.

It had room for sixteen, and those sixteen had the shiniest teeth, the best hair, the fastest cars, and the sleekest abs in the eleventh grade. The table almost glowed with promise. We, the non-sixteen, couldn't help staring at it. And there, right in the middle of that shining table, was my old ex-best friend, Abigail Kenner. She sat among them, ruling them, passing notes down the table, planning her stupid parties, and laughing her braying laugh that swept over the room, reminding the rest of us that she was in and we were out.

I had never heard that laugh before in our years of best-friendship. It was something she put on for her junior year, along with her penchant for illegal party planning. This was not the Abigail I knew and loved like a sister, but an entirely different person. Her kinky red hair was smoothed down, and she apparently used some kind of chalky camouflage makeup to hide her freckles.

I missed that kinky red hair. I missed those freckles.

Back in middle school, she had once shown me in a notebook her ten-step plan for gaining social acceptance with that upper strata, which at the time she claimed was just an exercise, as she didn't care about those kind of kids, what with her future soccer fame and all. I remember glancing over it, but I only remember one of the steps:

4. Treat them with contempt.

One day last fall a skinny, quiet kid whose name I never caught and who sat at the loser table must have gone crazy, because he got his tray and, instead of heading over to his table, made a beeline straight for the popular table, which was filling up with cool people. He sat down with them and then just froze.

I don't know what the poor kid was thinking. He must have missed the science class where the cause-effect relationship was explained—too much sunlight and the avocado plant wilts! Too many electrolytes and the cell buys the farm!—and he thought that sitting at the table would lead to his acceptance instead of the other way around. Or maybe he was protesting this whole unfair structure where you had to sit according to popularity. Maybe he was the modern version of the Buddhist monk pouring gasoline over his own head and setting himself on fire.

But I think the Buddhist monk suffered less.

At first, the other kids at the table just reacted in shock and confusion. Like a wolf pack that Bambi has stumbled into and asked, "Hey, anyone seen my mother?" They tried to ignore him, but as the table filled up and left one angry popular person circling without a seat, some of the kids at the table started glaring at him and mumbling things.

It was a train wreck. And the kid whose name I can't remember was the one perched frozen on the tracks.

But none of us knew how to stop it. We just stared as the whole sad drama played out. The kid was just sitting there. I'm not sure whether he was making a last stand or was just unable to move. His hands gripped his tray. He stared straight ahead, saying nothing. The clock ticked, and the horrible chicken on our plates began to congeal.

No one knew what to say or do, although I suspect most of the people felt what I did: the helplessness of the onlooker. I fought the urge to get up and pull him back to where he belonged so we could all pretend this never happened.

But I didn't move. Nor did anyone else.

Finally the popular kids stood up and went over to the drama kids' table and kicked them out of their seats and took over their table, leaving the poor unnamed kid sitting at the popular table all alone—except, that is, for Audrey Curtis, the saint.

She really belonged at the Christian table, but her great beauty, grace, and fantastical cheerleading abilities let her crossbreed with the populars. On this day, she chose not to follow the other kids but instead slid her tray down next to the frozen kid and sat beside him.

Perhaps it was her kind gesture that broke him, or perhaps the fact that everyone knew Audrey was a saint, and he suddenly felt like a leper now that Mother Teresa was in such close proximity, delicately peeling the skin off her baked chicken, because suddenly he jumped up and fled the cafeteria and never came back.

We heard he was transferred to another school. Staring at that golden table, which was shimmering like some mirage in the desert, it was easy to empathize with the poor skinny kid, name forgotten, maddened by the thought that he could be one of those chosen few.

Audrey was later killed by a baby grand piano, but I digress.

Where was I? Oh yes, the moment my life changed. The moment when I began to believe that something better lurked within these repressive walls.

Mistake.

Just a little trick played by Fate, so Fate could laugh with his asshole friends and go get a hooker for the night. Yes, that's right. Fate went and got a hooker because Fate plays by no man's rules.

Fate sent me Croix Monroe.

Of course Croix was a football star. He also sang in the choir. And he acted in plays. But he was neither a jock nor a choir guy nor a drama kid. He was his own man, handsome in a new, strange way that broke the handsome mold, with one green eye and one blue one and a habit of wearing vintage shirts and Indian bracelets. Once he wore a feather in his hair for a week for no reason at all. But he could get away with it. He was Croix.

Croix was nice to me. He said hi. Like the new Pope, he made divinity accessible. Last year I was in algebra class with him, and he was the one x and y added up to. Everyone knew it. Even the teacher. Once he asked me about homework . . . what pages were assigned again? I think that was the relevant question. And I repeated the page numbers and he listened, he really listened and smiled his dazzling smile. I know it's not much, but it was enough to deepen my infatuation.

This year, my junior year, we had Spanish class together. And those wily verbs and nouns that changed for no reason and pissed me off and made me swear to never go to Acapulco and ride one of their cheap barge cruises and drink their cheap tequila and throw up into their salty waters were suddenly golden in his mouth. He spoke like a native. A godlike native. And every girl in class, all of them—the geeks and the snobby bitches and the crop-top skanks and the quiet, shy girls—imagined him naked in the sand, washed up on the beach and asking for lemonade in a language we vaguely understood but suddenly loved.

Ah, the trills of his *rrrrrrr*'s.

I could stroke them.

Croix sat at the end of the cool-person table in the caf-eteria. On that fateful day, as I was navigating my way to the various uncollected bits of humanity table, balancing a tray on which sat the horrors dreamed up by the cafeteria cooks, Croix turned around and smiled at me.

It wasn't a polite smile. It was THAT smile, the one a lonely girl waits for.

I froze.

The sell-by date of the chicken on my plate retreated

farther into the rearview mirror as the seconds passed. It couldn't be true. He was Croix and I was me. I looked behind me, back at Croix. He was still smiling. I went to my table, set down my tray, and didn't eat. My face was flushed red. My heart beating fast.

And somewhere out off the shores of LA, down deep where the crabs skitter, deeper still to where the plates rumble and move, something shifted. Something started the mechanism that would later erupt into the undersea earthquake and cause the great wave that wiped out some of these very princes and pawns.

But right then, of course, I didn't know it. In the blink of an eye, my goal in life had flip-flopped. No longer did I want to just survive high school. Maybe I could actually make something of these miserable circumstances. Be invited to all the cool parties. Be respected, noticed. Bounce off Croix's perfect ass into a stratosphere where I could never have hoped to go before.

I know, I know. All from a look.

But things got better. Way way better. Or way way worse. To put it algebraically: way (squared) worse.

TRES

Spanish class.

For everyone but me, a minor California earthquake was like a shot of dopamine. It was like seeing a celebrity on the street or eating a handful of M&Ms at once or noticing that ten people just liked your Instagram selfie. It was a mild, welcome respite from a day that, since California has no seasons, would pretty much be like any other day.

But I was from solid, unmoving Wisconsin, and I was terrified of earthquakes, and four years of LA had not dispelled my fears one bit. When I first felt the tremor, I was staring at the back of Croix's head, desperate to find out if his meaningful look in the cafeteria had been some kind of cruel accident, that he had been staring into the middle distance and I was some kind of fixed point to orient him and he was smiling, actually, at a daydream or a girl whose breasts were bigger than the first two letters of a love note in Braille.

Our Spanish teacher, Mrs. Paltos, was mentioning that *la mano* was a combination of a feminine determiner with a masculine subject and wasn't that special? Then the floor beneath our feet started to rumble. A shudder ran through our desks, and the big window that looked out on palm trees and jacaranda rattled, and the lights swung ever so slightly. The class went *Ohhhhh*. Mrs. Paltos stopped the motion of her marker against the Smart Board and waited for Earth's outer crust to stop hogging the spotlight.

But I was speechless with terror, my hands gripping the sides of my desk, my heart pumping madly.

"Earthquake!" I managed to sputter, before springing to life and ducking underneath my desk, where all I saw were skinny-jean legs and overpriced shoes.

I heard laughter. The trembling had stopped, but the laughter went on. I was no longer invisible. I was the class joke. But I didn't care. My hands were still wrapped tightly around the chair legs. The earth had betrayed me, and I wasn't taking any chances.

Mrs. Paltos came over to me. I could tell it was her because the shoes were old-fashioned, the dress was too long, and the legs had veins that don't spread that far till way after college. She crouched down.

"*¿Que pasó?*" she demanded, leaning hard on the accent to reaffirm that she was indeed the Spanish teacher.

"Earthquake," I explained, because she was obviously some kind of idiot who needed things spelled out.

She shook her head, and I realized I had just violated her "no speaking English in Spanish class" rule.

"*¡Español solamente!*"

"*Earthquako,*" I said.

She scowled. "*¡Levántate!*"

But my body was not in the mood to *levántate* or, for that matter, do jack shit. It was in the mood to stay, crouched and trembling, right where it was.

"*¡Levántate!*"

The class had stopped laughing at me and was listening intently. Something intriguing was going on—direct defiance to a teacher. Suddenly, though, she moved, and Croix—yes, Croix—took her place. He wore jeans and a Billabong shirt and looked even more stunning now that he was close. His hair was cut to a perfect length. His strange eyes sparkled, and his cologne made my soul want to grow nostrils.

"Hey," he said. "It's all good. Just a little tremor."

I was so shocked, I let go of the chair legs.

"Right," he said, nodding. "Nothing to be worried about. Though I don't blame you. Best to be prepared for the worst."

I found myself crawling out from under the desk and taking my seat again, my heart still beating fast but totally ditching earthquake for sun god as inspiration for that rhythm. Croix gave me a thumbs-up and went back to his own seat, and that was that. The drama was over. The teacher made us go back to Spanish, which is what every survival handbook will tell you to do after an earthquake.

Abigail turned her head, looked at me briefly, and went back to her notes.

That's right. Abigail was also in my Spanish class. You're probably wondering if she ever acknowledged me, being my ex-best friend and all. Yes, she did. Sometimes she glanced at me and looked away. Not exactly Ariel and Flounder, but whatever. She was the one who had all the parties to which people like me weren't invited. Of course, she didn't use her own house. Her specialty was breaking into other people's houses to have the parties. People away for the weekend, or a house that was still sitting on the market after months of some Realtor trying to sell it for two million dollars over value.

She'd leave the trashed property for someone else to deal with. The police never showed up. She was never caught. Some said her father was friends with someone high up in the DA's office who would divert the LAPD. That was the rumor, at least. LA was the place where your connections got you everything: your script funded, your jury duty excused, or someone else's house to ruin in the name of a good time.

And evidently the minor earthquake had inspired her to throw another party, because she straightened up, turned, and whispered something to limber stick-bitch Sienna Martin. Sienna said something a bit louder that jumped the heads of two nobodies and landed safely in the ear of Madison Cutler, budding alcoholic, probable bulimic, definite boob-jobber, and total cool kid. She smiled a smile that welcomed chilled Jell-O shots and passed on whatever party message she'd received to the next cool person, who leaned back and whispered it to Croix. He nodded politely, still taking notes.

How did I know that a party was brewing when the words never reached my ears? I just knew. It is a skill common to people who are never actually invited to parties, and it brings on a kind of secondary reaction, spontaneous pain in the heart and a spasm of gut that was made of jealousy and longing and what the cliff divers of Acapulco would call *tristeza* when they missed and hit the rocks.

And why did I want to be invited to a party full of people I thought were assholes celebrating a seemingly C-list seismic event in LA? I don't know. It was some kind of hardwiring in the brain somewhere. That human desire to belong. But what could I do besides raise my hand and, when the teacher picked me, call out to Abigail instead: *"Hey, need any outcasts at this wonderful affair? You could set your drinks on my head."*

But of course I did not. I didn't want to give Abigail the pleasure of knowing I wanted to be included. I couldn't help wondering if she gave these parties just to punish me. As if I hadn't been punished enough.

After the bell rang, I happened to enter the bottleneck at the doorway with none other than Croix again.

He smiled at me and said, "Doing okay?"

My face flushed. "Oh, you mean that little earthquake? Barely felt it."

"Ah, no worries. You're probably smarter than the rest of us."

"At least it broke up the monotony of class. And I'll treasure the memory of Mrs. Paltos trying to get me to say *earthquake* in Spanish. She's so determined to weave conversational Spanish into the fabric of our lives."

Out of the corner of my eye I could see other kids

22

glancing at us. Wondering what was up with this rarely sighted loser/golden boy coupling.

"Some of these phrases, though," he said. "Are we ever really going to use them? I mean, *Mi amiga esta en la playa.* When would I ever say that?"

Talking to Croix was surprisingly easy. We were doing this. We were having a conversation, and it wasn't awkward, and I hadn't vomited or screamed, "I AM TALKING TO CROIX MONROE, AND IF A BLACK MAMBA SHOULD FALL OUT OF THE CEILING AND BITE ME ON THE NECK, I WOULD REFUSE ALL ANTI-VENOM SO I COULD DIE HAPPY!"

"My theory is that we should learn everything possible on the chance that at any given moment, something's going to matter," I said. "We just don't know what that is. And yes, one day you might have to inform a nonnative speaker that your friend is on the beach. Or if that nonnative speaker is a member of the Mexican paparazzi, you could say, '*La Kardashian esta en la playa.*'"

He laughed. "You're Denver, right?" he asked.

He knew my name. GOD SPEED, BLACK MAMBA FANGS ON THE WAY TO MY JUGULAR.

"Yes."

"I'm Croix."

"I know."

"So, are you coming to the party tonight, Denver?"

And that's what made him special. That complete and awesome, genuine or beautifully acted belief that an inconsequential girl like myself would be invited to one of Abigail's illegal parties.

"Sure," I heard myself answering. So casually, as if it were true.

"Great. So am I. Got to celebrate the earthquake, right?"

"Exactly."

Something of a more plate-buckling nature was happening inside me. For I was deciding that I, charter member of the invisible club, was going to go to that party to which I was not invited. And at that party, I was going to talk to and continue my impossible flirtation with Croix Monroe.

I walked around the rest of that day with an earthquake named Croix roiling inside me, wondering what I would wear and how I'd get out of the house and what lie I would have to tell my mother? I had gotten in big trouble my sophomore year, and she still didn't quite trust me, even though—again—not my fault. I didn't know if the cool kids had to lie to their parents or if their parents let them do stupid and illegal things because their parents were awesome or uncaring or high. Anyway, I was stuck with my visibly nonawesome, caring, unstoned mother, who was also pretty smart.

My only alternative was to sneak out. Easier said than done, because my mother was a night owl. I decided I would exit the house out my second-story window and then drop into the bushes below. I explained my plan to my cat, Sonny Boy, who I could tell anything to because he didn't give a rat's ass. I could escape successfully and go to the most important party in my life. Or I could die. It was all the same to him.

I had this thing I did where I talked to Sonny Boy and then answered myself in a high-pitched voice that was supposed to be Sonny Boy talking back. Try this someday when you find yourself friendless.

Me: Sonny Boy, guess what?

SB (high voice): *I don't care.*

Me: I'm sneaking out tonight.

SB (high voice): *I think I have a crust of cat litter stuck to my butt. Could you check?*

Me: I've been invited to a party by this dreamy guy named Croix, and this could change everything.

Sonny Boy stared at me with his golden eyes and then licked his paw pads and smoothed down the sleek fur on his small, uncaring head.

Our talk was over.

I waited until ten o'clock and then went downstairs, where my mother was reading a book from self-help guru

Robert Pathway while someone on TV interviewed a Cal Tech scientist about the earthquake we'd had that afternoon. The scientist was pointing to a digital chart and didn't seem alarmed. No one was, because the killer version of the quake hadn't struck yet, and the scientists and everyone else were just alarmed by everyday things like, would not finishing your antibiotics kill you or is the world running out of helium or is your teenage daughter about to sneak out to an illegal party in the name of some desperate, delusional love?

My mother was kind of an earthy type or maybe just the type who struggles with details. She had longish brown hair that never looked quite combed. Her eyebrows were always grown in because she'd forget to pluck them until the job got too big and then she'd just say the hell with it. And her clothes had apparently never read a color chart together. I thought her look was refreshing in this town full of phonies. I suppose my father once did too.

"Hey, Mom," I said. I bent to give her a hug, and she hugged me back with one arm.

"How are you?"

"Good."

"You'll be even better tomorrow." She'd been reading Robert Pathway ever since the divorce and forbade any negative talk in the house. Which was fine, because that kept my conversation to a minimum.

"Okay, Mom, if you say so."

"You feel that earthquake?"

"Yes. I hid beneath my desk, and everyone laughed at me."

"Maybe you were the smart one."

"I felt like a genius."

"You know," she said, "there may have been a gift in that earthquake. Always look for gifts, even in things that seem . . ."

Her voice trailed off. The look in her eyes said she wanted to pull a blanket over her head and wait for a better feeling. She hadn't had too many gifts in a while, and we both knew it. And I wanted to comfort her somehow in that curious way daughters are sometimes called on to comfort their mothers. I wanted to stroke her arm or rub her shoulders or give her that awkward hug you give when one person is standing and the other sitting. But that would take away the lie that was keeping her going: that circumstances didn't matter, they could be banished by the right thoughts or the right words, and she was getting better every day.

So I settled with a "Well, I'm off to bed now" and a kiss on her cheek.

I went upstairs and found my very best outfit. I put on my makeup carefully, screwing up the eyeliner and having to start over, all the while not talking to myself, because if I did, I'd be trying to talk myself out of this crazy plan, and I already knew I was going through with it. I felt bad about sneaking around on my mother, but not bad enough to just go to bed and wake up to the same dismal life.

Sonny Boy watched me impassively. If Sonny Boy were a human, he would be at the cool table in our cafeteria, because he was beautiful and confident and a douche bag. He would have snubbed me in the halls, perhaps making some cruel joke at my expense, and broken the hearts of cheerleaders who couldn't see beneath his sleek, purring facade.

Me: What are you looking at, Sonny Boy?

SB (high voice): *A dipshit who has never seen a YouTube makeup tutorial.*

Me: I think I'm getting really nervous because I'm abusing myself while pretending to talk in your voice.

SB (high voice): *Then can I paw at the butterflies in your stomach?*

Finally I was finished. I gazed into the mirror. I looked good. As good as I was going to look. My brown hair, although not a particular flashy color, was looking extra-shiny tonight. I had what were considered delicate features,

with a nice jawline and eyebrows that never needed plucking because they were born behaving themselves. And my
nose was a perfect size and shape—at least, it had been,
until Abigail punched me in the face. Now I imagined one
nostril was slightly deformed. Probably all in my head—
just part of the trauma of the memory.

And what made me think I could show up at the party
of my greatest enemy and she wouldn't throw me out?
I had no idea. And yet I took the chance. I opened the
window and slid out and fell into some bushes, and I was
free. It took a few minutes to extricate myself and pull the
leaves from my hair and check to make sure the branches
hadn't ripped my shirt. Sonny Boy gazed down from the
window at me, his eyes glowing bright in the moonlight.
Had he the power to lug his litter box to the window
and dump its contents on my freshly blow-dried head, he
would have. That is the kind of cat he was.

I crept over to the garage, opened the door as quietly as
I could, and started up my mother's Subaru. She had given
me a spare set of keys so I could drive myself to work.

I think we've already established that I was a terrible
person.

I took Santa Monica Boulevard west to the Pacific
Coast Highway. The window in the back of my mother's
Subaru had some kind of electrical short in it, and she was

going to fix it but used the money for a Robert Pathway seminar instead; and now the wind whistled through that space and made a moaning, disappointed sound as I drove sneakily up the coast toward Malibu.

I let down my window so I could feel the ocean breeze. The water itself was flat and calm. I passed Sunset and Topanga and many Realtor offices and seafood restaurants and surf shops before I finally entered Malibu, which was lined on the ocean side by narrow wooden houses right next to one another, where people could walk out in back and stroll down the twenty-two inches of viable sand between high and low tides.

The night was particularly clear, and the stars were bright overhead. The moon at three-quarters. I had overheard the address of the party house by lurking around the popular girls in the locker room before gym class and then used the internet to track down the location. According to Zillow, the Abigail-blessed party house had lingered empty on the market for the past eleven months at 2.4 million dollars—enough to buy a mile of bait shops in South Carolina but not enough to make a splash in California real estate.

I was a bit of a real estate freak. Not just because my mother worked in a Realtor's office but because lonely people need a hobby, and that's what I picked, along with my other two hobbies: watching the Discovery Channel and grooving alone to Just Dance 4 on Wii, my movements imitating that of a giraffe floundering in a vat of gelatin.

Zillow had displayed interiors of the house. The owner had staged it with tacky furnishings and even a baby grand piano. It was the perfect house for a group of entitled teenagers to destroy. I felt sorry for the owner, but not sorry enough to turn around.

When I was almost to Cross Creek I took a right and drove up a short road, and there it was, on a small bluff overlooking the Pacific Coast Highway and the ocean itself. Cars were parked tight all along the road, so I had to walk a bit.

I was wearing a pair of skinny jeans, a long-sleeved shirt, a light sweater, Converse sneakers, and an eternity scarf, and thought I looked reasonably attractive. I saw windows lit and heard the faint sounds of music. Something quirky and contemporary and subdued. Abigail was no dummy. Loud music made neighbors mad. And mad neighbors called police. And police were even less welcome at parties than me.

I stopped and straightened my shirt. Stopped again and smoothed my hair. Stopped again and just stopped. My armpits were sweating. What if a special black light had been installed in the doorway to pick up the telltale armpit sweat of the uninvited loser? And what if some loud buzzer went off, and everyone froze and stared at me just before a wild purse-dog hired just for the occasion buried its tiny fangs in my ankles as a subtle hint for me to go?

My feet wouldn't move. There was nothing wrong with a change of heart, right? I could just turn around right now and backtrack all the way up to my window and crawl into my bedroom, and no one would be the wiser.

But I would be the same, and I'd had a brief, wild hope of being different. And that hope, like an insane Pomeranian, had buried its teeth in my soul and wouldn't let go.

I took a deep breath and walked up to the house.

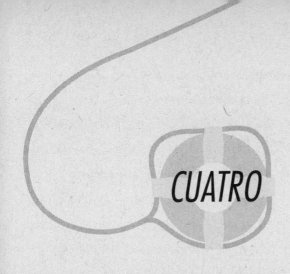

CUATRO

THE DOOR WAS UNLOCKED. I PUSHED IT OPEN AND FOUND that the poor bastard who owned the house must have had good insulation, because the music was turned up loud. Kids were drinking and talking and making out all around me.

The house was huge. The bad artwork looked expensive, and the floors were marble.

I wandered into the living room, then the kitchen, with its clean, steel lines and center island and perfectly stained cabinets. More kids were in there, some already drunk, all of them in clusters.

Croix was nowhere in sight.

Sienna Martin was lounging by the refrigerator, her hair swept back in a ponytail. She wore a long shirt, a pair of black leggings, and short boots. She had added clunky power bracelets and a bubble necklace. Her eyelids were in crazy peacock hues. She was smoking an e-cigarette.

She took a long drag and then expelled the nicotine vapor. "What are you doing here?"

"Same as you. Crashing a house whose owner suffers from the delusion that it should sell at twice its value."

The tip of her e-cigarette glowed blue. "You're always saying things like that."

"Things like what?"

"Big things you have to think about to understand. Why don't you just talk normal?" She looked over at her sidekick, high-strung simpleton Hayley Amherst, who drove a Mercedes. "Hey," she said to Hayley. "Look who's here." She had that tone of voice that meant "Look who's here who's not invited."

Hayley was dressed like a cover model from *Teen Vogue Idiot*. She slithered over and looked me up and down.

"Why would you want to be here?" she asked. "I mean, who do you think is going to talk to you? Why should anyone talk to you when no one here is your friend? I'm not being a bitch or anything. I'm just telling the truth and honestly I'd really like to know, because everywhere I go

I'm invited, so I've never been someone like you, I'm just saying."

Hayley liked to talk in a spray of words that always reminded me of the aggressive mist of Finesse Extra Hold aerosol that Abigail once used in a desperate attempt to keep her springy hair in place.

"What was the question again?" I asked.

Sienna was there to helpfully translate word-spray into bitch-stick. "What would make you come to a party where you aren't invited?"

I didn't like the way this was going. "I was actually paid to do a strip show here. Where's my pole?"

Hayley nodded as if that made sense. Sienna just stared at me and blew some secondhand vapor my way.

"Why would you want to hang around with us? Don't you have any friends?" Sienna asked.

"I have a ton of friends, especially if you count friendly carbs and friendly bacteria."

Sienna kept up the blank-bitch stare while Hayley cocked her head slightly.

I moved over to the refrigerator, grabbed a beer, and tried to open it, but it wasn't a twist top. So I just stood there trying to pry off the cap with my thumb. They were still looking at me like I needed to further explain myself, or beg for their mercy, or ask for a razor blade so I could start cutting myself, but I couldn't think of anything else to say. I thought it was somewhat funny, in a sad way, that I actually was at a party and actually talking to people but that the subject of our conversation was how crazy I was to think I belonged there. Sonny Boy would have said in his high voice: *"Well, now you've done it, dipshit."*

I felt a presence in the room and looked over. There was dear Abigail, head intruder herself, wearing jeans, a T-shirt under a rumpled sweater, and a pair of cowboy boots, because her reinvention of herself had never quite reached her clothes. Her hair was sprayed down hard, the camouflage was chalky over her freckles, and she had evidently been plucking her eyebrows and penciling them in too heavy, giving her a slightly deranged look.

She looked me up and down. "Well, well, well," she said in her fake Texas accent. It came out sounding like *Way-ull, Way-ull, Way-ull.* "Have we got a trespasser here?"

A knot of anxiety was growing inside me. The last thing I wanted was a confrontation with my former best friend.

"All of us are trespassers," I said.

"Oooh," said Abigail. "Good one. Knee slapper."

I was starting to feel like it was a very, very bad idea to come to this party.

"Where's your video camera?" Abigail asked. Some

people have inside jokes. We had an inside worst-memory-in-the-world.

"Decided not to bring it," I said.

"You know what happened last time!" Hayley piped up.

Abigail gave her a withering look, and she made a squeaking sound and took a gulp of her beer.

"Is she allowed to be here?" Sienna asked. "Shouldn't you throw her out?"

And that's what made Sienna such a bitch. She wasn't content to be unfriendly. She just had to take it to the next level. And what was it to Sienna that I was there? No one was supposed to be there.

I almost said that Croix had invited me. Then I decided I wasn't going to give them the pleasure. Ironically enough, this would be the second time Abigail threw me out of a party. And if I was made to leave before I got to see Croix, if this dream died right here, then I was going to pull Sienna's ponytail really hard before I left. Give it a kamikaze yank and watch her eyes bulge out. I could almost feel her salon-slickened ponytail grasped in my palm like a pelted salamander.

Do it, I thought, now glaring at Abigail. *Go ahead, Texas witch.*

Abigail shrugged. "Whatever," she said. "I just think

it's kinda sad that you want to come to a party where no one wants you around."

I wanted to respond, "I think it's kind of sad you think that fake Texas accent is cool," but I said nothing. Tried to feel nothing, but that was impossible.

And that was it. Sienna and Hayley shrugged too because they were obedient robots. They lost interest in me and went back to talking. Abigail turned her back to me, and there I was. At the party but not of the party. Allowed to stay but completely unwelcome.

"This is the best party ever," Sonny Boy said sarcastically in my ear. *"Well done, loser."*

I left the kitchen and wandered through the living room, which was furnished tastelessly—lots of fake gold inlay and faux French art. The beer bottles strewn everywhere and people making out on the couch could only have added to such tacky decor. I decided that since Croix wasn't here and no one else seemed interested in talking to me, I'd give myself a lonely little tour of the house, maybe read some books from the bookshelf, and stare out the window and pretend I was a friendless, invisible old lady just waiting to kick the bucket, like I would be in about sixty years.

I wandered down the dark hallway. The walls were

lined with paintings of people from another century. They looked rich and pissed off, like they had somehow anticipated this night while sitting for their portraits. The hallway still had a new-house smell, and I wondered if anyone had ever lived here.

I found a bathroom and went inside. It had two vanity sinks and was bigger than my entire bedroom. A cocker spaniel could have done laps in the Jacuzzi tub. The track lighting and fixtures were tasteful, and the marble floor had subtle flecks of silver. It was surprising to find such a stylish bathroom in such a tacky house, but the trusty purple shag bath mat was there as a reminder that the exception proved the rule.

I sat down cross-legged on the bath mat and closed my eyes. This wasn't so bad. You don't necessarily have to be with other people to have fun at a party. The bathroom had a pleasant, just-cleaned smell even after all these months. It was sad, in a way. This house, for all its splendor, had a lonely, hopeful vibe to it. Just wanting to be wanted.

I was meditating on this when someone pounded on the door. The doorknob turned and then jiggled.

"Hey!" a muffled voice called. "Let us in! Emergency!"

I jumped up and unlocked the door. It burst open, and in came Sienna, supporting a very wasted Madison Cutler, whom I hadn't seen yet, possibly because she was off somewhere getting drunk enough to look like she did now, which was a hot mess.

"Get out of the way!" Sienna ordered, and I stood aside but didn't leave, because I had nothing else to do while I waited for Croix to appear, and watching a drunk bitch taking care of a drunker bitch was better than the mother-gorilla-and-her-young videos on the Discovery Channel.

"Hey!" Madison mumbled, smiling at me, and I realized she had reached the point of drunkenness where snob functions begin to shut down. Possibly twice the legal limit, I estimated. "How's it going, Phoenix?"

"Denver," I said.

Madison's eyes went big and her hand flew to her mouth, and Sienna hustled her over to the toilet, where Madison collapsed and began heaving her guts out as her friend held back her hair.

"Nice," I said before I could stop myself.

Sienna's head snapped back. "What do you mean, nice? She's very sick."

"I think you mean, drunk."

"At least she was invited to this party. At least she wasn't pathetic enough to come uninvited."

"Yes, her dignity is an inspiration to us all."

Madison heaved again, and Sienna shouted, "Get out

of here!" Her eyes were on fire, and her teeth were bared, so I supposed our conversation was over and it was time to move on. Just before I shut the door behind me, Madison's hand came up and grabbed Sienna's ponytail, perhaps mistaking it for the toilet handle, and yanked it down hard, and I was given the pleasure of seeing Sienna's wild-eyed silent scream.

I decided that moment was worth the whole party and wondered if I should just leave. It hadn't been a terrible party, by pariah standards, and maybe I should quit while I was ahead. But something stubborn in me—something that refused to believe this was a fluke or a trap—made me decide to stay a while longer.

Once when I was very young, my family took a trip to Portland. When it was time to go home, we took off from the Portland airport, the sky cloudy overhead. The plane rose up through the clouds, and suddenly I could see the blue sky and the yellow sun above us, and the clouds were now a blanket below the plane. There was a whole new world up there. And I guess that's what I think of all stories. We believe we know the limits of them and then we find out there's another story lying right on top of them. In my mind, which was stupid, I thought there was another, brighter story going on at this very moment, and I just hadn't broken through yet. So, instead of heading to the door, I went into one of the bedrooms.

Big mistake. Some naked monster made of two horn-dogs was humping itself on a four-poster bed.

The boy part of the monster rose up, his eyes wild.

"Get out of here!" he shouted.

"With pleasure!" I screamed, and beat a hasty retreat.

I decided that each bedroom probably contained a similar scene, because the first thing that high school kids have to do at a party is soil a stranger's bed. It's a beautiful ritual, like a Japanese tea ceremony.

I decided to see what was upstairs. Maybe blue sky and a yellow sun.

The second floor was one big den and wet bar bordered by giant windows that looked down on the ocean, and was even more hideously furnished than the downstairs. Trevor Dunlap was drumming on the bar with a pair of empty beer bottles, gently enough not to break the bottles, hard enough to make the most obnoxious sound in the world. I knew he played drums in a band, but apparently he was going solo tonight. He wasn't talking to anyone, just gazing out straight ahead, nodding to the beat of his hellish racket.

A giant, never-ending sofa with leopard print and cabriole legs wound around the room, playing host to various people drinking and laughing. A group of guys surrounded a pool table whose felt covering was the color of those molten lakes you see in fantasy movies. A suit of armor stood by the bar as though it were waiting to check IDs. An ugly zebra rug covered the floor. A baby grand piano sat near a narrow set of stairs that led to the rooftop. The winding staircase, I had to admit, looked cool. It rose in a very tight spiral to the ceiling, where a small door had been placed. I thought about going up to the roof and looking at the stars or down at the sea, but I was afraid of interrupting some act of frantic humping, and I couldn't take that sight again. Still clutching my unopened beer, I took a seat on one of the sofas.

There I sat, holding my warming beer. All around me the party progressed, with people getting louder and rowdier, and guys shoving and roughhousing each other and screaming playful bro-insults. At some point, I heard the beer bottle drumsticks stop clinking and looked back to see Trevor smoking something that was not an e-cigarette, his hair hanging down in his face.

I was not even important enough to be challenged again. No doubt Sienna was giving clumsy, unnecessary CPR to her passed-out best friend in the first-floor bathroom, and Hayley was talking and talking, and Abigail was surveying her kingdom or breaking a window or whatever she did for fun these days.

Croix was still nowhere in sight.

I decided I was going to sit there with my beer and my invisible cat and outlast all of them. From what I heard, the coolest kids always stay to the end of the party because they don't care the most, and their parents are the most high on something and therefore the most permissive. I was going to be one of those kids tonight, clinging on to the good times around me like a barnacle.

I had just formulated this plan when something awful happened. Something that I did not realize was awful right away.

Audrey Curtis suddenly appeared in a blue dress and silver flats, with a purse that somehow matched both in a way that I could not have figured out if I had a million years and a team of physicists to help me.

"Hey, Denver!" she said, and I could not believe she knew my name. But I suppose it's like what they say about God, that no lowly sparrow falls without his knowledge, and no loser fluttered the halls outside of Audrey's sphere of awareness. Perhaps I'd even been the subject of her prayers before she turned off her Tiffany lamp and fell asleep under a coverlet made of angel socks.

"Hey," I said.

"How's it going?"

"I'm having a great time."

"I don't usually see you at the parties," she said, but her tone was nothing like that of Sienna and Hayley. It was kind, encouraging, as though my presence made this party everything it could be.

"Well," I said, "I tend to be quite picky over which party I attend. But this one seemed to have promise."

Audrey smiled and nodded as though I were perfectly serious. "Can I sit with you?"

"Sure," I said, grateful that someone actually wanted my company.

She daintily sank down beside me, crossing her legs at the ankles and sipping at her drink.

It looked like Coke. Or a rum and Coke. She followed my eyes.

"Oh, it's just Coke!" she said. "I like soda. It does fun things in my mouth." She wiggled her nose as if to prove her nose liked to party with the soda bubbles. She laughed at her own whatever and then looked around the room.

"I love the decorations!" she cried. "So cute!"

I didn't answer. I had a sudden pit in my stomach that was burning with a fiery heat. For I had just made two lightning-quick, stunning realizations:

Audrey Curtis had the personality of a slowly turning rotisserie chicken.

Audrey Curtis was a saint, and I was the leper to whose

sores she was applying her conversational iodine.

Now I knew exactly why the kid-whose-name-I-never-caught fled the cafeteria after that fateful day Audrey lingered with him at the otherwise-empty table. That emanating kindness she directed at him, and now at me, had a withering effect. For it was then that I realized just how sad and desperate and loser-y I was to merit her attention. It was a painfully dissolving feeling, as though I were a chord from Audrey's harp fading in the air of a chapel.

My face was hot. Tears flooded my eyes.

"Denver!" Audrey said. "What's wrong?"

I didn't answer her. I jumped off the sofa and staggered for the stairwell, the room gray and disorderly around me, the chaos of jokes and laughter and gossip and urgent whispering and some new Katy Perry song and drunken howls forming some kind of cool-kid white noise. I hurtled forward, trying to right myself, tripped over the zebra rug, and stumbled to the floor before quickly picking myself up, leaving my unopened beer behind.

People were drinking on the stairs, more people who belonged there, and suddenly it seemed as though the whole world, in fact, was there, not just the cool kids of my high school but from every high school in LA—no, every high school in the country, with more cool kids pouring in from Belgium and France, cool kids from Austria and Nepal humping each other in the bedrooms, cool kids from Denmark high-fiving cool kids from the Ukraine, more cool kids joining, cool kids from Venus and Mars and Jupiter and planets not yet discovered.

I elbowed my way to the bottom of the stairs and hurtled through the crowd, jostling people, knocking their cups of beer. I heard curses and annoyed mutterings, but I paid no attention. Finally I made it to the front door, grabbed the handle, and threw it open.

Croix Monroe stood in the doorway.

CINCO

HE LOOKED GREAT, OF COURSE, IN AN UNTUCKED BUTTON-
down shirt and faded jeans. I was so stunned to see him
that I just stood there in shock.

"Hey," he said. "You're not leaving, are you?"

"Well . . . it's getting kind of late."

He pulled his cell phone out of his pocket and glanced
down at it. "It's a little after eleven o'clock. The night is
young."

I didn't know what to do. I didn't want to go back
in there, but here was the reason I came, all friendly and
smiling and ready for the great time I had just been denied
for the last forty minutes.

"My mother really needs her Subaru back," I said, then flinched inside. I might as well have said, *"I have absolutely no social skills or way of relating to the world. I was raised in a basement by a madman with no human contact. I was fed Cheetos through an air duct, and my only companion was a termite."* But then again, "My mother really needs her Subaru back" was much more concise.

He smiled again. Neither one of us had moved toward the doorway. Small insects from the light above buzzed around his head but did not land on him lest they be zapped by his majesty.

"Your mother doesn't actually know you're here, does she?"

"No," I admitted. "She doesn't."

"You sneak out the back?"

"Out the window. I hurtled into some lantana bushes and broke several branches." (Sonny Boy's high-pitched voice in my ear: *"Shut up, idiot."*)

He laughed. "Good strategy. Glad you're still in one piece." He nodded at the door. "Shall we go in?"

I'd just escaped that horrific den of popularity, atmospheric salt for my invisible wounds, but now Croix was here, and everything had changed.

Something made me say, "Sure." We entered the foyer as the crowd parted. All the drunk guys were happy to see

49

him, and all the drunk girls were giving me icy stares. He gave out a few high fives and several fist bumps, and then guided me to the living room, into a corner where two overstuffed chairs faced each other by a bay window.

He gestured to a chair. "What would you like to drink?"

"Oh, anything."

"How 'bout a beer?"

"That would be great."

He took off, and I sat there waiting for him, my heart racing. The leper shame Audrey had given me was wearing off, and the lesions were fading. Croix's interest had not come from my desperate imagination. It was real. It was the top half of the story, the one above the clouds, the one I deserved. And all I had to do was not blow it.

Sonny Boy appeared at my elbow to say something about my chances, but I pushed his face away.

"Not now," I whispered.

Croix returned with two bottles of beer. He handed one to me and sat down.

"Do you have a cat?" I asked, adjusting my crown as the worst conversationalist in the world. I took a few gulps of my beer, hoping that would loosen up the conversation. The beer was so cold it hurt my throat.

Croix just smiled. "No. We used to have a dog, but he died of cancer."

"What kind of dog was he?"

Croix looked wistful. "A Lab." I suddenly imagined Croix crying, shirtless, over his Lab's dead body. Since it was my own inner fantasy and I could play God, I added some sunlight to flash across his abs. Not the dog's. Croix's.

"I'm really glad you came," Croix told me, and flashed his dazzling smile. He really was a handsome guy. *El chico esta muy guapo.*

This was swiftly turning into the best night of my life.

"I've been wanting to talk to you," he added. "Get to know you better."

"Really?" I said. I took another couple of nervous gulps from my bottle. "Why?"

He took a sip of beer as he considered the question. "Well, because you're different from the other girls. You're really smart. And funny. And ordinary things don't seem to matter to you."

"What things?"

"I don't know." He searched for the words. "Girly things."

Girly things. I wasn't sure what he meant, but his tone of voice said it was a compliment.

"Thanks." I wondered if he'd heard the rumors about me that Abigail had spread around, and I wanted to tell him I wasn't a traitor or a terrible friend, just an innocent victim. But I decided not to say anything. Why ruin a great conversation with unfair gossip about myself?

"So, anyway," Croix said, "I thought tonight would be a good chance to find out more about you."

"We could talk in Spanish," I suggested, hoping he knew I was joking.

"Sure," he laughed. "*Mi amiga esta en la playa.*"

"*¿Por qué?*" I asked.

He shrugged. "*No se.*"

"Well, that's it for me. We've come to the end of my Spanish vocabulary."

He took another sip of his beer and nodded. "Mine, too."

Just then the house moved.

The paintings on the wall rattled, and the chairs shivered. Someone had turned off some lights in the few minutes Croix and I had been talking, and in the dimness around me, I heard cheers and shouts. Instinctively I grabbed the arms of my chair, fighting the urge to cry out or dive into a corner.

But suddenly Croix reached over and took my hand in his, and I was just frozen there, frozen by my fears and my amazement at his touch.

He raised his eyebrows at me. "It's nothing," he said. "Just like last time. Just the earth not ready to sleep yet."

"It should sleep," I said weakly. "It's a school night."

He kept looking at me. My hand was still in his. My face flushed hot, but my heart rate slowed until it was just in the infatuation zone. I drank the rest of my beer and Croix got me another, and I was halfway through that one when the next earthquake hit.

It was sudden and violent. My beer fell out of my hand and rolled on the floor. Paintings fell from the walls, furniture fell over, glass shattered, girls screamed, guys went "*Dude!*" and the house rocked and shook. It was like God took his big finger and thumped his planet over and over again. And I found myself in Croix's arms as he pulled me down from the chair and into a corner as the furniture slid around and the plasma screen fell on the marble floor with a huge crash.

"Whoa," Croix murmured in my ear. "Got a wild one this time. Just ride it out. We're good."

Finally the shaking stopped, leaving Croix and me still wrapped around each other in the corner of the room.

"It's done now. It's done," he said. All around us people were talking excitedly and stepping over broken glass and getting online to see what number the earthquake had hit.

I could barely breathe. I was scared but in kind of a murky way, because I'm a lightweight, and the beer had started taking effect. I disentangled myself from Croix and tried to stand up.

"Where are you going?" he asked.

"I need to get back home. My mom's gonna check my room now that we've had this quake to see if I'm okay."

"And you'll be in trouble, right?"

"Yes." Trouble meant looking into her sad, disappointed eyes. I hadn't exactly lied to her, had I? Just neglected to mention that instead of going to bed, I was sneaking out to a party. Okay, fine. I had lied.

"You don't want to be on the road during an aftershock. It's not safe. Also, you seem a little drunk. Just stay here for a while and sober up and then call your mother."

"She'll be worried," I said. "I should call her now."

"Wait a few minutes."

"Okay."

I sat back down on the floor next to Croix and he took my hand, and we watched people stepping around the broken glass and fetching themselves new drinks and shrugging and going back to being idiots. They were probably sad that the earthquake had wrecked the house and would now get all the credit. We started talking again, leaning in close to whisper to each other. Just ordinary things you'd say in a tipsy state after an earthquake, about aftershocks and wood-framed buildings.

I wasn't sure how much time had passed, but I was thinking about calling my mother again when I suddenly realized Croix's lips were getting closer and closer to mine, and things were going my way, the sky opening up over Portland, the sun shining down. Below us was fog and a blanket of nothing, but here the sky was blue, so blue, and his lips came ever closer; they were going to touch mine in a moment, a blink. . . .

A girl screamed.

Then another.

Croix and I stopped and looked toward the sound. Everyone was crowding by the windows.

"What's going on?" I asked.

Croix stood and pulled me up, and we rushed over to join the screaming, pointing kids at the window. I looked out and couldn't believe what I was seeing.

The ocean was eating California.

A wall of water had rushed over the Pacific Coast Highway. Cars were being swept away. Houses that lined the beach were crumbling, and the water was racing up the short bluff toward us.

"Oh, my God," I said.

"It can't possibly come this high," Croix murmured.

More people were screaming now, even guys. I simply watched, stunned, as the water rose higher and higher, uprooting a row of ornamental palm trees that were arranged near the back deck. I saw things floating in the water: cars and bicycles and surfboards and kayaks and couches. Another surge came, and the water rose up to the bay windows.

"It's going to get us!" someone cried.

I felt something wet. I looked down at the floor. I was standing in a puddle spreading out from the wall. The water rumbled outside the windows. It was churning, terrifying, roaring like a train.

Moments later it broke through the windows and poured into the house.

People were stampeding for the stairs now. Croix grabbed my hand and pulled me along with him. We joined the bottlenecked crowd trying to get up to the second floor.

"Hey, don't panic!" Croix shouted, but no one paid attention. People shoved and swore and banged into one another. Someone's elbow caught me in the ribs, and I gasped. The people from the bottom pushed us along, and we tried to keep from falling down and being trampled.

When we were halfway up the stairs, I looked down and saw water continuing to pour through the broken windows, filling up the room, sweeping away chairs and tables and bookcases and lamps. Some of the kids who were still on the first floor were frantically moving in slow motion, waist deep in the swift and rising waters, trying to get to the stairs. Some still held on to their drinks, trying to keep them above the water, displaying a human tendency to save small, ridiculous things when their lives are at stake.

A girl fell under the surface of the water and a guy pulled her back up, and she gasped for breath. The water was rising so fast that some of the kids were swimming now. Swimming in a room where just ten minutes ago they had been drinking and laughing.

"Come on," Croix urged in my ear. "Keep moving."

Finally, we reached the second floor, where water-logged kids were waiting, some of them frantically texting as though somehow that could save them. As if the reporting of the wave were stronger than the wave itself, and the act of seeing and witnessing was somehow going to make everything okay. But all the texting in the world didn't stop the endless water from pouring in and taking anything it wanted.

"Are you okay?" Croix asked me.

Before I could answer, I heard a deafening crack. A sickening, unforgettable sound. The sound of a house losing. A wave winning. A monster come to visit. A pariah called death invading a party that was supposed to be about living as much and as fast as you can.

The upstairs windows all smashed at once, and a wall of water rushed through, picking up the baby grand piano like a five-pound weight and hurling it across the flooding room. Out of the corner of my eye I saw Audrey rushing toward us. She had her mouth open to say something when the piano flew into her and smashed her through the back window, and she was gone.

I tried to scream, but I was pulled under the cold, dark, rushing water that dragged me down and held me as the sounds and the sensations around me extinguished. No more music. No more popular kids. No more Croix. No more fizzy beer. No more ins and outs and cool and not-cool and dreams and hopes. Just water. Strong, merciless, unrelenting, terrifying water.

I couldn't see a thing. Furniture and people bumped against me. I felt the brush of fingers and the hard edge of a chair.

I was drowning.

And it was interesting, drowning. Not what I'd thought. Not desperate and flailing. Not like high school. Just quiet, sort of. Like being trapped inside an echo of something that was horrible when first spoken but now, hundreds of years of echoes later, was just a vague rumor. I didn't flail and kick. My body went limp, and I got the feeling I was headed somewhere new. I closed my eyes and got ready to accept death, here at the height of my popularity, forty minutes into the only date of my life. On the night of my first deviation ever from the game plan of survival, I was not surviving. I was dying. Drowning. And it was okay.

That is, it was okay until I felt a wet, warm paw against my face and heard a high-pitched, disembodied voice in my ear:

"Kick, you idiot. Kick!"

SEIS

HOW I GOT FROM MOSTLY DYING TO BARELY LIVING IS STILL A mystery to me.

I woke up cold and dripping wet, one foot bare and head pounding, my scarf and sweater gone, clinging to what I supposed used to be the roof of a Malibu mansion. The invading teenagers were now the least of the doomed structure's problems. An invading wave had come and wiped that much smaller trouble away.

I heard someone breathing next to me, and I knew I was alive. I didn't turn to see the source of the breathing. Just concentrated on steadying my own.

"Hey," said a voice in my ear.

I looked over. It was Croix Monroe, next to me, holding on to the roof. He had a cut near his eye that bled in a slow trickle. Looking around, I made out some other faces.

Sienna. Hayley. Trevor Dunlap. Matt Riley, football star. And . . . my breath caught . . .

Abigail, dazed and clinging on for dear life.

I know I hated her, but in that moment I found myself strangely relieved that she was still among the living. Her hair was straggly and wet around her shoulders. Her basecoat makeup had washed off, but the stronger camouflage around her freckle zone remained, glowing ghostlike in the moonlight.

We exchanged a look of stark terror.

I heard screams around me in the darkness but was not sure where we were floating. On the sea or on what used to be land? I couldn't tell. I was about to say something when suddenly our piece of wreckage reversed itself, and we started traveling, faster and faster, toward the horizon line.

"Hold on! Hold on!" Croix shouted. The line of blood from his cut had reached his jaw.

Sienna screamed, "Oh no oh no oh no!" with the cadence of one of the cheers she used to chant during varsity games. But these words were filled with horror, and they weren't going to rhyme with anything.

I dug my nails into the shingles, but I was losing my grip.

Matt Riley was sliding away. I'd seen him earlier, and he was drunk and having a great time. Now he was in shock.

"Matt, hold on!" Croix ordered him. "Come on, dude. Don't give up!"

"I can't hold on!" he murmured. "It's taking me."

The roof was rotating as it rushed toward the sea.

Croix grabbed on to Matt's wrist.

"You've got to—"

A palm tree came sideways out of nowhere and smashed into Croix's head with a sickening thud, and scraped Matt and him off the roof and into the rushing water.

Now everyone was screaming. We were a horrified choir now, our cries in perfect synchronicity with what we'd just witnessed. The roof spun and moved out past a small family clinging to a floating door, and past all kinds of debris, and people trying to swim or holding on to trees and light poles and pieces of furniture.

My mind just could not believe I had gone from near-kiss to almost certain doom in the blink of an eye. Sights and sounds swirled around me with no meaning. They were like a slow-motion dream, and I understood nothing except the need to hold on.

My nails dug in. Fingers straining. I coughed salt water

as we rushed out to sea.

"Croix is dead!" screamed Hayley. "And Matt! And we're going to die, too!"

I turned toward her and screamed back, "No! We are not going to die. We're going to live, so shut up and believe it!"

TIME HAD PASSED. How much, I didn't know. Out here, slumped on the roof with the other dazed survivors, no one could be sure. Our roof had borne us far out to where the water was calm and the stars were bright. No one had spoken a word. We were all in shock. Every few minutes I had to convince myself that this was real, that in fact I was floating on the Pacific on a roof instead of at home safe in bed. I had never made that call to my mother, and my phone was somewhere in the dark and endless water. I hoped that she was okay and wasn't too afraid. But of course she was.

I couldn't believe that Croix had been killed right in front of my eyes. I didn't know how much of him I had the right to mourn. I only knew that I had liked him for almost two years and had almost kissed him on what, at one point, was a magical night, and now he was gone. Just ripped away right in front of me. I could still see the look on his face.

I wondered who was dead along the Malibu coast and who was still alive. I mourned the loss of saintly, boring Audrey, who had made time to validate one more pariah before her untimely end. We had released our death grips and were now sitting cross-legged on the roof. I removed my remaining shoe and threw it into the water, where it made a distinct splash. The others regarded it silently.

Abigail's hair was almost dry, springy and wild again without her trusty hair spray. Sienna's hair had escaped her ponytail and lay around her shoulders in half-dry straggles. Hayley's bangs had dried straight up like a horn. She kept stroking her horn of hair and sighing. One of her dangly earrings had been torn away, but I noticed with astonishment that she had managed to hold on to her purse. Abigail was missing her cowboy boots, but Sienna was still wearing her short boots, and Trevor . . . had probably come to the party barefoot. There was a cut near his lip and a swelling under his eye. His hair had dried in a pompadour. He was the first to break the silence.

"Holy shit. That was a big-ass wave." He began to drum his fingers on the surface of the roof. "But we're alive, though. Right? Unless we're dead, and this is how they take you to heaven."

"We're alive," Abigail said in a distant voice.

"But our friends are dead," Hayley whispered, and started to cry.

No one said anything. Her crying was like her speech, going on and on and on. Finally it faded out, and we were left in silence again.

"Maybe some of 'em made it after all," Abigail said.

"Lots of those dudes were friends of mine," Trevor said. "And Croix . . . we went all the way back to third grade." He shook his head, stopped drumming, moved his hands through his hair. "Croix . . . this can't be happening."

Sienna looked at me. "I saw Croix with you at the party."

"Yeah," I said. "We were on a date." Tears came to my eyes. "And it was going pretty well."

Sienna's bright makeup was gone, except for the mascara smudged all over her eyes. Astonishingly, she had a supply of emergency bitchiness accessible. "Right. You were on a date with Croix."

"I was! We were in the living room in the corner."

Hayley shook her head. "Lying about dead people is breaking one of the Ten Commandments."

Trevor sighed. "Dude," he said, as if that explained everything about life and death and sudden loss and whether I was lying or not.

I looked out toward what I thought was the land. I couldn't tell; there was nothing but water and moonlight all around us. "My poor mom," I said. "She didn't know I was coming to the party. She has no idea where I am. I had a chance to call her after the quake, but I didn't."

"Well, I called mine right after the earthquake," Sienna chimed in. "She knew I was alive, at least at that point." Her eyes watered, and she wiped them.

"I thought tidal waves were supposed to hit countries over there in China or somewhere," said Hayley the genius.

"Well, that's the way life goes, girl," Abigail said. "Sometimes what's supposed to happen to someone else happens to you." A few more strands of her kinky hair had dried and risen, making a metaphorical statement about rebuilding and carrying on. "Haven't you seen all those tsunami evacuation signs near the beaches? Did you think they were a joke?"

I remembered that Abigail herself had once declared them a joke, but I kept quiet. It was slowly sinking in that I was trapped on a roof with my worst enemy.

"I don't want to die!" Sienna cried suddenly.

"We ain't gonna die. We're safe right now. Everybody just calm the hell down," Abigail said.

"The roof is probably gonna sink soon," I said.

Abigail gave me a look. "Unbelievable," she said. "I let

you stay at the party, and now here you are. I suppose this is God's little joke."

"She's saying that you're not even supposed to be here," Hayley explained.

"Thanks, Hayley," I said. "I was feeling so welcome."

Hayley combed her straggly hair with her fingers as she fumbled with some invisible gate latch and then freed the beast of another run-on sentence. "Everyone remembers what you did to Abigail and no one wants to be around you and this is like the worst moment in my life and half my friends are dead and I'm cold and I'm not like that girl Anne Frank who's just like 'Everything's okay' when it was totally not and here you are with your big words and all the weird stuff you say and we're all stuck with you and that is not fair it's not fair at all."

I glared at her. "You're right. I'm going to just swim away and die now since I don't have a Fendi purse. Which, I see, you managed to save."

"It's a gift from my mother!" Hayley protested, and began to cry again. "I wonder if my mother's dead!"

"It's hard to say for sure how far the water went," I said, "but I imagine everyone who lived more than a couple miles inland is probably alive."

"Probably?" Hayley cried harder.

"Dang it, Hayley," Abigail said. "Calm the hell down."

Hayley stopped crying, but her face stayed red and her mouth stayed all crumpled, just in case she needed to burst into tears again. My eyes moved from her face down to her purse, a black shoulder bag with a fold-over flap.

"Hey," I said. "Do you happen to have an iPhone in that purse?"

"Of course," she managed to sniff.

"Maybe it still works."

She opened her purse, pulled out her phone, and tried to turn it on while we waited, all staring at the same dark screen.

"It's useless," I said.

"They say that you can put an iPhone in a bowl of rice when it gets wet, and the rice will suck out the water," Hayley said in a trembly voice.

"Good to know." I couldn't believe that a tsunami would be that cruel, to force me to talk to people that stupid.

Sienna put her hands to her face. Her thin, limber back slightly humped and straightened with each sob.

"What is with all the crying?" Trevor remarked. "I wish I had some damn dudes on this roof, but they're all dead."

Abigail looked at Sienna with undisguised annoyance. "What the hell is the matter now?"

Sienna cried harder.

"What?" Abigail asked impatiently.

Sienna took her hands away and threw her anguished face back to the sky. "I left her!" she wailed.

"Left who?"

"Madison! She was throwing up again in the bathroom downstairs, and the water came in, and I tried to get her out of there and she wouldn't go. I just left her slumped over the toilet!"

For once I really did feel sorry for Sienna. She looked miserable. She wiped her eyes and spread more of the mascara around. What I wouldn't have given for a quart of baby oil and a bag of cotton balls so I could fix the spectacle.

"Oh no!" Hayley shrieked. "Madison's dead, too?"

"Stop it," Abigail ordered Sienna. "You did your best, right? What were you supposed to do, stay in there with her and drown?"

Sienna sniffled and wiped her face on her wet sleeve. "But . . . when I think of what happened to her . . ."

"She died doing what she loved," Abigail said.

Hayley hummed sadly in agreement.

"Audrey is holding her hair back in heaven," I added.

They all turned to me, shocked.

"Back that horse up for a second," Abigail said. "Audrey's dead?"

"I saw her get smashed by the baby grand piano."

My roof companions all drew in their breaths. Hayley's eyes filled with tears.

"That can't be true," she whispered. "Audrey was a saint."

"Saints die," I said, "just like the rest of us."

"But Audrey was special!"

"I know," I said, but I didn't know. Not really. I didn't know Audrey or any of these people, except for Abigail. And maybe I never really knew her at all.

Trevor drummed on the roof. Nine Inch Nails? Taylor Swift? Hard to say.

"Stop drumming," Abigail said. "Ain't respectful."

"Audrey was supposed to be the designated driver tonight," Sienna said. "She was going to make sure Madison and I got home safe." She pointed at me. "That's what's so unfair. Why did you get saved and not Audrey or Croix or Madison or Matt? They should be on this roof, not you."

"She's right," said Hayley. "She sounds mean, but she's just saying what's true."

What they were saying was not true but totally unfair and mean, but I knew Abigail wasn't going to defend me. All the rules and roads were gone. We were washing slowly away from land, having just undergone a disaster of epic proportions, but our social strata were still in place. And I was at the bottom with the shellfish.

Oddly, the hatred for Sienna flooding my body made me feel alive. That brisk, cold rage resuscitated me, brought me to my senses like a mermaid pressing on the chest of a half-drowned sailor until he drooled out seawater and breathed pure air. "It's not based on how popular you are or how good you are. Look at you, Sienna. You're a terrible person. And yet you lived."

Sienna drew in her breath. She looked at Abigail. "Did you hear what she said to me? Are you going to let her talk that way to me?"

Abigail considered this. "She's got a point, Sienna. You're kind of a bitch. But she's a snake and a traitor, so she ain't one to be talking."

"Thanks, Abigail," I said. "Your grammatically compromised defense of me is inspiring. And I'm sorry I was saved over worthier, more socially acceptable kids. And if it is helpful for you all, I will die first."

"If you bitches are going to fight, then I'm going to drum," Trevor said, drumming.

"I can't wait till we're rescued," Abigail said to me. "Then I won't have to talk to you anymore."

"Think about it," I told her. "It's the middle of the night. There are probably thousands of people dead or missing up and down the coast. We have no working phones, no GPS. There's no way to get in touch with us, and even if all your parents knew you went to a party, I'm sure none of them knew you broke into a house in Malibu that isn't there anymore."

"They'll send choppers, dummy," she said.

"Choppers? Don't you think there might be other people who need choppers right now? I know all of you think you're everyone's top priority, but you're not. No one from the Coast Guard is running up and down screaming, 'Who'll save the cool kids?'"

"You don't know anything, so stop pretending you do," Hayley said.

"Or what, you'll burst into song?" (Hayley once tried out for *American Idol* and made it through the first audition. No one had ever heard the end of it.)

"Okay, okay, you're giving me a headache," Abigail said. "I suppose we've got to try and be a team."

"Right," I said, looking at Abigail pointedly. "A team."

"Yes," she said, glaring right back at me. "A team. For now at least. Once we're rescued we can go on about our lives."

"Ironic, isn't it?" I said to Abigail, but also to the others.

"What?" Sienna asked.

"Here I am, trying to survive *with* you, when before

my whole plan was just trying to *survive you.*"

"I'm not sure what that means," Hayley said. "And I wish you'd stop talking in puzzles and just say normal things, because I've had a big shock. This morning I was looking at a YouTube video of a hamster eating a tiny burrito and now I'm floating on this stupid raft and my friends are dead so just keep that in mind."

I CAN'T RECOMMEND apocalypse in the springtime highly enough. The night was clear, and the nearly complete moon shone down on water that grew calmer the farther we drifted. A couple of seals surfaced. Our possibly sinking rooftop gently rocked us. Trevor drummed, and slowly the others stopped talking and sank back to lie on the roof and stare up at the sky, each to her own thoughts. It was strange. The reality of what had happened seemed to hit everyone in waves. It was just so preposterous that this shallow, glitzy town would serve as the landing place for something as ancient and terrifying as a monster wave. Such a wave seemed to demand a primitive tribe shaking its spears and calling out to its gods and fleeing, not the people of Malibu. And not us.

I turned my thoughts to my mother. My poor mother, last seen reading the affirming words of Robert Pathway under a swag lamp she'd bought off Sky Mall. She had probably gone to bed before the earthquake hit. Bolted wide-awake and tried to make her way to the stairs with the house still shaking. Calling my name: "Denver! Denver!" Finally arriving at the doorway to my room to find the furniture moved and photos down, and my bed perfectly empty and made, while a shaken-awake Sonny Boy perched on my pillow, one front paw pointing straight at the damning evidence of the open window. She must have stuck her head out that window and spied the broken bushes where my ungainly, hurtling body had landed. She must have rushed to the garage and discovered the missing car and realized that her daughter was unaccounted for, possibly dead and certainly a liar.

In my imagination, I watched her as she ran back inside and grabbed the phone and coded my name, seeing it rise ghostlike on the screen . . . DENVER . . . the phone ringing and then connecting to a cheerful voice saying, *"The liar you have reached cannot be located, as her phone is turned off right now so she can talk to the man of her dreams before the tsunami hits and washes them both out to sea. Please leave a message at the sound of the beep."*

At this very moment, she was probably calling police and firemen and relatives and officials and news stations and hospitals and everyone she could possibly think of. And since she had no car to look for me, she might, in her terror and desperation, be on foot right now, trying to flag down a ride through the chaos of that damaged city, because what choice did a mother of her quality have?

I should have called her. She'd still be terrified right now, but at least she would have a lock on my last location. At least she would have the sound of my voice one more time. At least I could tell her I loved her, something I didn't say so often anymore.

I was lying on my back at this point, the roof feeling rough against me, my bare feet cold in the night air, looking up at the stars.

"I'm sorry," I said to my mother, wherever she was.

I heard Trevor's drumming stop and felt the roof shift as he settled himself for the rest of the night. Then all was silent but for the sound of breathing and the occasional sniffle or cry as someone woke up and remembered that the world was both a whirling sphere and a cruel inflictor of sudden and staggering loss.

Croix. He had been breathing beside me hours earlier. And then he had died. Just like that.

My eyes welled up as I thought of him. I knew that our time together was short, too short to sit in the front row of his funeral and accept the flag, but that was the worst part of the whole sad tale to me—we had something. Maybe it had taken him a year or two to get up the nerve to talk to me, but he had, hadn't he? And the way we had connected in that living room with voices and music all around us as a sneaky wave crept up the coastal shelf—that was real.

His lips so close.

I cursed this wave for undoing what should have been done long before. Because I deserved to have a boyfriend like Croix. I deserved to walk down the hallway holding his hand. I deserved to be popular, and known, and seen, because if popularity was something bestowed on the dipshits at that party, then it was all a game, and I deserved to play.

I HAD ALWAYS been unsure about God, who he was and what form he took. Did God have a beard? On which side did he part his hair? Was his hair white, and would he ever consider using Grecian Formula? That was the problem with God. I couldn't think of him without thinking of a million questions. Like, why did he make the color burnt orange, the ugliest color on Earth? God could have prevented burnt orange, but he just stood by and let it happen.

Sometimes I had said disrespectful things about God and gotten absolutely no reaction from him. Did that mean that God was quietly pissed off and waiting for a chance to get me back? The giant wave may have pointed to option B, though I couldn't see why he'd punished a whole part of a coastline just to smack one whippersnapper. And didn't God make me that whippersnapper? If God didn't want me to make fun of him, why wouldn't he have made me a saint like Audrey?

I imagined that after all this doubt and sassiness, I would get a nosebleed seat in heaven at best.

That night on that slowly moving roof, I asked God to welcome Croix into heaven, because if there was a heaven, that handsome dead boy was surely a candidate. Next, I asked God to please save me, and though I knew there were many souls out there worthy of saving, I had dreams and hopes and a straight B+ average and would have written a short essay on my qualifications had I any paper. I also apologized for all the jokes I had made at his expense and said I hoped he didn't hold it against me. *"It's human nature, God,"* I said silently, *"to taunt the larger mystery. And you are very large."*

I asked him to watch over my mother and Sonny Boy, and keep them safe and dry, and to watch over and protect all the people affected by the wave (although I felt guilty, because I didn't care so much. I mean, I did in a theoretical way, but it is hard, I found, to care for people you have never met while you are slowly drying out on a rooftop drifting farther and farther away with a bunch of assholes who hate you).

Speaking of which, I prayed for the assholes on the rooftop with me because, I admit, I thought God would look favorably on it, and besides, it seemed selfish not to. So as sincerely as I could, I prayed for their lives, too. Their entitled, arrogant, somewhat useless lives. Then I went back and prayed again and took out *arrogant* and *useless* so it would seem softer.

I even said a special prayer for Abigail, because I was the better person.

SIETE

TSUNAMIS GIVE YOU WEIRD DREAMS. IN THE DREAM, I WAS floating on the roof with Sonny Boy, and it seemed perfectly reasonable that he was there, never mind that he was a cat and hated water.

He said, *"How's it going, dipshit?"*

But here's the strange part. His voice was, like, an octave lower.

I said, "Sonny Boy, what happened to your voice?"

"I got my balls back, no thanks to you."

He lifted his leg so I could see them. They were huge— the size of golf balls.

"You touch them again and I'll kill you." I woke up, and

there was no Sonny Boy in sight, just a rising sun and a bunch of sleeping cool kids. I lay there for a minute, my cheek against the shingles of the roof, just letting my senses return to me. There had been a tsunami. A lot of people had died. And I might die, too. My eyes stung and tears ran down that funny way when you cry lying on your side, and a deep sniff drew seawater snot to the back of my throat and I sat up. Sienna and Hayley spooned each other. Abigail slept in a vampire position, her arms crossed over her. In her sleep, she looked so young, and I wondered what plans, if any, were forming in her dreams. Trevor also slept on his back, his fingers cupped and resting on his chest. Occasionally his fingers twitched and tapped. I noticed he had very long eyelashes and wondered why I'd never noticed that before.

I looked out to a flat, endless sea.

And something else.

A boat.

I rubbed my eyes in case my dream wasn't over, and Sonny Boy was going to rise out of that boat and flash his newly restored balls at me.

But no. It was a real boat, bobbing about a hundred yards away. It didn't look very big, but something told me that roofs don't float forever. And perhaps there was food on the boat. Water. A radio.

"Hey!" I shouted. "Wake up, wake up!"

Abigail lifted her head up. She looked confused.

"Where are we?"

"We're on the ocean. The tsunami, remember? Now look! Look over there."

She shielded her eyes and straightened.

"Wake up!" she screamed to the others. "It's a boat!"

The others slowly came to.

"Shit!" said Trevor.

"It's drifting away from us!" Abigail said.

Let me just take a very brief moment to tell you something about lonely girls. While other girls are flirting and texting and listening to whatever they listen to or shopping or telling their parents to go to hell without getting grounded, lonely girls swim. At least this one did. Every afternoon from three to five. I used to be on the swim team in my neighborhood in elementary school, and I was competent at butterfly and breaststroke, but a total badass at freestyle.

So I did what any other lonely girl did who had swum countless hours until the chlorine was a trusted confidant and red eyes were an ordinary thing. I dove into the water and swam toward that boat.

The water was bracingly cold, but I warmed up quickly. Even in my clothes I was quick as a seal as my body recognized the water as an ally and immediately fell into synchronicity, my bare feet kicking.

The boat had drifted another ten yards or so by the time I got to it. It was an old boat. Either the tsunami or someone's neglect had done a number on it. Its side was dotted with scrapes and dents, and the plastic awning had seen better days. The entire sunshade, in fact, was bent so that it covered the front of the boat rather than the back.

"Hello!" I called, treading water.

I waited, but no answer came. The boat was abandoned. I moved around to the back and was hoisting myself up the ladder when I noticed Abigail and Trevor swimming toward me. Abigail was a pretty good swimmer herself. I know this because she had a pool in her backyard in the Palisades, something we enjoyed together back when we were best friends.

Sienna and Hayley were still waiting on the piece of roof. I motioned for them to come, too, but they just shook their heads at me.

I took a look around the boat. First of all, and of paramount importance, there was no engine in the back. Just a few wires where an engine was supposed to be. The deck was covered with wet, stinking carpeting that squished under my feet. There was a captain's seat, two seats built into the back, a swivel seat in the middle of the boat, and a raised, carpeted place up in front where more people could sit. The cracked leather cushions spilled wet foam.

Of course God would answer my prayers with a boat like this.

Abigail climbed up the ladder in back and stood dripping beside me. Her hair was slicked to her head again.

She looked around, studying the boat, holding on to the rail for balance. "What a piece of shit."

"Agreed."

This boat wasn't taking us anywhere, but it was at least a little bit better than a floating roof.

Trevor climbed into the boat.

"It's beautiful," he breathed.

Abigail shot him a disgusted look. "You're joking."

He flipped his wet hair out of his eyes. "You should learn to appreciate things."

I looked over at Hayley and Sienna, who were still staring at us from on top of the roof. Hayley had her purse over her shoulder like she was ready to go.

"Why aren't they coming?" I asked Abigail.

"They can't swim, that's how come."

"They're drifting farther away. We've got to do something!"

I opened a hatch and found some supplies and a coiled-up rope. I quickly uncoiled it.

"It's not going to be long enough," I said.

"Shit," said Trevor. "Well, we tried."

Sienna and Hayley were looking worried.

"Come get us!" Hayley called.

"We can't," I shouted back. "There's no engine!"

I opened another hatch and searched around frantically. "Great. No life preservers."

"Help us!" Sienna called.

"Don't leave us!" cried Hayley.

"Why don't you get off my ass?" Trevor called back. "You're the ones who can't swim."

"Hold on!" Abigail shouted. "I'm comin' for ya!"

"What good is that gonna do?" I asked her. "You can't haul them one by one to the boat."

"You just watch me."

"Don't be stupid. I have an idea."

Abigail gave me a sneering look. But she was listening.

"Take your clothes off," I said. "Down to the underwear. You too, Trevor. Do it now." I was busy peeling off my clothes myself. I had no time to be embarrassed. I just knew that we were going to go back in the water, and we didn't need to be weighed down by our clothes.

Shockingly, they didn't question me. They obeyed me as Hayley and Sienna watched us from the drifting rooftop.

I tied one end of the rope to the rail of the boat. "I'm

not positive, but I'm guessing the boat is more buoyant than that roof. So it will be easier to bring the boat to the roof than the roof to the boat."

I threw the other end of the rope into the water.

"Get in," I said. "We're going to tow this boat over to the roof."

We jumped overboard and arranged ourselves with me in front, then Abigail, then Trevor. We grabbed the rope and began to pull.

It was harder than we thought. A lot harder.

"Pull harder!" I said. "Harder!"

My arms ached. My back hurt. My feet kicked in the water. Sea foam went up my nose. A couple hundred feet below me were probably the bones of other idiots who had seen this in a movie and had also tried it.

Finally the boat slowly began to come our way.

Hayley started singing an encouraging, up-tempo Miley Cyrus song in an attempt to give us strength.

"Shut up!" Abigail shouted at her. "We're trying to concentrate."

The warbling annoyance ceased, and we kept pulling. Slowly, slowly, we closed the distance to where the others stood, waiting anxiously. After about half an hour, we finally got the boat over to the rooftop, and Hayley and Sienna clambered aboard, then the rest of us hoisted ourselves up the ladder and pulled in the rope. We watched as the distance increased between our new floating device and the rooftop that had once served as our savior.

Trevor, Abigail, and I slumped down on the gross carpeting of the deck. We were exhausted. Hayley and Sienna looked much more refreshed, having done nothing but add "Can't Swim" to the history of their utter uselessness.

"It stinks in here," Hayley said.

"Smells like a bunch of dead fish," said Abigail.

Sienna paced the boat. "I need an e-cigarette," she said. "I'm getting twitchy."

Trevor stared at me. "I can see your boobs," he said.

I looked down. Of course I'd had to wear my thinnest underwire bra to the party, and indeed my nipples showed through. I put on my wet clothes, discovering in the process how hard it is to put on wet clothes.

"Hey," Abigail said to her friends, "we figured out how to save you. The least you can do is thank us."

"I think she means," I said, "thank me. Because it was my idea, not hers."

Abigail smirked and rolled her eyes. "Well, aren't you the credit hawg," she said.

"Thank you," Hayley said suddenly. She still had her purse and was nervously touching her dangly earring.

Sienna gave her a look.

"What?" Hayley said. "I know she's unpopular but she just saved us and I didn't even have to get wet, you know I hate getting wet so anyway I was raised to be grateful so there you go."

I shot a cold glance at Hayley. "I don't need your charity. I helped save you because it was the right thing to do. I don't need a medal every time I do something right."

The last of Abigail's camouflage had come off in the water, and now her freckles stood out in the light. Her shirt was still half on, and more freckles showed on her chest and arms. She took a hank of her wet hair and squeezed it. Water dripped onto the deck.

Trevor had taken a seat and was leaning back in his wet underwear. I dragged my eyes away from the somewhat large bulge that I would later find out was named Ranger Todd.

"No use fighting," he said. "We're stuck with each other unless we all die."

He began to drum.

OCHO

I FIRST MET ABIGAIL WHEN I KICKED HER IN THE FACE.

I didn't mean to do it. I wasn't born with face-kicker tendencies like Bruce Lee or a kangaroo. It was a total accident. And there was more to the story than you'd think. But there was always more to the story when it came to Abigail.

My family had just moved from Wisconsin to West LA when I was about to enter the seventh grade, suddenly friendless and angry. The new city filled me with contempt, those countless nail salons and fancy convertibles and shiny round sunglasses. And sushi. How that city loved to cut up fish. And there was no slowness, no realness. I never saw a kid roll a tire down the street. I never saw an American flag in a front yard or heard the clanking sound its pulley chain makes when the wind blows. I never saw neighbors gathered on a porch. I never even saw an ice cream truck. All the ice cream truck drivers had probably become movie stars or written songs that were used in commercials, and now they were too rich to drive ice cream trucks.

It was a totally different world. In my little protected neighborhood in the Midwest, kids could ride their bikes to one another's houses. Here you had to get a parent to drive you, because LA was spread out and choked with traffic, and no one walked anywhere. Everyone drank weird brands of coffee, and was skinny and perfect. I didn't even trust the flowers. Their colors seemed fake and showy. They paid no attention to the blooming seasons of the Midwest, just bloomed whenever the hell they wanted to. I wanted to slap those flowers.

I missed my friends from Wisconsin terribly, and Skyped and texted them every night, complaining about my terrible luck in moving to this place just because my father lost his teaching job in Oshkosh and now taught at UCLA.

"You'll make new friends," said Jessica Altvine. She was my most positive friend and therefore my least favorite.

"I don't WANT new friends," I hotly replied, leaning in to the light of my computer. Jessica's skin had a pink, unflattering tone to it over Skype. "I want my old friends. The ones I grew up with. Not these dopes in this town."

"Don't worry. You'll make a ton of new friends, and before you know it, you'll be glad you moved there."

I decided that should I ever return to Wisconsin, I was going to replace Jessica with a more cynical and less pink-toned friend.

"Come on," my mother said. "Give the West Coast a try. I am." Indeed, she was trying. And it was hard for her to make friends with a bunch of women who went to Spinning class and talked about cultured goat's milk. My mother totally didn't fit in here, but it was her nature to be a good sport about everything.

"You know your father needed a job," she said, "so let's make the best of it."

I didn't want to make the best of it. LA was full of people hungry for something. They didn't grow up with this town wrapped around them. Most of them came here to make something of themselves, and that failure was written all over their faces.

They wanted to be famous. They wanted to be stars. They wanted paparazzi to follow them around, and they wanted to sing or dance or act or just be important. It was a strange feeling. Like a bunch of shipwrecked sailors competing over one bottle of water.

A prize example was my new gym teacher, Ms. Hanson. She had blindingly white teeth and a fake smile, and her forehead didn't move when she got mad, and she didn't wear a bra, so when she led us in jumping jacks, her breasts would fly around and it was weird and gross. And she was always talking about her "auditions." About how she had been an extra in the movie *Titanic* when she was twelve years old, and any day now she was going to get her own show or be the star of a movie or move to Broadway or whatever. In the meantime, she was teaching gym class, but she reminded us often that it was only temporary before she got "the call," which could happen any day. In fact, she kept her cell phone on the bench next to the bleachers, and she'd glance at it often, just in case James Cameron thought, *Who was that sassy twelve-year-old sparkling like a lost diamond out of a cast of thousands who caught my eye? What's she doing? I need her.*

The way she looked at us was weird—as though she resented us for being seventh graders and loving things that had nothing to do with overnight success. She squeezed a stress ball when she talked to us, and it made the veins between her knuckles stand out. I thought her prominent knuckle veins might explain Hollywood's lack of interest, but maybe it all came down to plain bad luck.

I hated gym and I hated Ms. Hanson. The only form of athletics I liked was swimming. Everything about gym class made me miserable. There was even a knotted rope hanging from the ceiling that I knew inevitably we'd have to climb in that tired old cliché repeated since the first asshole decided to string a knotted rope from a gym ceiling and make some ungainly loser climb it. I'd fall to the floor and break my neck, and they'd put my framed picture in the hallway.

I also hated the uniform I had to wear. The T-shirt was too tight, and the shorts were too high in the waist. I tried to get my mother to sign something that said I had asthma and couldn't participate in sports, but she told me she'd had to take gym class and I had to take it, too.

Everyone was supposed to partner up to learn the handstand. How the handstand would serve me later in life was still a mystery, in the same way that how anything would serve me later in life was still a mystery. Ms. Hanson told everyone to "pair up," which was the cue for all the best friends to run shrieking toward each other and the leftover girls to look around shyly.

Out of the corner of my eye I saw a girl with springy red hair coming toward me. I'd noticed her in class. Who could not notice that hair? It went out in all directions and was parted on the side, and a single barrette had the laughable job of trying to contain it.

When she walked, the barrette flapped and trembled.

She had rosy lips, pale skin, and a splash of freckles, which spread out across her cheeks and then abruptly ended. Her eyes were blue, dark and deep. She had a studied, wise way about her.

"Hey," she said when she reached me. "Wanna pair up for this dumb-ass exercise?" Her accent startled me. I hadn't run into too many Texans out here.

"Sure, I guess. But I have to warn you, I'm terrible at handstands. And cartwheels. And doing those stretches where your chin touches your knee."

She nodded. The barrette bobbed. "I'm Abigail."

"I'm Denver."

"Don't recollect hearing that name before. I thought you'd be a Jessica. This school is crawling with Jessicas. Of course, back in Texas we had our share. Lotsa Ashleys too. Rancher friend of my dad named his cow Ashley. I don't see the specialness about it myself."

"My mother wanted to name me after a city. It was that or Paris. She said Cancun was in the mix, but I think she was just trying to be funny."

"Well, parents trying to be funny are a burden we all bear, ain't it?"

I liked the way she treated the English language so casually and brutally, like swinging a cat around by the tail. And I liked her easy way of making conversation.

Ms. Hanson's stress ball sat on the bench next to her cell phone. Those two objects, banishing anxiety and welcoming fame, were what got her through the day. "Okay," she announced, "one of you is going to try the handstand, and the other will catch and hold your ankles."

The class groaned collectively.

"Now, girls," she said with barely disguised contempt, "this will teach you balance and flexibility."

"And failure," I added softly.

Ms. Hanson clapped her hands together, a motion that caused her unharnessed breasts to jiggle briefly. "Let's go, girls. Pick which one is going to do the handstand and which one's going to help."

"You do the handstand," Abigail told me. "I'll grab your ankles."

"Like I said, I'm terrible at this."

"Just fake it."

"I hate gym class."

"Right there with ya."

We watched as Ms. Hanson demonstrated with a bored-looking girl named Sienna Martin. Yes, that Sienna. She had not yet grown the breasts that would serve her so well in grope sessions in high school with any guy who moved, and it would take another few years to perfect her bitchiness and master the dark science of her true calling: snubbing those outside her circle and holding back the hair of her drunkenly vomiting friends. But she had the lips. Thin on the top, fuller on the bottom, and always slightly curled, as though the smell of rotting pariah had just come wafting down from the vents.

Here she was now, curl lipped, bored, a bitch in training and as limber as a snake.

"Everyone, watch Sienna," said Ms. Hanson. We watched as Sienna did a perfect handstand, her top lip fighting gravity to stay snarly, and Ms. Hanson caught her by her ankles.

They stood there frozen for a moment, like a fisherman and her skinny swordfish trophy, and we were not sure what to do. Clap? Take notes? Marvel?

Finally the moment ended. Sienna was released. Her long legs came down again, one after another in perfect succession. She bounced up, as did her bouncy hair, and gave us all a quick, bored, smug glare.

"Now you do it!" Ms. Hanson ordered the rest of us. She glanced back at her phone.

"Here goes nothing," I said to Abigail.

I backed a few feet away from her, hurled myself at

the floor, and flung my feet up in the air. Predictably my body rebelled, immediately collapsing as momentum carried my legs up and then down the opposite way, my big feet gone rogue and ready to inflict collateral damage. I could do nothing but scream "Get out of the way!" at my new partner, whom I couldn't see because I was facing the opposite wall.

I felt the impact of my feet hitting Abigail's flesh, and I heard her pained little scream. Then we both fell down in a heap.

The girls let out a collective "Ahhhh."

"Abigail!" I cried as I extracted myself. "Are you all right?"

She didn't answer. She was sitting with one leg beneath her and the other straight out. Her hands covered her face, and she was making gasping sounds. Ms. Hanson wandered over, bored with our catastrophe, which I suppose was completely dwarfed by the trauma of her post-*Titanic* career. "What seems to be the problem?"

"That big girl flipped over on her. That's the problem," sneered Sienna, folding her stick arms and curling her lip.

Abigail exhaled a breath of pure agony. Her muffled voice came through her fingers. "I think she broke my nose."

It was hard to tell where her pain began and her accent ended. As it was, they seemed to intersect. Ms. Hanson sighed and rolled her eyes. She clenched and unclenched her absent stress ball. Her breasts had clocked out for the day and were pointing at the floor.

"Let me see," she said without pity. "Take your hands away."

Abigail's hands came down, revealing a violently red face and eyes full of tears.

Ms. Hanson studied her nose while I stood there horrified at what I'd done.

"It doesn't look broken. But who knows?" She nodded at me curtly. "Take her to the nurse."

Everyone was staring at me. I felt like such a dope, having injured a potential new friend in just under two minutes.

I helped Abigail to her feet. "Can you walk?" I whispered stupidly.

More tears came out. She put her hands over her face again and nodded silently.

"Way to go," said Sienna, and some of the other girls snickered.

I led Abigail out of the gym. As soon as the door closed, she dropped her hands and wiped her face on her sleeve.

"Perfecto," she said.

Her face was flushed red, but her eyes were dead calm. Her barrette had slid down to the last two inches of her red hair, an innocent victim of the debacle. She stopped, removed her barrette, and then laboriously shoved it back into her hair, buckling it over as many springs as she could gather.

"What is perfecto?" I asked, confused.

"How that went."

"What do you mean? Is your nose okay?"

"Of course it's okay," she said as though impatient with the question. "I staged the whole thing."

I was completely bewildered. "Why?"

"I couldn't stand frigging gym class one more second, that's why."

"You're not hurt?"

"No." She began to saunter down the hall. I followed her. "I picked you out because you seemed like the most likely to flop over. I've noticed your big feet and lack of grace."

"Wait," I said. "Just wait a second. You just made me look like an idiot in front of the whole class."

She just kept going, paying me no mind.

I was growing furious. "So everything's okay now, huh? Now that your little plan worked?"

"My little plan *always* works. Now get off your high horse. We're free, ain't we?" She breezed right past the nurse's office and out the double doors that led outside.

The light from harsh LA flooded my eyes and then the doors shut in my face, and I was alone in the hall, fuming. I'd had just about enough of this town and all the dip-shit people in it. I burst out into the sunlight, filled with adrenaline and self-righteous anger.

Just ahead was a grassy area and a few plank tables. Abigail was already lounging on top of one of the tables, looking up at the drifting clouds. She glanced at me but said nothing.

"You know what I hate about this town?" I asked. "People like you. People just concerned about themselves. People doing whatever they need to do to get what they want at someone else's expense. You are LA. You are this gross desert with pumped-in water and fake teeth and shitty beaches."

She seemed unconcerned. "Well, in case you haven't noticed, I am not from this damn town. I am from the great state of Texas, where my friends would have slapped me on the back and said 'Good job' instead of whining and carrying on like I threw a rattlesnake on your grandma."

"I'm gonna go tell Ms. Hanson what you did to get out of class. Then you can go tell the principal and tell him how smart you are while you're getting a detention slip."

"I should have figured you for a dirty-dog snitch. Well, go ahead. Go back to gym class. But guess where you'll be? Back in gym class."

I turned to go, but I couldn't. I wasn't a dirty-dog snitch. I climbed on the table and sat down next to her.

"Okay," I said, "you win. You are less excruciating than gym class, but that's not much of a compliment."

"There are some things that should never have been dreamed up," Abigail said, sounding conciliatory. "One of them is the handstand. The other is gym class."

It was a glorious day—the sky so blue; lean, hungry-looking clouds drifting by. Clouds that went to Spin class.

"You know what's even worse about gym class?" Abigail asked. "They don't have soccer. How dumb is that?"

"You like soccer?"

"Hell, yeah," she said. "And I'm great at it. I'm gonna be a soccer star like Mia Hamm. I practice every day out in my backyard."

I pictured her and her family living in a barn in the middle of Beverly Hills with cattle and horses roaming the property as Abigail punted soccer balls, startling groups of chickens. She seemed pretty determined to make it big. My own goals were still a bit shaky.

"Don't we need to go to the nurse?" I asked. "I mean,

you're supposed to be hurt."

"Nah. The last thing I want to do is hang out with that nurse. She checked the whole grade for scoliosis. I still remember her cold fingers on my back. All she did was go on and on about the Atkins Diet, like I give a shit."

"But don't we need a note?"

"That gym gal probably doesn't even remember we're gone. She only cares about herself. So we can hang out here awhile and go back in, and she'll never even ask if I'm okay."

"I call her Swing Tits," I said.

She nodded, considering the nickname. "Swing Tits," she repeated, although she said it like "Swang Teyuts."

Her pale face was turning a bit red in the sun, and the freckles seemed to be multiplying. I wasn't sure whether to point this out or not.

"Where are you from?" she asked.

"Wisconsin."

Abigail pulled her gym shirt down to cover her stomach. "Let me guess. Wisconsin is the most beautiful place in the world, where life is real and you know your neighbor, not like this fake place."

"Exactly. I hate this horrible town."

"Well, you're stupid."

I stared at her. Her expression hadn't changed.

"LA and Wisconsin are the same place," she continued. "It's just a hunk of land. LA might be warmer with palm trees. Wisconsin might have more doughnut shops and cows. But it's land. You can't hate land. You leave LA alone and it will leave you alone. You can be whoever you want here. You can be whoever you want anywhere. You just need a plan. Like mine. Come freshman year I'm gonna be on the soccer team. Junior year I'm gonna make varsity. Senior year, captain of the varsity. And then on to fame and fortune."

"You seem very sure of yourself."

"I have natural talent."

She was silent for a moment. "Got any friends here?" she asked.

"My friends are all back in Wisconsin."

"How many ya got?"

"Four best friends. Jessica, Katie, Chelsea, and Emily." I said their names reverently, as though they had all recently fallen backward off the Grand Canyon attempting to pose for a group selfie and plunged to their deaths.

"Next year you won't even remember them."

"You're wrong. You don't even know my friends. They are funny and wise and wonderful, and we've known each other since kindergarten! We'll be friends all our lives."

"Okay, then lemme know when you're ninety years old and hopscotching through the nursing home."

Her tone annoyed me. "Well, who are *your* friends? I don't see you hanging around with anyone."

"I don't have any friends yet," she said calmly. "I am waiting for quality." She pulled up her gym shirt, exposing her pale, freckled belly and her bra, and wiped the sweat from her face with it. "I had a girl last year I was trying out. Name was Brittany. Big strike already with that name, but she had potential. Then her guinea pig went tits up, and all hell broke loose. She went mad over that varmint. I mean, she had three funerals for it. For months, she went on and on about it. And she made me do a séance with her and her parents so she could talk to it. She said the guinea pig wanted a Japanese marble lamp for its grave and would haunt her unless it got one. So her stupid parents ordered her one for the critter's grave, and then of course it was on the grave for two days and disappeared. Brittany kept it in her closet and took it out at night."

"So you dumped her for being a liar?"

"No, actually that made me think I'd made the right choice. Pure genius. The thing was, she never did anything smart again. I think that was just a fluke. So I dumped her."

"I once used my dead grandfather to get out of a piano recital," I offered.

"Did you kill him?"

"What? No!"

She snorted. "Then, lame."

I couldn't tell if she was kidding or not. I hadn't met anyone quite like her before. She annoyed me, but she intrigued me. I wanted to leave, but I wanted to stay.

"When will you know when quality has finally come along?" I asked her.

"I'll just know." She looked at me meaningfully and I felt flattered despite myself. "And by the way, I don't love this town. Ain't got nothing on any given town in the great state of Texas. But I like living here. It's too dumb to hurt you too much. You always hear about people who've had terrible childhoods. How they're screwed the rest of their lives, and they never do what they really want to do. LA is fine and my parents are fine and I hate my little brother, but that's fine too. Nothing's gonna bother me on my way to the top."

She pressed a finger to her face and announced, "I'm beginning to fry. Curse of the redhead. We should probably go inside now. Here's our story in case anyone cares: the Atkins nurse put ice on my nose and the swelling went down, and everything's peachy now. Got it?"

"Got it. I'm sure Coach Swing Tits will find that tale acceptable."

Abigail got up and headed toward the doors. I caught up with her, and we walked inside and down the silent hall together.

"Swing Tits," she mumbled. "Funny."

NUEVE

IT WAS SHOCKING HOW CALM AND CLEAR THE SEA WAS THAT morning. Like some monster that just ate a bunch of people then stuffed its hands in its pockets and whistled an innocent tune. Looking into the stretch of flat blue on all sides of us, it was possible to believe that nothing had happened at all, that we were just taking a leisurely ride on a boat with no motor. The boat also lacked a GPS system or a radio, but did have three flares. Whoever owned this boat was a schizophrenic who wanted to be found and wanted to be lost and wanted to sail the seas but didn't want to go anywhere.

Trevor inspected a flare. "How do these things work?

Oh, I see. You flip this switch and then just point and pull the trigger."

"Could you maybe not point that damn flare at me?" Abigail said crossly. "Put it down. Ain't a toy."

We hunted through the hatches of the boat for supplies. We found a gallon of water, two cans of Spam, and half an opened wax bag of crackers that looked really old.

Abigail took a cracker and bent it in half. It did not break but simply stayed in a U-shape.

"I'm not gonna eat that," said Sienna.

"You will if you get hungry enough," Abigail said.

"I'm hungry already. And I want a cigarette. Not an e-cigarette. I want a regular cigarette with real smoke."

"Gotta pee," Trevor announced. He turned around, unbuttoned his jeans, and whizzed over the side, his urine forming a lusty arc in the air.

"I've gotta pee too," said Hayley.

We all did.

"Well," said Trevor, facing away from us, his elbows shaking up and down to indicate he was finished, "you are SOL."

I'll spare you the details, but the girls had to lower themselves down the ladder one by one in the back of the boat while clinging to the rail. The ocean's not big on dignity. It goes flat, it gets riled, it kills things, it keeps things alive. But it doesn't care. The ocean is like a giant Sonny Boy.

A few minutes later the wind started blowing and the waves grew higher. Hayley suddenly rushed to the side of the boat and threw up. Finally she steadied herself, still gripping the rail.

"Try not to do that too much," I said. "Vomiting speeds along the process of dehydration."

She turned back to shoot me a disgusted look. The sunlight glinted off her earring.

"Why are you always acting like such a smarty-pants? And how can I help being seasick? I've never been to sea."

"But you live in LA!" I said.

"So?"

"Never mind."

"It's just that you're saying it like it's my fault I've never been out to sea just because I live in LA. Maybe you don't know this, but there are a lot of things to do in LA before you get to the sea (turns to throw up) and I just never got around to it, but it's not like it's a federal crime (turns to throw up) or it's my fault in any way, it's just a coincidence, and anyway (turns to throw up) maybe I'd get seasick anyway even if I had gone before, did you ever think of that?"

She slumped down, exhausted, into a seat.

Sienna paced and took drags from an imaginary

cigarette (e or regular, I wasn't sure). She looked dazed. Her makeup had finally worn off. It was weird to see her barefaced and her hair a mess.

Trevor leaned back in the swivel chair, eyes closed, drumming fingers at rest while we waited out the choppy seas, but now he opened one eye.

"I once did it with a chick on a raft," he said. "Not so easy."

Abigail was watching the sky and then staring out to the horizon.

"There's got to be a ship or a plane or some damn thing," Abigail said.

"Like I said," I told her. "We're not top priority."

"Well, maybe *you're* not top priority, but I consider myself pretty damn important."

"Great," I said. "The Abigail Navy will be here soon to pick you up."

The sun had brought out Abigail's freckles. Back in middle school, she had liked her freckles. Had gotten around to naming thirteen of them. She let me connect the freckles with a green Razor Point marker we thought was water-soluble. She found a picture of a spider on LSD web on the internet, and we used that as a pattern. I was very proud of my job, but when she tried to wash it off, the web stayed. Her mother flipped out, but Abigail took it well. She went to school with her face looking like a Just Say No to Drugs ad and people laughed at her, but she cared not. She had a best friend and a soccer dream, and life was good.

Now she caught me studying her face and ran her fingertip over her nose.

"What are you looking at?"

"Just the freckles," I said. "They're really starting to show."

"And your snakeskin is starting to turn red."

"And your hair," I said. "A total kinky mess."

She looked at me closely. "Ya know what? I know you used to be very proud about your nose, and I thought you should know. It looks a little crooked. Did it get hit by the roof, or is that where I punched you last year?"

My hands flew to my nose before I could stop myself. "My nose is *just fine*," I said, yanking away my hands.

Trevor took a big gulp of air and closed his mouth, and I was not sure if he was making a statement or what. But then he began thumping on his puffed cheeks and went back into his own world where he was drumming solo in front of the teeny-bopping whores whom he would later lure out to the alley, and I realized that Trevor and Hayley could start their own hellish band together and tour the country.

■ ■ ■

THE OCEAN GREW calm again, and we all quieted down, each to our own thoughts. That's something I had never learned about shipwrecked people, castaways, and generally people who had screwed up or been washed away and were now floating in some vast, lonely space. All the thinking they must do.

The other girls had collected under the dented sunshade to keep the bright rays off their faces. They spent a lot of time speculating over who had survived and who had not, who might still be out there clinging to something, and how lucky Nina Hanrahan was, because she'd pulled a tendon in drill team practice and stayed home from the party. They also went over every celebrity they could remember living in Malibu and even Venice, in case the wave stretched farther south. Once in a while, Sienna would burst into tears over the assumed fate of Madison, not the city in Wisconsin but the drunk. Abigail talked philosophically from time to time about the nature of fate, relating it somehow to the insemination of Brahman bulls, and Hayley responded with bursts of nonsense when she wasn't trying to pray her iPhone back to life.

Trevor lounged in the swivel chair, turning slowly with his shirt unbuttoned, exposing his tanned surfer dude chest, a shade very close to that of a Behr Premium Plus offering called Gobi Desert. I knew this because Abigail and I used to spend countless hours obsessing over which paint shade we were going to use on the inside of our solar-powered RV, in which we would ride around the country righting wrongs and rescuing strays while she demonstrated her soccer prowess to raise money for charities.

No one talked to me. It was shocking to me how fast cliques could re-form even on a lifeboat. Like wisteria vines, they could be cut and replanted and bloom their exclusive colors in some alien garden.

Nature was impressive.

Sometime in the early afternoon, Trevor said, "Hey, getting the munchies here, and I'm not even high, ya feel me?"

I went to get the crackers, but Abigail darted in front of me, grabbing them first.

"I'm in charge of food," she announced.

"Why are you in charge of food?" I asked.

"'Cause I'm the captain of this ship."

"You are captain of nothing, Abigail. But go ahead, if it means so much to you."

Abigail's bull-like domination of everything had once seemed curiously charming to me. But now it was just one of the many things that annoyed me about her.

Abigail got out the crackers. "Trevor," she said, "open the Spam."

Trevor stopped drumming and looked up. "I don't know what Spam is. Is it made from an animal with human-looking eyes? Because I don't eat anything if it has human-looking eyes."

"I don't know what varmint it's made from," Abigail said.

"Then I don't wanna eat it."

"Well, then you and Sienna can starve. That would leave more for us. We got to ration it. We only got two cans, and God knows how long we'll be floating around on this crate." She lifted up the gallon jug. "We got to go easy on the water, too."

"A gallon holds sixteen cups of water," I said. "That's a little more than three cups of water for each of us. And that might have to last awhile."

"How long is awhile?" Sienna asked. "I'm thinking we're gonna be rescued any minute."

"Seawater's not good to drink, right?" Hayley said.

Abigail was looking at Hayley's Fendi. "What have you got in that purse?" she asked.

Hayley started going through it. "My iPhone, two tubes of lipstick, two Kleenexes that are soaking wet, a pressed-powder compact . . ."

"Stop," I said.

"What?" asked Abigail impatiently.

"Let me see that compact."

"Why?" Hayley asked. But she handed it over.

I opened it, blew away the loose powder, and polished the mirror with my sleeve. I held the mirror to the light and watched it sparkle.

"So?" Sienna said.

"I saw this show on the Discovery Channel that said you can use a mirror to signal passing ships. It's much easier to see this over miles of water than our little boat. A ship might come and investigate. And then we can set off the flares."

Sienna sneered. Her nicotine withdrawal put an extra curl in her lip. "Useless," she said, meaning the compact and possibly me.

"Give me my compact back," Hayley said.

"No." I put the compact in my pocket. "It could save our lives."

"LISTEN!" Hayley shrieked, tears welling up. "I have been through so much and given up so much and so much has happened and I'm here on this stupid ocean in this stupid boat and I don't give a shit about your dumb Find Something Channel and you weren't invited anyway, why don't you just—"

She stopped talking and rushed at me, knocking me over onto the dried-out but still-stinky carpeting of the deck, and we struggled there, wrestling for the compact mirror as she screamed, "Give it to me! Give it to me!"

I felt someone grab my foot, possibly Sienna by the feel of her claws.

Hayley's crazy-eyed face was in mine, and she displayed surprising strength for a post-tsunami simpleton.

"Give it back!" she screamed.

Abigail stepped in and pulled us apart, also dislodging Sienna's talons in my foot. "Stop it, all of you. Break it up. Break it up." Her voice was loud and full of authority, and finally Hayley and I were extricated and faced off, huffing and puffing and glaring at each other.

"Let her keep the compact," Abigail told Hayley.

"What? Why are you taking her side? It's my compact and just because we're stranded out here doesn't mean I have to listen to some stupid girl and her science talk and there's something called property rights I think and I'm just saying—"

"Stop," Abigail said. "Sea Snake might have a point, for once."

"Thank you, Freckle Fish," I said.

"Don't call me that," Abigail growled.

Hayley looked crushed and Sienna shot me a look of

death and Trevor laughed, and that was that.

Our friendship was growing.

"What else is in your purse?" Abigail asked Hayley.

Hayley sighed, put-upon, and resumed her search through the open Fendi. ". . . a ballpoint pen, my dad's credit card—oh, God—he's going to kill me—a five-dollar bill, a lighter I was holding for Sienna, and a pair of toenail clippers with a built-in nail file."

Abigail considered the items.

"The credit card. Give it to me."

"Why?"

"We need something to slice the Spam."

"Gross," Hayley said.

Trevor did the honors, twisting the key around the side of the can and then carefully pulling off the top, leaving half a pink slab of potted meat glistening in the sun.

Hayley made a gagging sound. "Ewwwwww. That looks so horrible. I can't even tell you how horrible that looks. That can't be food. If I saw that on the street, it would look like someone threw up and the throw up was just like a block of—"

"Give me one of those Kleenexes," Abigail interrupted.

"They're wet."

"But they're clean, right?"

Abigail took the Kleenex and spread it out on the flat

area near where the engine used to be and laid the open can on its side on top of it and pressed the credit card into it, peeling off a thin slice with the skill of a surgeon. She took out one of the ancient crackers and handed it to Hayley with the slice of Spam. Hayley put the sad cracker/ Spam combo together and took a quick bite, making a face as though she'd just been forced to put on a belt that didn't match her shoes.

"Ugggg!"

She held out her tongue to reveal the shimmering wreckage of the cracker and the mass of deconstructed Spam, then the tongue slowly went back inside her mouth, and she swallowed with an exaggerated effort.

"Horrible." She gobbled down the rest and reached for the gallon of water.

"Just two swallows," Abigail warned.

Sienna, whose remarkable bravery about eating canned meat and stale crackers was an inspiration to us all, was next. Abigail gave me my Spam and cracker without comment. They weren't so bad. They tasted a bit like homework would taste if that homework would keep you from starving.

"Okay, Trevor," Abigail said, "eat the damn Spam and cracker. Forget about the eyes. It's all we've got."

Trevor stared at the food, deciding. I wondered if he'd

ever consider eating Hayley, whose round, flat eyes were more like those of a mackerel. Finally he took it and bolted it down.

Then Abigail at last took her turn.

"This is what leaders do," she announced. "Eat last."

I could only shake my head. Here she was, making sure she was boss, even on this rickety boat in the middle of nowhere. But I did recognize a certain irony: this was the first time I'd ever had lunch with the cool kids. And all it had taken was a devastating act of God.

Everyone got another cracker and another sliver of Spam, and that was it.

"Wait a second," said Sienna. "That's all we get? I'm still hungry."

"Oh, come on," said Abigail. "That's more than I've ever seen you eat."

She put the top of the Spam can on carefully and placed the container in one of the hatches. "None of you even think of sneaking in here. Anyone steals food, it's man overboard. Rules of the sea."

Sienna was giving me a long, hard look. Suddenly she pointed at me. "We'd have more food and water if it wasn't for her. Like Hayley said, she's not even supposed to be here. She crashed your party, Abigail."

"That's not true!" I protested. "I never wanted to go to her stupid illegal party in the first place. Croix invited me."

Before anyone could answer, Trevor let out a long laugh. It didn't end, just collapsed into smaller laughs that sounded like—if I remember right from that episode on Animal Planet—the tiny yips of a dingo pup.

"Croix did invite her," he said. "He told me he did."

I felt simultaneous pulses of relief and dread.

"Then why are you laughing?" I demanded.

He flipped his hair out of his eyes. "Because it was a bet."

"A bet?" A sinking feeling was forming in my stomach that had nothing to do with being marooned on a boat. "What kind of bet?" I insisted.

"There was a bet he couldn't get in your pants. And I guess he didn't, what with that big-ass wave and everything. Now we'll never know who would have won."

"That's not true!" I insisted. "He was a perfect gentleman. You're making that up!"

Trevor began to drum slowly on his legs. "He was just setting the trap, man. Like a rat sets a trap for . . . whatever rats eat."

"Shut up, Trevor," Abigail said. She actually looked a

little sorry for me. Amazingly enough, so did the other girls. "That was a mean thing for Croix to do," Sienna said.

Trevor shrugged.

"Yeah," said Hayley. "That was mean."

I really felt like crying, and I probably would have if my body's water supply wasn't busy just keeping me alive. I looked at Abigail. "Did you know about this?"

She shook her head.

"Then how do you know it's true?"

"'Cause I knew Croix. He was a dog."

The other girls nodded.

Everything was unraveling in me. Everything I thought I knew about Croix and gentlemen and luck and fate. I felt terribly humiliated. Now everything about that magical night fell into a different context. When he had smiled at me or laughed at my jokes, handed me a beer, it meant something else than I thought it had. And that almost kiss—that was just a strategy in Croix's ultimate goal to win a bet.

Perhaps the tsunami had come to save me.

The boat rocked gently, and there was silence for a few moments. Trevor didn't seem to notice all the trouble he'd caused. "Men are dogs," he said finally. "You can't take the dog out of the man. It's a lyric in one of our songs."

He began to drum and sing.

"You can't take the dog out of the man
You can't take the soup out of the can
You can't take the rice out of the bowl
You can't drink the Stoli you just stole.
You can't eat the doughnut without the hole . . ."

His voice trailed off, and he began to laugh that dingo pup yip of his, which grew in intensity until he began gasping and clutching his stomach. "Oh, my God, eating a hole, that gets me every time!" He collapsed on the deck, rolling around, still laughing, his open shirt revealing his tanned, hairless chest.

I had no idea how he'd managed to score cannabis on the high seas, but he wasn't helping.

"Croix was very nice on the outside, but he wasn't that good of a person," Sienna said. "He just pretended to be. He could fool you for a long time, but you can't fool people forever."

Trevor stopped laughing. He stared up at us, his expression turning hostile. He got to his feet. "You didn't know Croix. You didn't see him visit his grandmother every single week in the nursing home till she died. You didn't see him work that shitty job at the burger place to try to pay the bills after his dad left his mom. You didn't see him drive his little sister to school every day instead of riding with us because his mom had to work. Don't you judge him, you stupid bitches. Because that's what you stupid bitches do. You judge. Croix was a prince; now he's shit. Because, oh, my God, he tried to get in a girl's pants? No dude in history has ever done *that*."

We were all silent. This was the most I'd heard Trevor speak. I thought his psyche consisted of a drumbeat, a good wave, some high-grade weed, and a pair of fake boobs.

But Trevor wasn't done yet.

"That's the thing about guys that maybe you need to learn. We don't judge you. We accept who you are." He looked at Sienna. "You've got a great set of tits and you're a bitch, but I've seen you be nice a couple times and you're a good soccer player and that's cool." He looked at Abigail. "You've got a white-trash accent and no one knows why you're popular and you give great parties and that's cool." He looked at me. "You're weird and you use big words and I forgot your name and that's cool." He looked at Hayley. "You talk too much and you're pretty and that's cool. So shut up about Croix. He was good and bad and whatever, but he was Croix. He was Croix. He tried to save us. He loved his sister and his mother. And he was a dog. But he wasn't just a dog, goddamn it. He was my fucking friend, and now he's *dead*."

These last words came out as a sob, and we all just

stood there, stunned, as he turned and dove off the back of the boat with all his clothes on. We heard the splash of his pissed-off body, and we rushed over to see the roiling circle in the ocean where he disappeared.

Hayley turned to Sienna. "He said I was pretty."

We waited for him to come up for air. I imagined him crying underwater, his feet pointing toward the ocean floor, his hands over his eyes, concerned manta rays and gentle dorados approaching to bump his arms consolingly.

Finally he surfaced. He lay on his back in the calm sea, his face blank and his arms and legs moving slowly. I think he'd forgotten about us. He was alone with his thoughts and his grief and maybe with the lyrics of some new song his garage band could sing about Croix.

Abigail looked contemplative. When she spoke, her voice was oddly soft. "Men can let you down, Sea Snake. You of all people should know that."

A warm flush ran through me.

"Are you talking about my father?" I demanded.

Sienna and Hayley had both perked up.

"What about your father?"

Then it dawned on me.

"Oh, my God, Abigail," I said. "These are supposedly your best friends, and they don't even know."

■ ■ ■

TREVOR FINALLY CRAWLED back onto the boat, dripping wet, and sat down in his swivel chair and didn't say a word. Silently we watched the trickles of water run down his face and a stain spread out in the carpeting around his feet. I still believed that at least part of Croix's attention was real. Perhaps it had all started out on a bet, but either he had been the greatest actor in the world or something about me had charmed him. Anyway, I would never know for sure. It was another mystery in my life I could put next to the mystery of why loss is so sudden and so absolute.

"Abigail," I said, opening the compact, "I'm going to start signaling."

"Nah, I'll do it," Abigail said.

I should have known she'd take over.

"But first," she added, "I think we should take just a moment to remember our friends and say their names."

"Like a funeral?" Hayley asked.

"Yes. Like that."

Trevor raked his hands through his wet hair. "Croix Monroe," he said.

Abigail nodded as if in reverent approval. "Matt Riley."

"Audrey Curtis," Hayley said.

I noticed something over Hayley's shoulder way out on the horizon. I straightened my back and squinted.

Sienna took a deep, shaky breath and sobbed out the name. "Madison Cutler."

I stood up. "Ship!"

Abigail stared at me. "What?"

"Ship! Ship!"

Then we were all on our feet, jumping up and down, pointing. The ship was just a tiny, gray rectangle in the distance, but we were filled with a wild hope. Of course there was a ship. The ocean was full of ships. And of course we were going to be rescued. We lived in LA, the town of obvious resolution. Heroes were saved. Wrongs were righted. Sure, there would always be fires and floods and earthquakes and the threat of nuclear winter.

But a small band of characters you had grown to care for would always survive. And we were that small, chosen group. We were the ones still standing at the end of *Saving Private Ryan*. We were the ones the velociraptors of *Jurassic Park* did not end up having for dinner. We were the ones, at the end of *War of the Worlds*, who were left to start a new civilization.

Of course the ship would come.

Abigail grabbed the compact from my hand and held the mirror to the light, signaling frantically as the rest of us waved and shouted.

"We're over here!" Hayley shrieked.

We screamed ourselves hoarse. And yet the boat remained a gray rectangle on a giant blue page of a coffee table book called *Better Luck Next Time, Losers*.

"Damn it!" Trevor shouted. He opened the hatch and took out the signal flares and the gun. "Get out of my way!" he ordered us, taking a John Wayne stance and firing up in the air. We watched as the flare went off with a *whoosh*, shot up into the sky, and burst into an orange-and-red flash of fire.

We waited. The ship wasn't moving.

"It's hard to tell if it's coming this way," I said. "Let's just wait a little longer."

Trevor ignored me. He shot off another flare.

"Hold your horses, Trevor," Abigail ordered. "We only got one flare left."

"But it must see us!" Hayley insisted. "It must, it must!"

We clung to the rail, peering out into the distance, still waving and calling and hoping to bring the ship closer by sheer force of will.

But it was retreating. Growing smaller.

"No!" I said. "No, no!"

"Damn you, you stupid boat!" Trevor shouted. "You piece of shit!"

He grabbed the last signal flare.

"Trevor, don't!" Abigail hurled herself at him and tackled him. The rest of the girls piled on top of him, and we wrestled our wet friend over the flare, pinning down his arms. But Trevor gave a mighty effort and freed himself just long enough to point the flare gun at the sky and set it off. We stopped struggling and lay in a tangled heap with Trevor, looking up as the flare soared and burst.

Slowly, we picked ourselves up off the deck and looked over the rail.

The ship was gone.

"Well, that's that," said Abigail.

THE SUN SANK low in the sky on our first day at sea. We watched from different places in the boat, our gazes covering 360 degrees of empty sea. It was stunning, devastating, to watch it stretch out forever, confirming our solitude. It was strange to feel alone after four years of living in LA, where people were everywhere and impossible to escape. And yet, as the sea darkened, no one appeared. Abigail had signaled for a few hours and then, exhausted, finally surrendered the mirror to me. I was equally ineffective. We were going to spend another night as castaways.

My clothes were stiff and smelled like seawater and dead fish. My face felt dry and hot. And I was getting thirsty. We all were.

Abigail parceled out some more Spam and crackers, and then we passed the gallon jug around.

"Just two gulps," Abigail warned, watching Sienna very closely, no doubt realizing her penchant for selfishness.

"We should keep watch all night," I said. "Take turns."

"Okay," said Abigail. I was expecting her to challenge me, but she seemed subdued, tired.

"Crazy," Trevor murmured, shaking his head.

"What's crazy?" Hayley asked.

"This time yesterday, it was just a regular day. It was, what? Seven? Seven thirty? My mom had made me dinner, and I was hanging out in my room, getting high before the party."

"I had a fight with my sister last night," Sienna said. "It was so stupid. Over nothing."

She fell silent, and we each thought our own thoughts about how nice and orderly the world was twenty-four hours ago, like a row of pressed shirts encased in plastic at the dry cleaners.

This time yesterday Croix had filled up my head. He was in every thought. I had barely spoken at dinner although my mother had tried to engage me. Now I'd give anything to be able to go to her and tell her I was alive, that her world had not crumbled entirely, that Robert

128

Pathway was right to some extent and things you think are lost might just be under something else.

I knew she hadn't brushed her hair today. She could barely get that done on good days. Was she wandering the streets, the house? Bursting into tears at the sight of Sonny Boy curled up on my pillow? Of course my fate mattered not to Sunny Boy, unless my dead body happened to fall across his favorite shaft of afternoon sunlight on the upstairs carpet.

Trevor took the first shift of the night watch as the rest of us found places around the deck to arrange ourselves. My tongue was dry, but we had already drunk our rations for the day. I wanted to tell the others good night, but somehow it didn't seem appropriate. The expression was too familiar, too ordinary, not quite right to say to a group I didn't belong to on a salvaged boat in the middle of the sea.

The deck carpeting was wet against the back of my head. Stars crowded the skies, so absolutely crisp, like new crackers. My eyelids were heavy. I couldn't help but believe things would be put back in place. I pictured the water retreating from Malibu, the land drying, the dead being counted, the wrecked BMWs being towed to various body shops. And our parents, traumatized, clinging to hope and waiting for news. At what point would they give up on us, and have our funerals?

DIEZ

BACK IN MIDDLE SCHOOL, ABIGAIL AND I WERE OBSESSED with the science class pet, a parrot named Mr. Shriek. He was an odd-looking creature, with a blue head, a green body, yellow wings, and a tuft of green right above where his brow would be, if he had a brow. His feathers were slightly ruffled, as though someone had just pissed him off or held a blow dryer to his back. His eyes always looked vaguely startled, and his beak never completely closed. But his clawed feet were long and delicate—his best feature, in my opinion—and quite animated. He would lean back and lift a foot off his perch as though making some theatrical point.

Apparently Mr. Shriek was not that smart of a parrot, because he didn't know any words. And though Patrick Ryan would sneak in every afternoon and patiently teach him the dirtiest word he knew, Mr. Shriek could only get out a shrieking *FUHHHH!* sound that no one even recognized, despite Patrick's proud assurances that Mr. Shriek was indeed cursing.

Abigail and I felt terribly sorry for this ruffled, multicolored, stupid parrot, once proud and free, now locked in a cage, stared at and mocked by countless preteens, lacking the ability to defend himself verbally. We'd sneak in during lunch hour and visit him. He would lean in, and Abigail would reach her fingers inside his cage to stroke the side of his head.

"It's okay, Mr. Shriek," I'd say. "You are a beautiful bird. You just be you."

"FUHHHHHH! FUHHHHH!" His eyes would bulge, and he would lift one leg in the air.

"He's trying to talk, poor little winged varmint," Abigail said.

"I think he might be stupid."

"Maybe so. But even stupid birds have the right to blue sky."

Abigail was always saying cool things like that.

Right next to Mr. Shriek's cage was the window and

the prospect of freedom. A sky full of drifting clouds. Worlds unknown. A flock of lady birds somewhere, floating above some balmy island, waiting to greet him and worship him as their idiot god.

We couldn't stand it. The injustice of it all tore at our middle school hearts.

One day in spring when the sky above Los Angeles was a beautiful, evenly toned blue, Abigail watched the door while I opened Mr. Shriek's cage. I held out my finger, and Mr. Shriek walked onto it, gripping it with his long black nails, the warmth of his body spreading down over my knuckles.

"It's time to be free, Mr. Shriek," I whispered.

I opened the window, and Mr. Shriek took off into the world.

Abigail left her post at the door to join me, and together we watched him fly so far away that he became a murky stab of color, a darker blue patch in the sky. We both stood quietly, reveling in what we'd done for him. It was bird justice, and didn't that make for a better world?

I was just about to close the window when Abigail stopped me.

"Look up yonder." She pointed at the sky.

"What? I can't see anything."

But in a couple of seconds, I saw it too, and we could

only watch as Mr. Shriek flew back down, getting bigger and bigger until we stepped away to let him come through the open window and back into his cage, where he made himself at home, gripping his bar and shrugging at us.

"Mr. Shriek!" I said. "What's the matter? Don't you want to be free?"

Mr. Shriek stared at us with his bulging black eyes. *"FUUUUUH!"* he screamed. *"FUUUUUH! FUUUUUH!"*

We couldn't believe it. We let him escape this school where he was not free and where he didn't belong, and he flew right back into his same miserable life.

Abigail shook her head. "He's not the brightest parrot in the world, that's for sure."

I HAVE TO admit I was honored when Abigail chose me as her friend. It didn't happen right away. It came after a couple more escapes from gym class—once when she rubbed liquid soap in her eye and said she had accidentally stabbed herself with a pencil, and once when she dropped two Alka-Seltzers in a Diet Coke and drank it real fast to make herself throw up. True to Abigail's words, Ms. Hanson never questioned us. She did not care if we were sick or lying or whatever as long as her phone was all charged up and ready for James Cameron to call.

We were sitting outside on our favorite table in our gym clothes when Abigail said, "We're friends now."

"You mean, like just this minute we became friends?"

"Yep."

And that was that. I know it sounds ridiculous now, but Abigail made me feel like being her friend was something special and sacred, like having my birthday party inside Noah's Ark and eating cake off the hump of a camel. She was just that way.

My mom was very excited that I had made a friend. "That's wonderful, Denver. She sounds very nice." Then she said, a bit wistfully, "I need to make some friends, too."

When I first met Abigail's family, I expected a bunch of rednecks with Stetson hats and cattle prods singing Dwight Yoakam songs and doing the two-step. I was completely stunned to find that they were nothing like this at all. None of them had Texas accents. None of them wore boots. They spoke with perfect grammar. They were like every other family in LA. Only Abigail, it seemed, had taken that giant state and its way with words to heart.

Abigail's mother did ride a horse, but not a Texas kind of riding. More like a Pacific Palisades style. She had a toned body and a pretty face, thick lashes, high cheekbones, and short blond hair that was shaved high in the back and left longer in front. She had a palomino she kept in the stables at Will Rogers Park and rode in tournaments, so sometimes when I came over we found her wearing jodhpurs, and her little crop would be sitting on the counter ready to go, and she'd shake it for emphasis when she talked about how bad the traffic was or how she was sick of not having four seasons and wanted to move to Vermont. She also talked about something called "The Other Trail" a lot, which Abigail explained to me was a meditation retreat in Sedona run by a guy who had a sweat lodge in his backyard. But for someone who was so into meditation, Abigail's mother seemed kind of wound up about a lot of things. The height of the next-door neighbor's fence, for one thing.

"It's ten feet high. How do I know this? Because I measured it. It's only supposed to be nine feet. Why does this matter? Because of sunlight. My hydrangeas have never been as pink since that damn fence went up."

"What can I say?" Abigail told me. "She has periods when she's pretty cool with everything and then she starts complaining more and more about little stuff, and then my dad sends her off to Sedona to cram herself into a sweat lodge with all the other women who hate ten-foot fences, and the cycle repeats itself."

Abigail's lawyer dad had short, curly red hair and freckles and a beard he kept neatly trimmed. I thought he'd had Botox, because when he laughed, lines would form around his eyes but his forehead would never move. He was a nice enough man, although he said very little, and his mind always seemed to be somewhere else. Every time I saw him—even on the weekends—he was always wearing a suit.

Abigail had a little brother named Maxwell whom she hated for mysterious reasons. "I don't know," she'd said impatiently when I asked her. "He is evil and has many faults. Too many to mention, so just be glad you're an only child."

I didn't get why Abigail was so Texan and her family wasn't. "Oh," her mother said one day to me, "we were only there for three years, and I couldn't wait to get out of the place. So much humidity, and utilities were *ridiculous*. But Abigail really identified with Texas. You know Abigail. She goes a bit too far with things."

AS WE MOVED into the fall season, which LA did not acknowledge with a change in weather, I found myself Skyping my friends in Wisconsin less and less. They lived in a different world. A world where leaves turn colors and are raked into piles, and fathers crowd the televisions, obsessed with the fate of the Green Bay Packers. I continued on in

T-shirts as my friends to the east transitioned to sweaters and then coats. We tried to talk about the kids from my old school, but it didn't seem to matter anymore.

"You've got to keep the friendship going," said positive, pink-toned Jessica. "We'll be friends forever, right?"

"Right," I said.

But really, by that point, it was all about Abigail. We made a good team. I was consumed with learning about every little thing, no matter how seemingly mundane, on the chance that it might matter someday. Abigail was the master of the grand plan, but she hadn't bothered to learn much, as she was so busy sketching out her ten-point steps for soccer stardom. (Ex., *Beat old personal best record in fifty-yard dash. Practice kicking on the laces. Do balancing exercises.*)

We were happy. Absolutely content with each other's company. Abigail came to my house once or twice, but mostly I went to hers, which was nicer and had more cool things, including a swimming pool and a small balcony outside her bedroom whose rail we could use to climb up onto the roof and watch the exclusive Palisades world unfold below us, the beautiful lawns and the too-bright flowers and the swing sets and the biggest play houses I had ever seen.

"Look," Abigail said, sweeping her arm to the left. "It's

the ten-foot fence that puts my mother in the sweat lodge once a year. I don't really mind it so much myself. Gives us more privacy."

Abigail's bedroom was covered with posters of famous women soccer players. She made me watch endless videos of Mia Hamm, her idol.

"She's a forward," Abigail told me. "That's what I'm gonna be. She scored the most goals in soccer history. What a badass."

I spent hours kicking a soccer ball to Abigail, helping her practice her one-touch passes, shooting form, juggling, and figure eights. I wasn't that interested in soccer myself, but I was ready to be the good friend and help her attain her life's ambition. I noticed that Abigail wasn't very coordinated at all, and most of the balls she kicked went into the pool rather than the homemade soccer goal constructed from the cinder blocks her pale father had laboriously hauled in from Home Depot and set up for her near the back fence.

"You suck," Maxwell would announce, watching from the porch.

"No, you suck!" she'd shriek back at her tormentor, but then he'd cross his arms and stand there, staring at her, until she'd finally get unnerved enough to go fetch her mother.

"Little agger-vatin' son a bitch," Abigail muttered. "Brothers and dreams don't match up. They're like rain and suede."

We had two classes together in school—science and gym—and we met in the hallways after class and ate lunch together in a cafeteria that had not yet stratified into the social haves and have-nots. Back then, table space was on a first-come, first-serve basis. There were girls who you could tell would someday rule high school—like Sienna and Madison—but at the time, we barely noticed them.

One day in December I realized I hadn't Skyped my Wisconsin friends in three weeks, and they hadn't contacted me, either. They were there, and I was here. They were outside the Sphere of Abigail, and I was within it. They were not dead to me as Abigail had predicted, but they weren't quite alive, either. They had their coats on somewhere. Snow was falling.

And I was wearing shorts.

GYM CLASS WAS proceeding without much drama, with Abigail and me in the bottom twenty-five percent who failed everything from spiking a volleyball to throwing a basketball into a hoop to doing a cartwheel, and Sienna Martin continuing to exceed at everything, including kissing Ms. Hanson's ass. Apparently Sienna was the only person in class deranged enough to think Ms. Hanson was really going to make it in Hollywood and had some equally deranged idea her narcissistic gym coach would then be happy to open doors for her. We couldn't imagine Sienna had any acting ability, but she could put her natural bitchiness to good use in a reality show called *My Useless and Delusional, Smug Life*.

"We'll pitch it to Lifetime," Abigail said. "Everybody wins."

In early February, the Great Rope-Climbing Campaign of Swing Tits began, a regime of terror and dread, where gravity became a subject awkward girls were doomed to fail.

Fail we did, over and over, and we had company, although of course Sienna hauled her stick body right up that knotty rope. We shouldn't have cared. But Abigail and I wanted to climb it. We wanted to do it because it could be done, and if it could be done, why couldn't we do it?

"We need a plan," Abigail said. "Stage one, the will. We've got that. Stage two, greater upper-arm and leg strength."

"Pilates?" I asked. "Don't make me do Pilates."

"Nah. We'll go traditional. And we need to do brain exercises, too. Picture ourselves climbing it easy-peasy." She closed her eyes. "I'm climbing it now. It's so easy, like hating my little brother. I can feel the rope in my hands. I can feel myself rising. My body suddenly is light as a feather. And now I'm at the top. And now I'm letting go. I'm falling on top of Sienna. Crushing her as Swing Tits screams."

"That's beautiful," I said.

She opened her eyes. "Now you try it."

"You know what?" I said after a month of summit attempts. "We're not meant for climbing that stupid rope. And what's the point, anyway? Is the world out there full of knotty ropes you have to climb? Do you have to climb one to drive a car? Get a credit card? Go to heaven?"

Abigail gave me her half-smile-and-nose-twitch combo that signaled disapproval. "Aren't you the one who said you need to learn everything, on the chance that something could be important?"

"I changed my mind. There is nothing about this stupid rope that could ever be important in any way."

"You've taught me lots of stuff, like big, important words I'll never use and highfalutin grammar. And that you just never know what might come in handy someday."

"I'll take my chances."

"Nah, don't give up. That rope is what you call a metaphor."

"For what?"

"For something we want to do but can't yet. But we will someday. We just can't give up."

There was one girl who was even more hopeless at climbing the rope than we were. Her name was Stephanie Caldwell, and she was one of those miserable, overweight, dejected-looking girls who are scattered through this land, populating gym classes from LA to Pittsburgh and beyond. Surely there are Stephanie Caldwells in Russia, Denmark, and Uganda, and their purpose is to make everyone else feel superior and sad. Her inner life meant nothing to us: whether she stepped on spiders or let them go, or if she liked frozen yogurt or had a natural sense of direction or sang into a hairbrush. We didn't care. She was a type, there for a Hollywood script to find and usher in the captain of some mythical football team who would love her for her heart. Some talent agent who would hear her sad, mournful song in some lonely park and make her into a world-famous pop sensation. But for now she was Stephanie Caldwell who couldn't climb the rope.

She'd take a few great lungfuls of breath, as though preparing to go underwater, then grab the rope and take a little hop, briefly positioning herself on the first knot before falling flat on the mat with a terrible thump while Ms. Hanson sighed and the other girls looked on, stone-faced.

One time Abigail caught Sienna smiling, moved over close to her, and whispered, "What's so funny?"

Sienna's lip curled. "Nothing. Mind your own business," she said, and then Ms. Hanson said, "Less talking, more climbing," and broke them up. But before they moved away from each other, Abigail whispered to Sienna, "You laugh at her again, and I'll punch you in the face."

We kept trying to climb that bastardly rope, symbol of everything wrong with school and LA and the world. The knots were only there to taunt us, pretending to give us an advantage. Abigail made me call them "why knots." She said this would encourage us. Something about rope and girl still would not communicate. But we were inching higher and higher.

Meanwhile, Ms. Hanson got an audition. She wouldn't say what it was, but the first week in March she was on a high so high she completely neglected us, her day job, these students that she would jettison and forget in a second for the right role. Or any role. Nevertheless, her excitement was contagious. The glow on her face was hard to resist, and we cheered her on.

She was absent one Wednesday on a trumped-up medical emergency we knew meant "possible sitcom." We got a substitute who was a monster at volleyball and whose boobs didn't move when she jumped for the spike. She had gray eyes and a square jaw and a faint, blond mustache.

"I will suffer no bullshit!" she'd scream for no reason before making us do laps.

Abigail and I found her refreshing.

"I bet she traps feral cats and then sedates them and spays them herself in a lab in the basement, for the good of the community," I said.

The next day Ms. Hanson was back and full of hope. The audition had gone well. She had a callback on Saturday. She smiled at us, was nice to us, remembering at least half our names. If all went well, she could forget us by Sunday.

Monday morning she came in with a blank and distant stare. They had given the part to another woman, a younger woman. Someone without even half her talent. Someone who was not funny, had not memorized her lines, and did not have that special charisma that everyone had noticed all of Ms. Hanson's life, from her sixth-grade drama teacher on. She was too depressed to lead the class and so we spent the time making a big poster out of glue and different colors of glitter that said WE BELIEVE IN YOU, MS. HANSON, which we did not, as she slumped on the bench, staring at her cell phone.

The next day she was back and ready to be an angry, discontented bitch again. It was rope-climbing time, and damn it if we weren't all going to climb it, because life was full of ups and downs (i.e., her disastrous tryout), but the best of us (i.e., she) would overcome adversity (i.e., her shitty job as a gym teacher) to triumph (i.e., forget us all).

Sienna dominated the rope easily, as did a few of the others. Then it was Stephanie Caldwell's turn. She did her usual halfhearted routine and then gave up with a heavy sigh.

"No," Ms. Hanson said. "Do it again."

Stephanie Caldwell looked at her in surprise. This was not the routine. The routine was: try, fail, and then slink back to the shadows. We all exchanged glances, because Ms. Hanson had an edge to her voice, an edge meant to cut the flesh of chubby girls, and it made us all feel a bit nervous.

"Again?" Stephanie Caldwell asked. I don't remember her ever speaking before. Her voice was faint, uncertain.

"Do it again. You can't just quit, Jennifer."

"Jennifer?" I whispered to Abigail. "She's not even close."

Stephanie looked to the rest of us as if we could do anything about her situation. She grabbed the rope again and tried to climb it. Cords stood out in her neck. Her arms shook. She made it up two feet and then she let go, landing in a heap on the ground.

And this is when you quit. This is when you call it a day. This is when you realize that you are perhaps not cut out for the rope, that you have other things to give the world besides the red, ugly stripes on your palms.

But Ms. Hanson wasn't buying it. Hollywood had been cruel to her, so she was going to take it out on Stephanie.

"Again!" she barked. "Again!"

"Really?" Stephanie asked in a whisper. Her eyes were red. Tears welled and began to fall down her face, and we all cringed a little.

"I don't feel sorry for you, Jennifer," Ms. Hanson said, repeating the same speech Hollywood had given her. "And you shouldn't feel sorry for yourself just because you're overweight."

An audible gasp went through the room. Swing Tits had gone there.

"Now get up and get back on that rope!" she ordered.

"I can't," Stephanie said, and now she crossed the line into ugly crying, the kind you see on babies. A line of spit formed an unclimbable thread from her upper lip to her lower. Her face crumpled up, and she began to sob. "I can't I can't I can't!"

"Leave her alone, Ms. Hanson." I turned around to find the idiot in the gym who had dared challenge this moody Hollywood also-ran and found it was myself. "Who cares if she climbs this stupid rope? It's all bullshit, anyway." I was horrified at my words, yet I couldn't shut up. "You're just being mean to her because your audition didn't work out, and that's bullshit, too."

Stephanie gaped up at me, openmouthed, her saliva rope broken by the shock of it all.

Ms. Hanson seemed shocked herself. Her eyes burned. "What did you say to me?" she asked as a murmur rippled through the throng of girls.

Before I had a chance to answer, Abigail appeared at my side. I had forgotten about her for a second, but suddenly, as Stephanie crawled away, there she was.

"Ms. Hanson," she said. "I'm awful sorry about my friend. She did not mean to be so rude. She was kicked by a milk cow in Wisconsin when she was eight years old, and it kind of tilted her brain all catty-whumpus. I would like to volunteer to climb this rope for Stephanie."

"There are no substit—" Ms. Hanson began, her world collapsing, little gym bitches being sassy to her and James Cameron turning his camera on someone else. But Abigail had already taken the rope and started climbing, and suddenly the drama went vertical again.

We all stood watching as Abigail struggled up past her last high-water mark and kept inching upward, not effortlessly like Sienna, but huffing and puffing and turning red as she paused to look down at me and see my encouraging thumbs-up.

"I'm coming, Abigail!" I shouted. I ran to the rope and began to climb it too.

"Get down here, both of you!" Ms. Hanson protested.

But we paid no attention. We inched up the rope, determined to succeed for Stephanie and every single Stephanie in the world.

I was sweating. My hands and shoulders ached. But I kept going, inspired by the efforts of my friend, who huffed and puffed above me.

Abigail reached the top first. She looked down.

"Come on, Denver!" she called to me. "You can do this! Easy-peasy!"

Ms. Hanson had abandoned her efforts to stop us and was staring up at us, arms crossed, wearing a furious expression.

I kept inching toward Abigail, who was anchored at the top, waiting for me. "Ya got this, cowgirl!" she called. "You got it, you got it, you got it. . . ."

Suddenly I was there. At the top. The class broke into a cheer. Abigail and I let one hand go of the rope long enough to high-five each other.

"Get down here," Ms. Hanson called up crossly as we

clung together, looking down at the class. "It was not your turn."

But Abigail wasn't done. Maybe it would have been better if she had been. She took something out of the waistband of her shorts and held it out so everyone could see it.

My stomach lurched.

I looked down at the bench. Ms. Hanson's cell phone was gone.

"Is that my phone?" Ms. Hanson demanded, her voice rising into a shriek.

"Call from James Cameron!" Abigail announced, her distinct drawl carrying through the gym.

"Abigail," I whispered. "What are you doing?"

She just smiled.

"You give that phone back to me!" Ms. Hanson shouted.

Abigail looked down at her. "You want it? You want it?" she taunted.

"GIVE ME BACK THAT PHONE RIGHT NOW!"

"Sure," she said, "I'll give it to you, since that's all you care about. You sure don't care about being no gym teacher, that's for damn sure." She threw the phone as far as she could. It soared and fell in slow motion, Ms. Hanson diving for it, but too late. Gravity sucked it down,

149

completing the betrayal, and it hit the gym floor and shattered. I heard the entire gymnasium draw a collective breath as time stopped and everyone froze in place, staring at that useless phone.

"Maybe we should just live up here," I whispered.

The aftermath? Not good. Abigail was suspended for a week, and I was given five hours of detention for swearing at a teacher, even though, if you wanted to get technical about it, I was swearing at a rope.

"Are you in a lot of trouble?" I asked Abigail over the phone.

"My parents are stirred up good. On the one hand, they are proud that I took up for 'the fat girl,' as my ma calls poor Stephanie. But my daddy the lawyer says I was legally at fault, and 'willful cell phone destruction is actionable.' That's a quote straight from him. Legal bullshit. My mother is headed for Sedona next month. The neighbors have a really loud lawnmower man, and our property taxes went up, and I suppose this was a rope too far."

The shop teacher, Mr. Crower, was in charge of my detention class. His feet were up on the desk, and he was reading a book with a bare-chested Jim Morrison on the cover. I walked in, and a bunch of loser-weirdo-criminal types looked up at me. I dropped the detention form on Mr. Crower's desk.

"I'm not supposed to be here," I announced.

He glanced up from his book and read my detention slip.

"Says here you are."

"I'm a political prisoner. I'm not like these people. I was protesting the treatment of a member of our society who—"

"Sit down."

I found an empty desk as the losers continued to stare at me. The guy across from me, who had sideburns and a yellow tooth, leaned over and said, "You think you're better than us, don't you?"

"Yes, I do. All I did was say 'Bullshit,' and you probably blew up a bus, so leave me alone."

OUR PARENTS HAD met once, on a Saturday when my parents had dropped me off at Abigail's house. But now, of course, they had to schedule a dinner to talk about what delinquents their two daughters were and figure out which one was the bad influence on the other. The four of them hit it off and started going to each other's houses and playing cards. But that was only the beginning of a much less happy story. Like an earthquake that shakes the coast. And you think it's over, but it's not over and the wave it causes just keeps coming and coming and coming.

ONCE

thing in the sky. I jerked my head up and moved the compact around, flicking my wrist frantically.

"Do you hear that?" I asked Abigail.

"No."

"Listen."

Then it came into view. "Look!" I shouted, pointing. "It's a plane!"

It was very high up there, in between the clouds, but we were all full of hope despite being abandoned by the ship. I continued to signal some desperate code of sun and mirror that was meant to say, "WE'RE DYING

DOWN HERE," as my companions waved their arms and shouted.

But the plane kept going higher and higher until it disappeared into the clouds.

I slumped, defeated, into one of the seats at the back of the boat.

"That mirror thing didn't work," Hayley said accusingly. "Again."

"Yes, I think we can all agree on that," I said. "Thank you, though, Hayley, for pointing that out."

"The plane was too high," Trevor said helpfully. His fingers went up to his tanned chest, but he was too languid to drum and let his hands fall back down into his lap. "We're screwed, man, screwed."

"Well, I don't know about you guys, but I'm not going to die without a fight," I said. "I'm going to keep trying to live."

Abigail's face was a bright red, and all her freckles were back, including backup freckles I'd never seen before, freckles that had lurked beneath the surface for years, little understudies waiting for the stage. The wind and sun had done terrible things to her hair. Her eyelashes were crusty, her lips dry.

"Well, I'm gonna live too," she said. "I just don't rightly have a plan this exact minute."

"Well, I do," I announced, as Abigail gave me the evil eye. "Everyone look away."

"Why?" asked Sienna.

"Never mind." I went to the other side of the boat, turned toward the sea, and took off my shirt.

The warm sea air hit the bare skin of my arms and belly. I took off my bra.

"Dude," Trevor said. But then he resumed his drumming and the others fell silent, waiting to see whether or not I had gone mad.

It was an old underwire bra I never wore unless I wanted my boobs to look perky. It was the one I had chosen for the fateful meeting with Croix at the Malibu house, and it had served me well.

I put my shirt back on. Then I ripped at the fabric of my bra with my teeth.

"She's eating her bra!" Hayley cried, and I wanted to turn around and remind her she was an idiot, but decided that would be a waste of energy. I wrestled with the wire on one of the cups, savagely bending it back and forth until I could finally separate the wire from the fabric. I began working the wire into the shape of a hook. Finally I turned back around and showed it to my fellow voyagers.

"What is that?" Sienna asked.

"It's a fishhook. Or it will be when I'm finished."

"What are you going to use as bait?" Trevor asked.

"Spam."

"But we need to save the Spam!" Hayley cried. "Abigail, don't let her use up our Spam supply."

I gave Hayley a withering stare. "I'll use a piece of mine."

Abigail was watching me. Processing everything. "Hell, let her try," she said at last. "Unless you got a better idea."

"Hayley," I said. "I need your nail clippers."

"Give her the nail clippers," Abigail said.

Hayley didn't even argue this time. She fished around in her purse and handed them over. I used the nail file part as a tool to bend the wire and completed the process with my back molars, grimacing with the effort and feeling like my enamel would crack any minute. But finally the wire bent double, and I had a crude loop through which to run a string.

I sat down, put the other end of the wire against the metal side of the boat, and pressed down hard, laboriously scraping the tip of the wire back and forth. The others were quiet, intrigued. Even Trevor stopped drumming. It was peaceful work for someone who didn't know what she was doing, and I imagined that's how midwives must feel their first time around. Just faking everything, pretending to be in charge.

Ten minutes later I had a point that felt sharp against my fingertip. I looked around for some line.

"Give me the rope," I said.

"I have a question," Hayley said, almost sounding polite.

"Yes?"

"What's the use of catching a fish if we run out of water?"

"Fish have water in their bodies," I explained. "Next to the spine, and in the eyes. Might buy us some time."

"Discovery Channel?" she asked, breathing the words.

"*National Geographic.*"

Abigail handed me the rope. I unraveled a few strands of it and used Hayley's clippers to cut them at a length of about five feet. I twisted the strands carefully. They kept unraveling, and I had to start over again. Finally I had what looked like a long piece of string having a very bad hair day. I forced the string through the hook I had fashioned and tied a quadruple knot in it.

"Dude," Trevor said, "you could have used this." He reached into his pocket and drew out a pocketknife.

"You have a pocketknife?" Abigail snapped. "Give me

that! You're a jackass, Trevor."

He handed over his knife and shrugged. "No one asked."

Hayley already had a tiny piece of Spam cut and waiting for me. She handed it to me with a look that didn't necessarily mean anything.

"I don't want to suck a fish eye," Sienna said.

"I'll bait the hook," Abigail offered. "I used to catch catfish out of a pond in Texas. I was a pro."

"Fine," I said. "Bait it."

I lowered the baited hook over the side of the boat into the water, wrapping the other end of it around my wrist. The others crowded around me, watching. Trevor moved in so close to me I could smell his underarms where the Old Spice deodorant had jumped ship long ago.

I waited for what seemed like an hour. The others moved away, bored, and started talking among themselves. My arm ached and then went numb. I felt my breasts falling forward now that their underwire support was tempting some unseen fish in the ocean depths. The sun was hot on the back of my neck.

At last I felt a tug. Then a distinct, hard pull, so hard it almost drew me down into the water.

"I got something!" I shouted.

"No shit?" Abigail cried.

"Help me! This thing weighs a ton!" Trevor reached

down and grabbed the line just below where I had it, and the two of us struggled together.

"Damn, that's a big fish!" he exclaimed.

Slowly we dragged in the line as sweat poured down our faces and the others urged us on.

A giant fish head came out of the water, mouth gaping open and the hook stuck inside it. Its eyes bulged. It shook itself, and suddenly the line went slack.

We pulled the line out of the water, and there was no bait left, no hook either, just a few rope strands unraveling in the sunlight.

I heard the collective sigh behind me, the auditory equivalent of the empty weight in my hands, that tactile, real, perfect defeat, that sinking heart of a moment. Suddenly I was so angry at that fish that I wanted to smash in its face. And I was going in after it.

Nobody had time to stop me. I dove off the back of the boat into the shocking chill of the water and down under the sea, my bare feet kicking, my arms moving, my teeth clenched behind my closed lips, my blood boiling.

I was looking for that fish.

That was my fish, my reward for learning and trying and caring more than the others. For my ingenuity and craftsmanship and grit.

Underneath the sea, the water was surprisingly clear. I saw pools of fish around me, little stripes on them, blue and red, beautiful and just out of reach.

I took a swipe at them, causing them to scatter, but still I swam farther down until I ran out of breath and my lungs felt tight, leaving me no choice but to rise, kicking my feet, following the sunlight that shimmered on the water and pointed the way back to temporary survival. I kicked harder as I swam upward, my lungs aching and crying out for air. Panic taking hold of me, until finally I broke the surface and took a deep, angry, jagged breath as the others watched, mouths agape, from the back of the boat.

"Hey!" Abigail shouted. "Get back in the boat!"

"Dude!" Trevor called. "You'll drown!"

Even Sienna and Hayley were gesturing at me as though mine was a life worth saving. Finally I began making my way back to the boat, my strokes still strong despite two days of Spam and crackers.

I reached the ladder and began hoisting myself up. Trevor and Abigail caught my arms and hauled me aboard, where I collapsed in a heap on the deck, breathing heavily, water running off my hair and clothes and soaking into the rotted carpeting.

"See him?" Hayley asked.

I was too exhausted to answer her or even sign the word *idiot*. After several moments, I caught my breath and managed to make it onto one of the back seats. I moved my wet hair out of my face but said nothing. I felt angrier than I remember ever being, but I wasn't sure at what exactly. There were so many potential targets for my rage: God, tsunamis, the sea, cool kids, underwire bras, fathers, ex-best friends. And the music of Nickelback.

"Well, dude," Trevor said. "You tried."

"Yes," Sienna said with surprising kindness. "You tried."

Hayley wiped her eyes. "That was the bravest thing I ever saw. Braver than when Jennifer Gilmore had eczema all over her face, but she still tried out for drill team."

I felt moved by their reaction. Surprised by it, too. I'd expected to be scorned. Called stupid for trying. But I was a tiny, fractional bit of a hero. I looked at Abigail and saw grudging respect on her face.

"Yeah, well, you almost got that slippery bastard," she said. "Ya came real close, anyway."

I couldn't help basking in her words. But I was too tired to enjoy the moment for very long. I sank down on the deck, lay back against the carpeting, and fell asleep in my wet clothes.

■ ■ ■

WE SAW NO more boats or planes that day. Just ocean, end-less sea, there to taunt us with fish that we couldn't catch and water we couldn't drink. The gallon jug was getting lighter, and we cut our rations to smaller gulps. The Spam was salty and worsened our thirst, but it was the only food we had. A seaworthy misery had begun to set in. That feeling of being helpless with nothing to hold on to, tired, salt encrusted, sunburned. We had no idea how far we'd drifted, but the initial relief at surviving the tsunami was ebbing, and the water level in that jug was as scary as a monster. My tongue felt swollen and my eyeballs dry. But the few clouds overhead were fluffy and white and had nothing to give.

That night Abigail took first watch as the stars came out in the sky. One by one, we lay down on the deck to sleep. Hayley inched over toward me until we were lying face-to-face.

"You were brave today," she whispered. "I wish I was brave and knew how to do things and had all this knowl-edge like you do and it just goes to show sometimes you don't really know about a person that you ignore 'cause you don't know them and they're not in your group and then a tsunami comes and washes you out to sea and you discover something about that person. . . ."

"Thank you," I answered. I wondered if Hayley were whispering to me to avoid being heard associating with a non-cool kid, but that wasn't the reason, after all.

"Do you think we'll survive?" she asked.

I thought about this. In truth, I didn't know. But she looked so desperate that I said, "Sure we will. I mean, we made it this far, didn't we?"

Maybe it was a trick of the moonlight, but her eyes looked haunted. Less fish now, more mammal. Something warm-blooded that feels pain and fear and grief.

"I'm sorry," she said, keeping her voice low.

"Sorry about what?"

She tried to wet her lips, but her tongue no longer held moisture. "Remember when Sienna said that you shouldn't have lived?"

"Yes, I seem to recall that."

"Well, that was an awful thing for her to say. And I agreed with her, and that was awful, too. You're a good person and you deserve to live, same as anyone else, even if you're kind of a traitor."

"I'm not a traitor!" I protested.

"But you ruined Abigail's reputation and made her the laughingstock of the school!"

"You don't know the whole story." I started to pull

away, but suddenly she gripped my arm and drew me close to her, so close that her lips were inches from mine. She had a tormented look on her face. "I don't blame you so much for that. Really, I don't. And about what Sienna said? I'm the one who should die. I'm a bad person."

"No, you're not, Hayley," I tried to protest.

"Yes, I am." Her whisper caught in her throat. "I've done terrible things, Denver. Terrible things."

DOCE

OUR THIRD DAY AT SEA BEGAN WITHOUT INCIDENT BUT quickly went south. We got up, reality set in, we divided our rations and passed around the jug, arguing a bit more loudly over the difference between a sip and a drink and a gulp and whatever. . . . The water wouldn't last, and the fact was a fact.

Abigail and I volunteered to watch for boats and planes. She looked out one way and I looked out the other, while Trevor sat drumming on himself in his swivel chair and Hayley and Sienna took shelter under the sunshade. I flashed my mirror and let my thoughts drift as my tired eyes looked for something out there in the shape of a rescue. Below us was the natural habitat of fish and sharks and whales. Frantic thoughts were reserved for above the waterline, where five exhausted teenagers struggled through another day. If only to be a little fish, moving naked through the cool sea. I imagined them in those peaceful depths, so much like LA, no change in seasons, just one day after the other, their gills moving slowly, their eyes blank, empty of the concerns of linear time.

Oh to be like those— *Splash.*

Splash? It took a moment for my groggy daydream to twist and turn like a Rubik's Cube until it had reconfigured into a panic. That splash was substantial, ominous.

"Hayley fell overboard!" Sienna cried. "She was on the rail trying to adjust the—"

Abigail and I were still blinking when Trevor dove overboard after her. We rushed to the rail and watched as he swam toward Hayley, who floundered a few yards from the bow.

"I'm goin' in," Abigail said.

"No," I said. "Just wait."

"Hell with that. Git out of my way."

But just then Trevor reached Hayley, and she grabbed him by his wet hair and pulled so hard he winced in pain.

"Hayley, let him go!" Abigail shouted.

But she was fighting him, grabbing on to him and

trying to pull him under in her panic. Finally Trevor got behind her and put his arm around her neck. I could see him talking to her and even hear his soothing voice, but he was too far away for me to understand what he was saying. Probably reciting some lyrics designed to make teen girls lose their motor skills so he could drag them out into the alleyway, or rescue them from drowning.

Trevor tugged Hayley to the back of the boat, and Abigail and I reached down and pulled her to safety, while useless Sienna did nothing as usual except chatter excitedly about how terrifying it felt to watch her friend plunge overboard and how glad she was that Hayley wasn't dead.

We laid Hayley down on the deck and helped her sit up as she coughed and sputtered and gasped. Trevor crawled up the ladder and joined us in the boat, sinking to his knees in front of Hayley, who reached up and grabbed him and pulled him down to her. The two of them lay gasping for air on the deck. Finally they pulled apart, and the drama was over.

"You saved my life," Hayley told Trevor.

"Nah," he said.

That was it as far as excitement went for the day, unless you count hunger and thirst and desperation as action-movie fare.

We watched, and no one came. Not even a far-distant

ship or plane that was only appearing to tease us.

The last of the Spam would be gone by nightfall. Soon the water would be gone, too.

"Can't you think of something?" Hayley pleaded to me. "You're smart. You know things."

"Hey," Abigail said. "I know things too." But her voice was weaker, less obnoxious. "I just wish I could think of some of 'em now."

"I don't know how to invent fresh water," I said. "I wish I did." My tone was not sarcastic. It was gentle, regretful. I wished I did know how to make water appear like a magician. I would have traded that for any other trick in the world. The desire for water trumped even my hunger pains. All I wanted was a drink. All I imagined were cool, running faucets and waterfalls. Showers and rivers and geysers. Aquariums. The dripping of icicles.

And grapes. A handful of grapes in my hand right from the refrigerator, the seedless kind that take no effort. Green, fleshy, watery grapes. Peaches, oranges, Slurpees from 7-Eleven. I tortured myself with that last thought and then I said the word out loud.

"Slurpee," I said.

"Oh, God," said Hayley. "Slurpee."

"Beer," said Trevor. "Right out of the cooler, poured down my throat."

"Kool-Aid," Sienna murmured. "I used to like the orange kind when I was a kid."

"Milk shakes," said Hayley, and we kept going, a round-robin of imaginative torture. As we imagined this gallery of liquids, we were only too aware that there existed vast amounts of water beneath us, cruel, undrinkable, spreading out for miles and miles until it hit the rocks of islands we would never find.

"Ya'll stop it," Abigail said all of a sudden.

"Stop what?" I asked.

"Talking about cold liquid stuff. You're just making it worse. So stuff a cork in it."

Her face and arms had begun to blister and peel. All her freckles were present and accounted for. Her body had no more freckles to give. It seemed to me that the others on the boat had warmed up to me a little, but Abigail, while not as unfriendly as she'd been at first, remained distant. And even within the context of our dire straits, this made me sad. If an act of God and the prospect of dying couldn't bring us back together, what in the world could?

We all took turns under the shade, where three people could fit at once. We divided up according to what was fair, not who was who, and I thought, *Wouldn't it be great if every high school were drained of water, and all people were equal, all just trying to survive, just looking for a ship or a boat or a cloud full of rain?*

Trevor wouldn't sit under the shade.

"I'm a man" was all he said as he sat drumming in his swivel chair, his shirt open and the sun darkening the bare skin of his chest. If he felt like a hero for rescuing Hayley, it didn't show on his face. He seemed to have adapted to the vast, unknown jam session of fate and luck and circumstance, and was nodding his head to its beat. I wished I could be more like him, calm and seemingly unconcerned, because the terror in me was beginning to rise. That ever-growing prospect of dying out here on the endless sea.

Sienna thought she saw a boat, but it was nothing. Hayley thought she heard a helicopter, but the sky was empty. Abigail saw something dart across the boat and gasped, but it was a ghost that only she could see.

The day hours went on and on. The sky was a teal blue, the color of time running out. Clouds did not come with gifts of water. The rain poured only as a dream. The sun went down, and the stars came out, and the moon was waning like the water in the jug. Abigail settled down in the bow of the boat, holding the water jug in her arms like a baby, protecting it from some thirst-maddened thief who might grab it and drink it all during the night.

Sienna had first watch and so I lay down and looked at the stars and tried to sleep, but the night was warm, and my mind kept going back to cool things, wet things. Lemonade, shadows, drawn curtains. A coconut leaking milk. I imagined holding a candle to a snowman and drinking his face as it melted. I'd drink anything. Oil, syrup, the green blood of a moth. Cyanide tea, slaking my thirst before it turned me blue. My tongue kept sticking to the roof of my mouth, and when I tried to say the word *Mom*, no sound came out.

I woke up sometime in the night, star patterns as annoying as car lights through a window, a cramp in my leg. I sat up to rub the cramp away and saw Sienna asleep at her watch, draped over the rail of the boat. I was just about to stand and wake her when I noticed something a few feet away from me. I blinked and stared, focusing my astonished gaze.

Hayley and Trevor lay in each other's arms. His fingers moved through her hair. They stared into each other's eyes in the solitude they had earned by being awake while others slept. Their lips came together.

I couldn't move. I could only watch them, incredulous. The ocean had steadily subtracted from them, but this was some defiant algebra in which they gave integers to each other they no longer had to give. Though they themselves were parched and weakened, their silhouettes made something strong and whole and calm, like the ocean creatures that drifted beneath our boat.

I thought again of Croix, the way I'd felt with him the brief time we were together. What would have happened had the wave not come? Would he have tried to win his bet? Or had I won him over? Had I been talking to the true Croix, the sensitive guy, the nice guy, the one who thought I was worth talking to? Now I would never know.

They kissed again, and I sank back down. No one was watching the sea. No one was watching the lovers. So wrong and so right. But I kept quiet and pretended to be asleep, envying the fact that Trevor and Hayley each had someone in whom to confide. I looked over at Abigail, sound asleep, her freckles standing out in the moonlight. I still thought she was a pain in the ass, but when she complimented me on almost catching that fish, a little bit of the old Abigail came through. Now I found myself missing that old Abigail. And I wondered: Did she even exist anymore?

TRECE

ONE DAY DURING THE SUMMER BEFORE WE STARTED NINTH grade, I found a tiny, scruffy kitten crying in a drainpipe, nary a teat to call his own, no mommy's belly to knead with his poor, shivering paws. I put him inside my shirt and took him home, where my mother wrapped him in a towel and drove us to the vet as I held him on my lap, listening to his small, uncertain cries and stroking him, murmuring, "It's a cruel world, isn't it, boy? But you're with me now."

I named him Sonny Boy.

The vet said he was too frail and probably wouldn't live through the night, but I refused to give up. I got some formula from the vet and woke myself up every two hours to give it to Sonny Boy with an eyedropper. The dawn came and the kitten was still with us, and my mother and I did shifts. My father even joined in when he got home from teaching his classes, and the three of us nursed Sonny Boy back to health.

Abigail came over to inspect the tiny creature. She leaned over his blanket and moved the flap out of the way so she could look into his bright-yellow eyes. He blinked at her and stretched out a tiny paw to place on her wrist.

"He'll make it," she said as though she were a vet or a fortune-teller. "He'll grow up to be a spoiled jackass and not appreciate a single damn thing you did for him."

"What are you talking about? He's the sweetest kitten in the world. He just likes to lick my face and cuddle."

"Mark my words. I see dick potential. It's in the eyes. Also, he's a cat."

HIGH SCHOOL SOCCER tryouts were held in late August, so all summer long I helped Abigail with her drills. We juggled, we dribbled, we passed, we sprinted. We kicked the ball as high as we could. Used both sides of our feet. Practiced on grass, cement, wood, carpet. We visualized success. All the while, Maxwell taunted his sister from the sideline.

"You suck! You'll never make it! You look like a moose! Your feet are so big!"

"Shut the hell up!"

"I can run faster than you, and I'm a little kid!"

"Listen, you little spaz-faced son of a bitch . . ."

Abigail's mother would come out and separate the two, and the process would begin all over again.

"You're letting him get to you," I said. "Concentrate on your game."

"I can't help it," she said. "He gets me so riled up I can't see straight."

I had to admit, I was a little jealous of Abigail's dedication to her dream. I myself had no real dream beyond having a boyfriend someday, and a great career of some kind. Or maybe I'd get my real dream when I was sixteen, along with my driver's license.

Abigail, though, did give me a hobby. One day when I came over, a present was waiting on the counter: a video camera. It had a big, red bow on it. Abigail looked at me expectantly.

"For me?" I asked.

"Yep."

"But, why? It's not even my birthday."

"Well, I thought you could maybe film my moves from different angles and then I could study the film. If you want to, of course."

"Of course I do!" I said. "But this is a really expensive present."

She shrugged. "My daddy's a lawyer. Got to spend it on something."

Turned out I was pretty good at playing camerawoman.

"I like the way you frame stuff," she said in admiration, gazing into the computer screen at my clips of her floundering around her yard with the soccer ball. "You got some real talent, cowgirl."

"Thank you," I said, flattered. "I'm learning how to edit."

By the end of August, Abigail was not exactly lean and mean, but of medium weight and passably coordinated. And no one could beat her fighting spirit or dedication to making the team.

My parents invited Abigail's family over for dinner the night before the big tryout. Our parents had been spending more and more time together, though I still could not put my mother and her mother together as friends, or, for that matter, our fathers. My father was tall and professorial and athletic, and Abigail's dad was a kind of chubby, indoor, rich-lawyer type. My dad actually had more in common with Abigail's mom. He'd been on the polo team in college, and they spent a lot of time talking about horses.

My dad proposed a toast with our iced tea at dinner.

"The girls have been training hard all summer," he said. "This is to Abigail's success."

We all raised our glasses.

"She's going to fail," Maxwell said.

WE ARRIVED AT the tryouts the next day in fine spirits. Abigail's parents went with us, and Maxwell and his big, self-confidence-crushing mouth stayed at home with a sitter. Abigail was nervous but confident, springing into a spirited set of jumping jacks to warm up, which I dutifully filmed.

The coach came in and made the girls do sprints in groups of ten. Abigail was pretty fast, finishing near the front of the pack despite her weird gait and flailing arms.

Next, everyone got in a line and practiced passing and juggling—laces, thighs, shoulders, heads—as the coach watched. Abigail did pretty well, and I myself did a great job of catching her moves on tape. Later I was going to add music and slo-mo for dramatic effect. Abigail noticed me filming and gave me the thumbs-up. I was impressed by how much she'd improved over the summer.

Finally the coach had the girls put on pinnies and divide into teams and scrimmage, red versus yellow. Abigail was a yellow. She had asked to try out as a forward, and she took that position as the scrimmage got under way.

My dear friend was a disaster. She couldn't find her lanes, she kept missing the ball when she tried to kick it, and a skinny girl with a don't-mess-with-me expression constantly outmaneuvered her. Late in the scrimmage Abigail got an easy shot at the goal and hit the post instead, her feet going out from under her. She landed on her back in the grass with a thump. I put down my camera.

She trudged back to the car in utter defeat.

"You held your own," her father said, trying to be nice.

"Righhhht," she said. "Held my own. A cross-eyed cow could have done better."

"Have you thought about yoga?" her mom asked helpfully. "Not so competitive and no grass stains."

"Nah," she said. "Douche Face was right. I suck. But I'm not giving up."

NINTH GRADE. HIGH school. A totally different world. Gone was the relative peace of middle school. Now we were in dog-eat-dog land, popularity quotients being sorted, the golden table forming in the middle of the cafeteria whereas before it had just been a table like any other. Sienna Martin had blossomed into a bitch who wore lots of makeup and the latest fashions and was already on the varsity soccer team. A sidekick had materialized by Sienna's side:

Hayley Amherst, a high-strung cheerleader full of run-on sentences and nervous energy whose never-ending monologues about why couldn't cells multiply and make a handbag dominated my biology class.

Abigail and I were basically ignored. But we didn't care. We had each other's company and support and inside jokes and perspective on the world. We were our own clique of two, and it worked just fine for us. The drama filling the hallways and the constant jockeying for social dominance of that pack of wildly insecure teenagers didn't affect us at all. We ate lunch together, had geometry class together, and spent every afternoon together after school. I was a bit tired of Abigail's constant soccer drills and her dreams of stardom, but I had to admit she was getting better.

My parents were glad that I had a friend. But sometimes they tried to nag me into getting more—as though one was a good start but not enough.

"Don't put all your eggs in one basket," my father said. "I had a best friend since I was in first grade. Name was Danny. We did everything together. When he was seventeen, he skateboarded off a cliff and died."

"That doesn't seem very relevant," my mother said.

"I think it is."

"I don't want to hang out with other girls," I said. "They're boring compared to Abigail. And why should I take time away from Abigail and spend it with someone who would just waste it? Makes no sense."

"She has a point," my mother said.

"And besides," I continued, "you two don't seem to have that many friends other than Abigail's parents. You do everything with them. Why don't you make other friends?"

The question seemed to make my father angry. "Don't be sassy, young lady. We're adults. What we do is our own business."

My mother gave him an odd look. There was a mood around the table that I didn't understand. We ate the rest of the meal in silence, and I still kept all my eggs in one basket woven from Abigail's crazy red hair.

ALTHOUGH WE HAD advanced to the ninth grade, Mr. Shriek was still stuck in the seventh, where he'd been, supposedly, for the last decade or so. We kept sneaking back into his room to visit him, forgiving him for his unwillingness to escape or to learn any words.

"He is what he is," Abigail said. "He's not a parrot from the movies. He's a parrot from real life, and that's what we've got to work with."

One day, however, we were astonished to enter the class and find that Mr. Shriek's life had suddenly changed.

His small cage had been replaced with a bigger one, and he had a mate; another parrot, with a delicate beak and sensitive eyes, cuddled with Mr. Shriek on his perch.

They were completely immersed in each other when we entered. Mr. Shriek was nuzzling his mate's head and making some kind of cooing sound we'd never heard before. He didn't even notice us standing there.

"Oh, my God," Abigail whispered. "Mr. Shriek has his cowgirl."

At the sound of his name, Mr. Shriek swung his head toward us. His bug eyes stared.

"*FUUUUUUUUUUH,*" he said.

"Is he bragging?" I asked.

Abigail actually wiped her eyes, she was so overcome. "I've always felt so sorry for him. But now I know he's going to be all right."

Later we found out someone at the pet shop had made a mistake, and the female parrot the science department had ordered for Mr. Shriek was not a female but a male.

Abigail shrugged. "Who are we to judge?"

"I CAN'T BELIEVE you're making me do this," I said to Abigail. We were sitting in the front bleacher seats watching an Avondale girls' varsity soccer game, and I was filming

Sienna Martin run up and down the field, kicking every-one's ass.

"Sienna's the best soccer player out there," Abigail murmured.

"She plays dirty," I said. "Tripping and punching and elbowing people. She's a maniac."

"Whatever. She's finally good for something. I'm gonna learn from studying the tapes."

"Well, study them alone," I said. "I get enough of her in English class."

One night in November, when the LA air had cooled and we were slogging out of the stadium, we were suddenly confronted by Sienna, still sweaty from her brutal victory, hair wet but her mascara still holding up fine. Her best friend, Hayley, who did not play soccer and was immaculately dressed, was by her side.

"What are you doing?" Sienna asked Abigail.

Abigail fixed her with a steady gaze. "Nothing."

"You're a liar!" Hayley chimed in, her lavender cologne smelling considerably better than her friend's alpha sweat. "You're stalking Sienna and it's super creepy because we see how you sit real close and watch her and your weird friend is taping her, not anyone else, just her, and there are stalking laws in this country and you're just creeping her out, know what I mean?"

"Free country," Abigail said.

"Yeah," I said. "Free country."

I didn't like the look in Sienna's eyes. She was all pumped up from the game like a skinny, possessed jackal.

"Give me that camera," she told me.

"You leave my friend alone," Abigail said.

Sienna lunged for my camera, but Abigail stepped in front of me, and the two of them grappled and fell to the ground. I dropped my camera and dove in and so did Hayley, and we were soon a clawing, punching, screaming mass of indecorous loss of self-respect. I smelled jackal sweat and lavender and grass. Someone's fist hit me, and I tasted blood. I heard people around us, cheering and calling.

Finally an angry male voice broke through, that of our teaching assistant, Mr. Moore, who let us call him Rob.

"What do you girls think you're doing?" Rob demanded as he separated us and we crawled away into our separate factions.

I grabbed my camera and made sure it was okay.

"What's the problem here?" Rob asked.

We picked ourselves up. "Little misunderstanding," Abigail said.

"Right," said Sienna. The varsity soccer team had really strict rules, and fighting could get Sienna suspended for the next several games. She shot Abigail a look that said, *"Let's just forget this."*

"My nose is bleeding," Hayley announced, showing us a single red dot on the end of her finger, "and it's my best feature, everyone tells me I have a perfect nose and who knows now, maybe it's broken and that would affect my future singing career and modeling contracts. . . ."

"I ought to turn you in for fighting," Rob said.

"No, please don't turn us in!" Sienna cried. "We're sorry!"

The look on Rob's face told us he was fighting a great battle: whether to be a dutiful teaching assistant or whether to preserve his title as the coolest teaching assistant at Avondale.

Title won. "Shake hands," he ordered us.

Sienna gave Abigail a look of death and held out her hand. Abigail took it. I could see that each one had a tiger's death grip. Each one was hurting the other, but neither let go until Rob physically separated them. I shook hands with Hayley and she started to say something again, but Sienna shot her a dirty look and she piped down.

"Okay, that's enough," Rob said. "Now go home." He turned to the people still milling around. "Everyone go home."

Abigail and I limped toward the parking lot, where

my dad was waiting for us.

"Good fight," I said.

"I want her," Abigail said.

"Who?"

"Sienna. I want that crazy bitch to be my coach."

"You're insane, Abigail."

"She's the best, and I want the best."

"And exactly how are you going to get her to coach you?"

"I'll pay her."

"Sienna's dad is pretty well-off. She doesn't need your money. And she doesn't seem to like you."

"Well, we'll see about that," Abigail said.

I stopped walking. "Wait a second," I said. "I might have a little present for you, Abigail." I pressed the reverse button on my video recorder and looked into the monitor. "I forgot to show you this. I was doing a little innocent filming after the game a couple weeks ago, and I caught Sienna behind the stadium, smoking a cigarette."

"So?"

"Well, during halftime I was going over some old footage, and I watched that scene again."

I found what I was looking for, and zoomed in and pressed Play. Abigail and I watched silently as Sienna leaned against a wall and lit up.

"Does that look like a cigarette to you, Abigail?" I asked.

"Nope. Looks a lot more like the locoweed."

"Exactly."

Abigail glanced at me.

"Are you suggesting blackmail, Denver?"

"Yes."

She smiled. "I like the way you think, cowgirl."

ABIGAIL SHOULD HAVE been careful what she wished for. True, thanks to me and my tabloid cinematic skills, Sienna had no choice but to become Abigail's reluctant tutor. But she made Abigail pay. The taunts of Maxwell were nothing compared to what Coach Sienna put her through every Saturday morning: yelling at her, calling her stupid, and making her do endless and punishing drills.

"Why do you put up with her?" I asked.

"I'm getting better, that's how come," Abigail answered. "Can't argue with that."

"It's kind of like *The Miracle Worker*," I said. "Except you're not blind and deaf, and your teacher's a bitch."

OVER CHRISTMAS VACATION Abigail and I, and both sets of parents, went to Playa del Carmen. (Much to Abigail's delight, her little brother stayed in town with a friend's family.) Of course, I brought my video recorder along so we wouldn't miss a single memory of our dream vacation.

We sat together on the plane and looked out into the clear sky and ordered Cokes and put the seats back. Our fathers were decked out in Tommy Bahama shirts. Abigail's mother had on a sleek halter dress thing, and my mother wore a simple skirt with a sleeveless blouse, and brought along her favorite straw hat.

We flew in to the Cancun airport, and our parents rented a van to drive to Playa del Carmen as I filmed out the window. Finally we arrived at the little villa my parents had found, featuring huts with ceiling fans and wooden floors. Abigail and I got our own hut with twin beds, and we wasted no time bursting in with our suitcases.

"Look," Abigail breathed. "They folded the guest towels into the shapes of swans." She lovingly stroked the towel swan's head.

"This is going to be the best vacation ever!" I told her.

And it was, at least at first.

Abigail practiced her soccer moves on the beach while I filmed everything I saw. Birds in the sky. Children selling beads. The waiters bringing our parents their mai tais. The sun setting. The sun rising. Palm trees waving. Someone's pet goat running down a stone-lined street. Our parents taking a sailboat cruise at dusk without us, the sailboat getting smaller and smaller and then disappearing altogether.

On the fourth day of our vacation, Abigail came down with an affliction called Hot Red Face with Freckles from being in the sun too long and was hiding out in our hut. I was outside, filming a woman setting up a display of pottery on her stand. Then I felt sorry for her because no one was buying her pottery and so I bought a pretty cup that could be used for just about anything.

I walked around, shooting, as the sun started sinking in the sky. I passed by the pier and saw my parents out there alone, facing each other, talking. The lowering sun and the birds circling over their conversation made for a promising cinematic moment, so I stealthily walked down the pier with my video recorder, the wooden slats warm under my bare feet and the seabirds shrieking.

Halfway down the pier, staring through the lens and keeping my mother and father in the center of the frame, I began to realize something. This wasn't a conversation. It was an argument. It was something hostile and ugly, and I was filming it.

"Don't tell me you don't know what I'm talking about. I hate when you say that," my mom was saying.

I froze, not sure what to do.

"I've had about enough of this crazy talk," my father

snapped. "I wasn't flirting with her. She may have been flirting with me, but I was just being friendly."

"I'm not stupid," my mom said.

She glanced my way and noticed me standing there, no doubt looking shocked, my video camera still propped on my shoulder. She touched my father's arm. He turned, his face red, and shouted at me.

"Turn that thing off!"

I WAS NEVER told why we left Playa del Carmen early. My parents packed up and gave Abigail's family the rental car, and we took a taxi to the airport.

"What's going on?" Abigail asked me as I packed my suitcase.

"Hell if I know. They had an argument, and *boom!*"

"Well, what about?"

"She was accusing him of flirting with someone."

"Who?"

"Well, the only thing I could think of was that waitress at the Lazy Lagoon. With the giant boobs. She kept laughing and putting her hand on his arm. But I think my mom's overreacting. My dad's just not the horn-dog type."

"I don't think so, either," Abigail said. "But one thing I know for sure. This vacation just went to shit."

■ ■ ■

I DON'T KNOW how to explain it. Only to say that I had a strange feeling after we came back from Mexico, like things weren't so perfect and I couldn't exactly figure out why. My parents and Abigail's parents didn't seem to be spending much time together anymore. My father joined an advisory board that guided master's degree candidates at UCLA, so he was tied up a lot more than he used to be. When he did come home, he seemed tense, distracted.

In March, my mother went to the hair salon, and when she came back, she had a distinctly different look. Her mousy brown hair had been cut into a bob and bleached blond.

I was speechless. She looked about as different from my mom as a mom could be.

"What do you think?" she asked me.

"It's . . ." I struggled for complimentary words, then finally gave up. "Mom, why did you do that?"

"I just thought I needed a change. I looked too old-fashioned."

She also started working out at the gym. She'd come home and rub her legs. "I don't think I'm doing these lunges right," she'd say.

"My mother's acting weird," I told Abigail. "Changing herself and stuff."

Abigail pondered this. "How old is your mother?"

"Forty."

"Ah, women freak out at forty. Known fact. Like birds flying south."

THE WEEK BEFORE tenth grade started, Abigail again made her appearance on the field. Again she wore the yellow scrimmage pinny.

Yellow. Color of domination. Of revenge. Of badassery.

Abigail ran up and down the field, keeping the ball away from her unworthy opponents. She passed, she juggled, she scored. She was everywhere at once. Her blackmailed bitch of an instructor had taught her well. And I kept the film rolling when her name was called as a new member of the Avondale junior varsity soccer team.

To say that we were jubilant was an understatement. But Abigail's parents were strangely silent on the car ride home. When they reached our house, I turned to Abigail.

"I can't wait to tell my parents!" I said. "I'll call you in a little bit."

"Great!" Abigail said.

"Good-bye, Mr. and Mrs. Kenner," I said, still puzzled by her parents' gloom.

"Good-bye," Mrs. Kenner said, but Mr. Kenner didn't speak.

My parents were waiting for me on the couch in the living room.

"So guess who made the team?" I said in greeting. I noticed their expressions and knew that no one was about to celebrate anything in this house.

"Sit down," my dad said.

"Is Grandma sick or something?" I asked. Boring though she was, she was my last living grandparent, and I felt tears coming to my eyes, certain this was it.

My father glanced at my mother, but she stared straight ahead. Her new blond hair was showing brown at the roots. Her toenail polish was growing out. She had a balled-up Kleenex in one hand.

"Your mother and I are getting a divorce," my father said.

I stared at him, completely stunned.

"What?" I whispered.

I looked at my mother. She said nothing, but pressed the tissue against each eye.

"You guys are happy, aren't you?" I demanded.

"I was," my mother said tearfully.

"But what happened?"

"Apparently," she said, her voice evening out and turning less shaky but harder, like she was just now learning to ride a bike of hatred without the training wheels, "your father is in love with Abigail's mother."

"WHAT?!" I shouted. "You're kidding me! Of all the mothers in the universe, you pick my best friend's mother?"

"It just happened," my father said miserably.

"You can't do this, Dad," I said. "You can go to counseling. It worked for Jason Seeger's parents. They were going to split up but—"

He held up a hand to stop me. "I don't care about Jason Seeger's parents. This is about true love, and being happy."

"It's about *you* being happy," I said. "You don't care about our happiness."

My father looked tormented, but I didn't feel sorry for him one bit. "Things happen," he said helplessly.

"Yeah, bullshit."

"Honey . . . " My mother dabbed at her eyes. "Don't swear."

I WASTED NO time storming from the room and calling Abigail.

"Holy shit," she said when she answered the phone. "My dad is packing." She sounded all stuffy, like she'd been crying. Which made me tear up a little bit.

"My dad is packing, too."

"Well," Abigail said after a series of sniffs, "your dad's the

192

one who should be packing. He's the dog in this situation."

"Don't call my dad that," I said. "Even though it's true."

A short silence. "I'm guessing you're thinking my mom's a dog, too."

"No, I'm not thinking that," I said, although I kind of was. "I'm just trying to figure out how to fix this."

"I don't think we can. I mean, I begged and pleaded with my mom to give it one more chance, but it's like talking to a wall."

"My dad is equally stubborn or in love or whatever," I said.

We both fell silent.

"You okay, pal?" she asked at last.

"I just feel like I should have figured this out earlier."

"What good would it have done, though?"

"I don't know," I said. "Maybe I could have stopped all that horse talk between my dad and your mom that was bringing them together."

Abigail allowed herself a small snort of laughter.

"I'm pretty sure, cowgirl, there was more than horse talk going on."

THAT NIGHT MY mom and I had a dinner meant for three people. If we'd had a dog, we'd have shoveled him the leftovers in the hopes that he'd destroy the evidence that we had been abandoned. But no such luck.

We sat side by side, watching old movies on TV. We turned off a love story and switched to a documentary on oil production in the Arctic, which was a topic we found sufficiently far enough away from this house to be tolerable. Occasionally my mother would burst into tears, and I'd put my hand on her arm.

We forgot to feed Sonny Boy, and he reminded us with a series of loud wails that made my mother jump and had me scrambling for the kitchen. I thought at least one member of the household should be happy on this night and so I gave him a treat of tuna fish and watched him wolf it down, his appetite unaffected by the fact that his daddy had left the building.

"I just feel so stupid," my mother said before I kissed her good night.

"That makes two of us," I said.

I couldn't sleep. My anger at my father wouldn't let me. We'd been a happy family. No major problems. How could he throw that all away?

I felt even sorrier for Abigail. After the most triumphant moment of her life, a moment for which she had sacrificed so much and practiced so hard and endured the bitchery of Sienna Martin, she'd been hit with this news.

And her glorious acceptance to the junior varsity soccer team was forgotten.

Our own teams were beat up, separated, destroyed.

I looked at the clock and decided to see if Abigail had left her phone on. She picked up right away.

"I can't sleep, either," she said.

"I'm so pissed off."

"At least you're stuck with the good parent. I'm over here with my harlot of a mother. Maybe I should run away."

"Don't do that," I said. "That will only make things worse."

"Did you see any signs?" Abigail asked me. "I mean, I had no frigging idea this was going on."

"I've been thinking about that. Remember that time we went to the Blue Oyster?"

"Yeah."

"Well, my dad and your mom ordered the same thing. Same salad, same entrée, same dessert."

"Twinsies," she said. "Not usually evidence of hopping in the sack together, but it could have been a clue. How 'bout the time we went to the beach, and they wandered off together?"

"Right," I said. "They supposedly were planning my mom's surprise birthday party."

"Well, who knows what else they were planning?"

"Exactly."

"Doesn't matter," Abigail said. "They're together now."

A long silence.

"You were great yesterday, Abigail," I said. "You were a monster on that field. And if fifty percent of our parents screwed our lives up, that was still a victory."

"Thanks, pal."

"And no matter what," I added, "this won't come between us."

THE BIZARRE LOVE story moved like a shock wave through my world. Over the weekend, my father got an apartment on Wilshire Boulevard, and Abigail's father got a month-to-month in Marina del Rey, where all the sad, abandoned husbands go. My mother and I stayed in our home, but it didn't feel like home anymore. And Sonny Boy, sleeping on my pillow, did not give a shit about any of it.

I wished I didn't give a shit. Wished I had a cat's indifference to a family dynamic that was suddenly destroyed. But I did care. My mother was so hurt and stunned that my faithful dad could have run off with the jittery blonde from the Palisades.

Truth was, we didn't work well as a family without

him. We had just assumed he'd always be there, and once he was gone, the holes were obvious. All the conversations, discipline, advice, and philosophies had to be retooled, as well as the special pancakes, and no one had the energy to do it. So we just sagged, a waterlogged–paper–hat kind of a family.

My mother started going to a divorce group, but it seemed to depress her so she stopped and eventually discovered Robert Pathway. She'd sit listening to his CDs for hours, a faraway look on her face as though trying to learn a new language from a country where people bounced back from misfortune. She stopped cooking, and we began to eat a lot of Chinese takeout food. The fortune cookies were full of weirdly optimistic phrases, like "A stranger will make your day today," which never turned out to be true.

My father called from time to time, and when I did talk to him, the conversation was frosty on my part, pleading on his.

"I'm sorry," he kept saying. "I would do anything to fix this with you."

"How about fixing it with Mom? Don't you care about Mom anymore?"

"Of course I do. I still care for your mom. She's a great person."

"Then come home."

"I can't."

My good-bye was bitter and consistent. "Whatever, Dad." And I would feel catlike saying that. My Sonny Boy heart cold in my Sonny Boy chest. Before my dad had abandoned us, there had not been much wrong in our family. It was a unit of three, humming along just fine. Now suddenly I knew I could lose the people I loved at any minute.

For a time, Abigail and I were closer than ever, brought together by our shared family drama. I went to every single one of her soccer games, filming her and cheering her on alone as the LA sky darkened and Abigail, with her peculiar meandering gait and awkwardness, somehow managed to lead her team in goals. She was living her dream.

She'd managed to score a learner's permit, and after the games, we'd drive back to her house, which was invariably empty, as her mother was out with my father. Soon we began raiding the liquor cabinet, because we were teenagers and from newly broken families, and we had some acting out to do. We made vodka tonics and margaritas and watched movies and drunkenly danced in the backyard. We enjoyed the badness of it all. We couldn't control our parents—that was true. And it was liberating to know that they couldn't control us, either.

■ ■ ■

IT WAS A cold, clear night after the game. Abigail and I had climbed out from her bedroom on the second story onto her balcony, then onto the roof. We were supposed to be watching her little brother. Instead we were drinking tequila.

Three shots had made me dreamy. "So this is what we'll do. You become a famous soccer player, I become a famous filmmaker, and I'll make documentaries about you."

"Deal," she said, pouring more shots. "'Nother one? I got to have at least one more to stand the sight of my brother."

"Hey, you know what?" I said. "Maybe I'll learn soccer, too." I stood up. "I've got some moves."

"Whoa," Abigail said. "Watch yourself, cowgirl."

"Look at me!" I said, pretending to juggle a ball with my feet and weaving around in the process.

"Sit the hell down. You're drunk!"

"Goalllll!" I shouted, kicking my foot the way I'd see Abigail doing it, so the imaginary ball bounced off my imaginary laces. Suddenly I felt dizzy. I waved my arms, trying to restore my balance as I reeled backward.

"Denver!" she cried, grabbing for me, but momentum was carrying me toward the edge of the roof. "Denver, noooooo!" she screamed as I fell off, plunging down through the cool, thin air of the Palisades to the ground below, landing with a thump.

I opened my eyes. The world spun slowly. Abigail was standing over me in the grass.

"Denver!" she gasped. "Say something!"

My drunken, relaxed body had plummeted down onto wet grass, which helped to break my fall. I was unharmed. I sat up.

"I just feel like doing stupid things, you know?" I told her.

"I know."

MY FATHER AND my mother went out to lunch one day, and I had hopes they were about to get back together. Until Abigail called.

"You'll never reckon what they got planned now," she drawled.

"What who has planned now?"

"Those two dogs in heat we call parents! Your dad is moving into our house!"

"No way."

"That's what he's telling your mom, right this very instant."

"You're kidding," I said. "How am I supposed to come

over when he's living there? It's too weird."

"Hey, it's even worse for me. I have to live here. And see them every single day while my daddy rots in a corporate apartment in Marina del Rey."

Something about her voice was funny. Almost like she blamed me. Like I had brought my dad into the world instead of the other way around.

I DIDN'T WANT to go to Abigail's house anymore. I felt that it sent some kind of signal that my father had my approval to move in when he absolutely did not. Not that Abigail was inviting me over very much. She was hanging out more and more with the other members of the team, lean, athletic girls who loved nothing more than to kick around balls for hours after school. We'd make weekend plans and then she'd blow me off and not even call. We stopped talking on the phone every night. I was lucky to get ahold of her for a decent conversation once a week. She was living in her own soccer world, where me and my two uncoordinated feet couldn't follow. But I still went to the games, still filmed her. And I was still proud of her, despite the fact that I could feel her slipping away from me.

I didn't know what to do without Abigail. Having a best friend was like having a sister—you kind of take it for granted until it's not there anymore. I was so used to having a funny thought or a sudden memory or reading about something interesting and then immediately sharing it with her. Now I just kept it to myself. I didn't like this lonely feeling, the way I woke up with it in the middle of the night. I felt I'd lost both my father and Abigail within a few short weeks of each other.

During my free time I'd walk around my neighborhood, filming things that interested me and then putting them together into movies on my laptop in my bedroom while my mother studied Robert Pathway and his forced march into happiness downstairs.

I desperately wanted some alone time with Abigail. We still ate lunch together, but now I was forced to sit at a table full of junior varsity soccer girls and feign interest in the soccer small talk. Sometimes I didn't even get to sit next to her. It really wasn't like having lunch with her at all.

"Hey," I said into the phone one night when she picked up. "What's going on? Want to get together?"

"Huh?" Abigail said over loud music. "Can't hear ya."

"Where are you?"

"I'm over here at Pizza Corral with some gals from the soccer team."

"You know I love Pizza Corral," I said crossly. "Why didn't you invite me?"

"Ah, you know. Just didn't come up. But I'm asking

you now. Come on over."

"Nah," I said. "I'll take a rain check."

That's how the rest of the fall passed: Abigail turning into a stranger, my dad filing for divorce, and life just sucking. My answer was to film life as much as I could, as though I could shoot it into not sucking. I had gotten pretty good, though, not just at framing shots, but at editing them together, making something out of nothing. I felt peaceful when I was doing that kind of work. Then I'd switch off the laptop, and I'd be lonely again. I suppose I should have been making new friends, but I kept hoping that when the season ended and we adjusted to the new configuration of our families, Abigail would come back to me.

Then one day she sent me a text:

Got a grand idea.

How was I to know it was the beginning of the end?

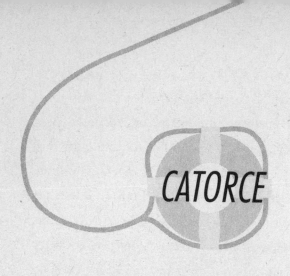

CATORCE

A NEW STORY HAD INTERSECTED OUR BOAT OUT OF NOWHERE, like one of the tiny fish that bumped it at night. Gentle, slippery, quiet.

A story called Hayley and Trevor.

I was the only one who noticed the glances they now exchanged and their tone of voice when they spoke to each other. I'm not sure why they chose to keep their attraction a secret. Maybe it was to have something to themselves. Maybe it was their way of feeling alive when hour by hour the prospects of our dying became more real. On land they'd be strolling to class together, texting each other, going to movies. Making out in the parking lot. But here their relationship was invisible to everyone but me.

There were no more planes and no more ships, not even distant ones. It was as if the earth had just re-created itself without the people. Repopulating the earth with Trevor and Hayley was a dicey thought at best, all those warbling, drumming humans unleashed on the world.

We had settled into a routine that grew slower as we weakened from thirst and hunger. We still watched for ships, still tried, still hoped, but we slept more and more in our designated places on the carpeted deck, which was dry now but still reeking of the dead organisms that had once swum through its fibers. Occasionally, we would lower ourselves into the water to try to cool off from the heat, Hayley and Sienna holding on to the ladder because they couldn't swim.

Small fish taunted us in groups, moving close to the boat and then darting away, stronger and faster and wiser than us. We hated the fish. Resented them for being so close and yet so far, and able to live in that water that would have poisoned us if we had taken it into our bodies.

Water. It was not in our world. It was in faucets and pipes and swimming pools. It shot out of drinking fountains in school hallways. Sprayed down on BMWs in the car washes of Venice. Poured down from clouds in Seattle. We dreamed about it, talked about it, cried inside for it, remembered it as though it were someone newly dead and still alive to us. But the only water we knew tasted of plastic and sloshed at the bottom of a gallon jug.

We talked occasionally among ourselves as the boat drifted slowly and the hours passed. The clique had dissolved in the sun. There was no more "us" and "them" by now. No ranking by how cool or pretty you were. We all looked like drowned rats, and we all wanted food and water and our families, and we all deserved to live, and we all were inching closer to death.

We learned a few things about each other.

When Trevor used to walk down Venice beach and saw a heart drawn in the sand, he was always careful to walk around it, because to him that was sacred ground. Hayley was terrified her earlobes were growing. Sienna had fallen out a four-story window as a toddler but was caught by a passing neighbor. And I loved American history so much as a child that I could look at Westerns on TV and tell if the Indians were dressed right for their tribe.

And Abigail? Well, Abigail wasn't sharing. She listened to the rest of us but offered nothing herself. This wasn't the Abigail I used to know. That Abigail talked of anything and everything. But this one was a stranger, even on this boat where we could barely sit cross-legged in a circle without our knees touching.

She had a hopeless, defeated look in her eyes. A look that no longer welcomed the future.

Occasionally someone on the boat would try to engage her or draw her into the conversation, but she would just gruffly say, "Leave me alone. I'm saving my energy," and that was that.

And while it was true that I still hated Abigail for ending our friendship and turning the whole school against me, part of me still cared enough to worry about her.

"Abigail," I whispered to her once when I was sitting close to her and everyone else was engaged in conversation. "Are you all right?"

"What do you mean? Of course not. Look at the mess we're in right now."

"No, that's not what I mean. You just look, I don't know, you just look very different than I remember you."

Her gaze was dull. "Then don't remember me."

WE ALL KNEW it was coming, but it still shocked us. We passed the jug around and took not even a sip, but a puddle the size of a quarter on our tongues, then the last of the water was gone. We had made it six days through careful planning, our bodies crying for it; but we were dogged in our persistence to stick to the sheer math of it, the divided gulps and then drafts and then sips.

We sat in a circle, staring at the empty jug, the boat bobbing gently. Hayley made a crying face, but the water had dried out of the recipe for tears.

"I don't want to die," she gasped.

Trevor reached over and touched her hair. "No one's gonna die."

Abigail and Sienna didn't notice the tender gesture. They were in their own worlds, deserts where everything moist was extinct.

Abigail stroked the jug gently.

"Well," she said, "we made it last a long time."

"Not long enough, though," said Sienna.

"We can't give up hope," I said. "We made it this far." I found myself looking at Abigail and speaking to her as a friend, forgetting for a moment that we weren't friends anymore. "Come on, we can do it, just like we climbed the rope! Remember the rope, Abigail?"

"Yeah, well," she said. "A rope is a rope. It ain't a big, blue sea."

Sienna suddenly cried, "Give me that mirror!" she shrieked, "Give it to me!" She snatched the compact and began signaling crazily into the horizon. Trevor jumped up and screamed at the sparse white clouds, "Rain, God damn it! Rain! Rain!"

Hayley joined him and, after a few moments, so finally

did Abigail. And we all screamed at the clouds with a fury and a righteous passion as if the clouds had lost a bet and owed us water. I went to the back of the boat and leaned down at a school of fish taunting me. Sacks of scaly fluid with eyes I would have eaten like tiny grapes. I swiped at them, and they scattered, and I screamed, "Come here, you bastards!"

And there we were, screaming at fish and clouds and signaling at passing nothings. Anyone who saw us would have thought, *That is so inspirational. Those kids are trying to live.*

THAT NIGHT THE dolphin came. We had seen dolphins jumping in the distance, but one had never come up close before. Exhausted and weak as we were, we still crowded the back of the boat to watch as it lifted its head out of the water, proving humans still love magic to the end. Parched, starving, dejected, we waved, and it disappeared and reappeared again.

"Maybe he's come to bring us good news," Hayley said.

It danced and chattered, moonlight shining off its wet skin, its smile meaning whatever a dolphin smile means, maybe welcoming us to a realm we would soon join, some kind of aquatic heaven where we moved in schools and were languid and weightless and free.

Trevor took off his shirt and unbuttoned his jeans, and they fell off his bony frame and piled at his ankles. Now he stepped away wearing nothing but his underwear, and hoisted himself onto the railing.

"Where are you going?" asked Hayley.

"I'm gonna swim with that dolphin."

"Don't go. You're too weak to swim," she said, clearly moving into the nagging phase of their tsunami-imposed speed romance.

But he had already disappeared over the side of the boat, emerging with his hair wet and plastered around his head. He lay on his back and faced the starlight. The dolphin vanished and then reappeared by his head. Trevor rolled over and swam a few strokes as the dolphin followed him, and they went back and forth that way, dying boy and living mammal, until Trevor suddenly went under and emerged near the back of the boat.

He held out his hand as the dolphin chattered behind him.

"Come here, Hayley," he said. "Swim with us."

"Oh, Trevor. You know I can't swim."

"I'll keep you safe."

She bent down hesitantly and put one cautious foot on the ladder.

"Come on," he said, his voice full of things only Hayley

and I heard. I came up behind her and took her thin arms and guided her down the ladder until she was close enough to drop into Trevor's arms. They went under the water. Hayley came up gasping, but Trevor spoke into her ear as he used his free arm for steady, even strokes. Hayley leaned back against him, floating, her knees, her shins, and then her toes bobbing up to the water's surface, the remains of her last pedicure visible in the moonlight. The dolphin circled and dove and flipped as the couple moved through the starlit water.

Abigail and Sienna and I watched them. There was something so lovely, so alive, so dying, so joyous, so tragic about it that we were able to leave our own selves and our own situation and become spectators to the magic of the sea.

"You know something?" Sienna murmured. "Call me crazy, but they would have made a nice couple."

EVEN AS WE waited for the end, I am proud to say that hope did not leave us. Increasingly disoriented and growing weaker by the hour, we still passed around the signal mirror. We still kept watch, although strange things were coming out of the ocean. A boy walking on the waves who would suddenly disappear. A hand coming up out of the water holding a bottle rocket that went off with a *whoosh* but never exploded. A teaming, swirling group of monarch butterflies. We reported these sightings to one another. Sometimes we all saw them at once.

Trevor seemed to be doing worse than the rest of us. His hallucinations were crazier than ours. Hayley stroked his hair.

"It's okay, it's okay, it's okay," she murmured, kissing his face with her parched, wrinkled lips. And I saw Abigail and Sienna narrow their eyes as if debating whether such open affection was real or just another crazy image thrown at them by the merciless sea.

I wondered what it would feel like to die.

I remembered a story my mother once told me about when I was a baby and got very sick, how she refused to sleep and stood guard over me, listening to my breathing all night long. I imagined that she was with me right now, listening again.

We dozed off one by one, slumping in our places.

I awoke to the sound of gulping. The others were still asleep, but Trevor sat in his swivel chair, his head thrown back, drinking out of the gallon jug. But that was impossible. There was no water in the jug. I was seeing things again.

"Trevor?" I whispered.

He stopped drinking and smiled at me. I reached out

and touched his knee to make sure that I was awake and sane and he was real.

"What are you drinking, Trevor?" I asked, a pit of fear growing in my stomach.

He smiled and took a deep, happy breath. "Seawater." He shoved the jug at me. "Want some?"

"NOOOOOOO!"

I grabbed the jug from his hands and poured out the rest over the rail. But it was too late.

"Trevor," I said, my voice breaking. "Why?"

The others woke up, sweaty, crusty eyed.

"What's the matter?" Sienna asked.

"Trevor drank seawater!"

"Oh, my God," Hayley gasped. "Tell me you didn't."

He shrugged. "I know they say not to, but there's a ton of things they say not to do, you know? Like don't surf after a storm 'cause all the shit from the sewers washed out into the bay."

"That's not a good idea, either," I said helplessly.

"This seawater is cool and refreshing," Trevor shot back, "and if you're too dumb to drink it, that's your problem."

"Oh no, oh no," Abigail murmured, her eyes filling with tears. "Your goose is cooked, Trevor!"

He laughed, and his laugh was warm and wet. For an

instant, I envied that dark, slick throat.

"Bullshit, dude. I feel fine."

Half an hour later, he was not fine. He was not fine at all. His face turned red, then a pale, slightly bluish color. He breathed in deep, heavy breaths. That's when, as Hayley sobbed her tearless sobs and hugged his knees, he started talking about Ranger Todd.

How Ranger Todd once caught a wave in Malibu so gnarly he almost drowned. And how Ranger Todd wanted to fight fires in Santa Barbara. And how only Ranger Todd had ever really understood him.

"Baby, please, sweetheart, please stop," Hayley begged him, and it finally sank into Abigail's and Sienna's brains what I already knew: Hayley had fallen in love with him.

But she could not save him, and neither could we. He and Ranger Todd were in their own world. We could do nothing but witness the horror until events played out and one thing led to another, and suddenly Trevor went overboard. He swam briefly, and then the water closed over his head.

"Oh, my God!" Hayley screamed. "This can't be happening! Abigail, tell me it's not happening, because if it is happening then this can't be real, and if in reality it's not happening then it must be a dream, and if it's a dream then I want to wake up and when I wake up I want to drink a pond full of water with a straw, not even one of those straws that filter out the yucky stuff, I don't care about the yucky stuff I just want the water. Trevor, oh God Trevor. . . ."

She tried to go in after him, but we held her back as we waited for him to surface. He never did.

Hayley went on and on and on, ranting and raving, and we all felt too sorry for her to tell her to shut up. Finally she collapsed on the deck and lay still. I would have thought she was dead, but she was still breathing. No one else moved. We were all stunned by what had just happened.

It was shocking to see Trevor day after day in the boat, all day long, so close, so real, and then not to see him anymore. The swivel chair sat empty. No more drumming. No more sudden, random thoughts. No more lyrics from Death Stare. And that's the thing. I couldn't say that I had liked Trevor, but he was familiar to me in the way that people are when they're in such close proximity. I had slept next to him. Inhaled his increasingly acrid body odor. And I had grown accustomed to this particular Trevor who was the only one of its kind in the world.

And now he was gone.

I think each of us had assumed that we'd all stay together, living or dead, and there was a certain comfort in that thought. But now we had realized that any of us could go at any time.

We huddled cross-legged in a circle around Hayley, barely able to move. An hour went by, maybe two. I glanced at Abigail and was startled to see a tear on her face, as miraculous as the bottle rocket or the boy who walked on water. Abigail, gazing off into the distance, didn't react when I reached over and gathered the tear on my fingertip, watching the tear quivering on its new perch, reflecting the world around us.

I knew that I was imagining things, but in that single tear I saw life, how it all went together, how it included all of us, a cafeteria where every table was in the center, and every person and bird and fish and plant and amoeba was invited.

I felt a tear on my own face, interrupting the reverie. It was a tear I did not remember crying. And then I felt another tear, and another, on my arm. I looked up at the sky, at the darkening clouds.

"Rain," I whispered.

For a few moments we remained motionless. We were shocked to the bone that the narrative had suddenly reversed like some crazy current running eastward that decides to turn westward and change the climate of some country on the other side of the world. The clouds overhead were heavy and dark and fat, and the rain fell, first in drops and then in sheets, as we turned our faces to the sky and let the water run down our throats.

Hayley stayed where she was, facedown on the deck as the splotches on her clothes bled together and she grew soaking wet, and I gently turned her over and prodded her until she opened her mouth and let herself live.

I wasn't going to let this surge of good fortune pass us by. After indulging in a few quick gulps of rainwater collected in my cupped hands, I got everyone right to finding every conceivable container—the Spam cans, Hayley's hastily emptied purse, Sienna's short boots. We even tore down the sunshade and stomped a dent in it large enough to collect more water until we had filled the jug.

We drank and drank and drank. It was the best drink in the world. It moved inside us, a beautiful flood turning our desiccated innards into Elysium again. Our lips filled, our wrinkly fingers swelled, and our tongues grew moist again. We drank too much, threw up, then drank more, relishing the act of gulping after the tortuous restraint of sipping. It was like a wild party where the liquor was water, and we could have wrecked that boat in our fervor, had there been anything to wreck.

Finally we stopped, and rested, and felt alive again as the boat bobbed in the short waves.

Hayley finally had the tears to cry over Trevor. "He died for us," she sobbed.

We all nodded politely, assuming Hayley had elevated her dead boyfriend to Christ position.

"No," she insisted. "You don't understand. He stopped drinking the water."

"What water?" I asked, confused.

"The water from the jug. He would pretend to drink it, but he wouldn't really. He was saving it for us."

"How do you know?" Abigail asked.

"He told me and I tried to argue with him, but he said, 'No, I'm a man. And I want you to live.' He meant all of us. He wanted all of us to live."

Hayley burst into tears again, and we all did too, even Abigail.

They poured from our eyes, and they meant we were devastated and lost and forlorn and human and vulnerable and that we had water again at last.

THAT NIGHT THE rain finally stopped, and there was a sweet smell in the air, as though a honeysuckle bush were blooming nearby. Who knows where such aromas come from, but out here, where supplies were so scarce, any sensory gift was welcome.

I lay on the wet deck and looked up at the stars, thinking

about Trevor. There was more room on the boat without him, and no drumming; but there remained a deep sense of loss now that he was gone. And it was weird to know someone else who was now dead. I had shared a boat with him, shared hopes and dreams, and watched him fall for Hayley. I wasn't sure how to mourn him.

We had talked about him earlier, the four of us, because that is what tiny reemerging societies do. They bury their dead, unless the ocean does it for them, and they remember those dead friends and family. They must mourn before they can go on. Of course, the others knew him better and told stories from back on dry land: party stories, hallway stories, beach stories. I told the stories I had gathered from our days on the sea. I had misjudged him in the same way they had all misjudged me. Maybe he would have outgrown certain faults. Gotten better. Less douchey. Less dudey. Less drummy. And maybe Ranger Todd would have matured into a more thoughtful, wiser man part. An elder statesman. A poet laureate.

It was nice to see Hayley's love for him out in the open, sad and ill-fated as it was. She even sang a song she'd written in her head for him the night before, and the song was surprisingly sweet and haunting and lovely and made us all cry again.

The stars came out, and the night deepened, and

Sienna and Hayley fell asleep. Their clothes were turning into rags. Their hair was tangled. Their lips were burned, and their faces thin. They did not look bitchy, or popular. They just looked like teenage girls who had been through something grim and were trying to restore themselves in sleep. I had almost a sisterly feeling for them, watching them. Not that I liked them, necessarily. Only that I was starting to know them up close, their little habits and expressions, many of which were annoying but some that were just human. Just ordinary.

Abigail was standing watch, her hands resting on the railing as she gazed out to sea. The wind was so calm that the rat's nest her hair had become didn't even move. I wondered if she hated being cooped up on this boat with all the things she'd tried to banish in this life: her freckles and her hair and me.

I studied the way her shoulders stayed so straight, and the slow, steady movement of her head as she looked right and left. Abigail would never fall asleep on her watch. It wasn't in her nature. She would have made a great prison guard. I wanted to tell her everything was going to be all right. But she didn't want to hear from me any more than she wanted to hear her freckles talk. I was probably just a part of the catastrophe, right along with the lack of water and food and the blistering sun and the lonely days.

Maybe it was the late hour and the sentimentality brought on by my fading strength and the prospects of death, but I wondered if our old friendship still stood a chance despite all that had happened. And while Abigail had been so mean to me, so unfair, I couldn't help wondering if my old best friend still lingered there under the blistered skin and the sea of freckles.

It was hard to forget the things I knew about her. Those little details. Her habit of dividing her meals into three sections. Her disdain for Los Angeles rainstorms that came without thunder. Her favorite song, "The Eyes of Texas," and her various nicknames for her little brother—Douche Face, Felon Boy, Maggot—and how they seemed to change with the seasons: Douche Face in the summer months, Felon Boy in fall and winter, Maggot in the spring. And the mantra she would mumble when she went in for a practice goal: *Toes-pointed-down hit-the-laces follow-through-with-power.*

All details that stayed with me even when Abigail disappeared from my life.

It made me sad that these long, fearful days at sea had not made us any closer. Part of me—a small part—was willing to try and be friends again, or at least not enemies.

I got up and made my way over to her, stood next to her and gazed out at water so clean and flat it seemed to invite us to walk across it to the safety of some distant land. Starlight shone down on the water's surface, reflecting itself, the moment perfectly frozen.

Finally, Abigail spoke.

"Your cat still a dick?"

The sound of her voice startled me. I tried not to show it.

"As far as I know. I don't think he's mellowed over the last week or so. That is, if he's still alive. And I'm sure he is. My family"—I stumbled—"I mean, my mom and my cat are far enough inland, I think. And your family is too."

"Well, ain't no doubt my little brother survived. He's like a cockroach."

"Everyone would be pretty amazed to know we're together."

She stiffened, and I thought it was in response to what I just said until I noticed she was peering intently at the horizon. Finally her shoulders slumped. "I thought it was a ship. But it was nothing. It's always nothing."

"One of these times it might be something."

"Well, that time better hurry."

We stood in silence as the wind began to pick up. I felt

my own hair flying in my face. A strand of it went into a corner of my mouth, and I pulled it free.

"Wonder what my ma's doing," Abigail said. "Probably gone loco. She ain't so great in a crisis."

I didn't know what to say. Despite everything that had happened between us, I was glad to be addressed in this manner and was afraid I'd say something to make the spell disappear.

"My mother is probably losing her mind, too," I said. "She didn't know I was sneaking out the night of the party."

"Missing her, huh?"

For some reason, the question made my eyes water. Robert Pathway had failed her. I had, too.

"Yes," I said.

Silence. Just the bobbing of the boat and the wind.

"You think we'll make it back?" Abigail said.

"Sure we will." I wasn't actually so sure. "What do you think?"

"What difference does it make?" Her tone had shifted, turned mean. "Ain't got nothing to go back to. All thanks to you."

"Bullshit," I said, annoyed now. "You could try out for the soccer team again if you wanted to."

She kept looking out in the distance.

"That's all over."

"Right," I said. "Because I ruined your life."

"Pretty much, yeah."

"So you had nothing to do with it? Nothing at all? It was all me?"

Abigail turned and looked at me. Her eyes were cold.

"Yes, ma'am."

It was so unfair. If I thought that a tsunami would have smoothed out the blame shifting in Abigail's brain, I was wrong. I almost said, "No, Abigail. You did this to yourself." But a slowly drifting boat in the middle of the ocean seemed to be a poor place to have an argument. I went back and sat in Trevor's old swivel chair, turning around and around and around.

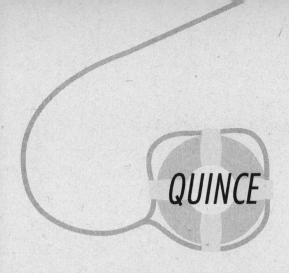

QUINCE

GOT A GRAND IDEA.

Those words still haunt me.

"What's your big plan?" I asked Abigail when we sat down to lunch. Her soccer friends hadn't yet arrived, and we were alone.

Abigail looked excited. There was a certain gleam in her eye. "Well, our cheating parents are gonna be out of town this weekend, and Douche Face is at some kind of spazz camp, so we got the house to ourselves."

"Abigail," I said. "You know I don't like going to your house anymore."

"Well, guess what? I got to go there every damn day

and see your damn dad. I'll hide all his shit so you won't even know he lives there."

I said nothing. Any idea of hers that took place in that house didn't sound like such a great idea to me. I speared a green bean off my plate and sniffed it, enjoying its cardboard bouquet.

"Anyway, I'm almost sixteen now, and my mom's dumb enough to think I can be on my own," Abigail continued. "So I thought, Saturday night would be a fine time to throw a shindig. What do you think? Are ya with me?"

"My mom won't let me go over there if there's no adults around."

"Well, your mom don't need to know that."

I sampled a green bean, tasting fiber and water. Julia Child rolled over in her grave.

"Come on, cowgirl. I need you."

I looked at her. She hadn't said those words in a long time. In fact, I'd been wondering lately if Abigail needed me at all.

"Bring your video camera," she added. "Make a party film. Hit the highlights. We can pass it around later."

A soccer player came over and put her tray down.

"What's up?" she said.

"Party," Abigail said.

Her eyes brightened. "Party?" she said.

What could I do but climb on board?

"Party," I said.

I TROLLED THE big lie past my mom that night about having an innocent sleepover at Abigail's.

"I thought you weren't going over there anymore now that your father's living there," she said.

"He won't be there," I said.

"Why not?"

"I don't know." She and my father didn't talk at all these days, unless it was absolutely necessary or involved me. I was counting on this fact to help me get away with my lie.

"Won't it be a little strange for you?" she asked.

"Sure. But I never get to see Abigail anymore. She's always with her soccer friends. I want to spend some time with her alone."

Still, she looked doubtful.

"Her mother will be there," I lied.

Her eyes darkened. Abigail's mother wasn't her favorite person, that was for sure.

"It's just one night," I said. "It's not like I've been having a great deal of fun lately and there's a chance I'm going to get poisoned with fun intoxication and have to go to the hospital."

"There's no need for sarcasm, Denver," my mom said, sounding hurt. "I haven't been exactly having fun myself."

"I know, Mom," I said, feeling bad now. "I'm sorry." I tried one more time. "But, please?"

She sighed. "Oh, I suppose it would be good for you to get out of this depressing house. But promise me you won't stay up all night."

"I promise," I lied.

ABIGAIL HAD VOLUNTEERED to pick me up Saturday afternoon, but my mother didn't trust her learner's-permit skills, so she took me herself, dropping me off and getting out of there quickly lest she catch sight of the woman who had ruined her life.

Abigail answered the door. Her hair was combed and sprayed, her freckles were covered by makeup, and she was all dressed up in a terrible-taste kind of way, with a cute skirt matched with colored leggings and a plaid shirt and her cowboy boots. She looked like Texas was trying to go to a fancy club with the other states but got turned away by the bouncer. I myself had dressed plain so as not to attract my mother's suspicion. My favorite outfit—black jeans and a black top—was in my overnight bag.

"Is the coast clear?" I asked.

"Yep," she said. "Come on in."

I hesitated.

"Oh, come on," she said. "The house is not gonna bite you."

I walked in slowly, glancing around. The place looked exactly the same. And yet it no longer felt welcoming. "This is creepy," I said.

"Ah, stop it with the creepy talk," Abigail answered. "We got a shindig to get ready for. Everyone's bringing food over, and we're going to have music, and it's gonna be a barn burner. Now help me go through my playlist."

We sat together on the couch and went through her songs. "Oh, my God," I said, a row of country and blue-grass songs staring back at me, "no one wants to listen to your shit-kicking music. What are you gonna do next, spread a little sawdust on the floor and have a mechanical bull?"

"Fine," she said, handing me the laptop. "You're in charge of music, Miss Mainstream America. I'm gonna go open up some chips and nut mixes."

We spent the rest of the afternoon cleaning and vacuuming my adulterous father's new love nest. I enjoyed the feeling of scrubbing out every trace of him from this place, my once-sanctuary. I wanted to write a bestselling book called *Cheating Ruins Your Best Friend's House*. But now that I was here, I was determined that I could be a fun party person like the rest of Abigail's new friends.

As night fell and Abigail was scurrying around with last-minute preparations, I began to film her.

"I'm thinking about maybe doing a before-and-after motif," I said. "Might be interesting."

"Okay," she said. "Whatever. Just make me look good."

When everything was ready, I went upstairs to change and put on makeup. "Wow, you are all gussied up," Abigail said admiringly when I came downstairs. "Maybe you'll hook up with some feller tonight."

"That would be fine with me," I said. I was actually looking forward to this party. Kind of a big FU to my father. I too could cause mayhem in this house. I too could break social rules. Besides, my mascara was perfect, and my video camera was ready to go.

Nine o'clock came and went, and we were still sitting there on the couch, waiting for our first guest.

"Are you sure anyone is coming?" I asked.

Abigail snorted and gave me a look. "Of course they're coming. The team wouldn't let me down. I hear even some senior varsity people are showing up."

"I didn't mean anything by it," I said, although I kind of did. Historically, neither Abigail nor I could drum up enough friends to have a party. What if she was wrong, and we ended up sitting in the dark with just each other? Not that I would have minded some Abigail time to myself. But she'd be crushed.

"Just hold your horses," she said. "You'll see."

Five minutes later the doorbell rang, and it kept ringing for the next thirty minutes, with more and more people piling in until a party was in full swing. Loud music played. Beer and drinks were passed around. But I made myself useful, tearing open chip bags and answering the doorbell as it rang and rang and rang.

"Hey, Denver," Abigail called to me from the den. "Don't forget to film."

I began answering the door with one hand and filming with the other.

"Come on in," I'd say. "It's Abigail and Denver's Party Event! Wave at the camera!"

Everyone was really cool about it until I opened the door and there, standing in front of me, was the stick-beast, Sienna Martin, and her idiot shadow, Hayley. They were both dressed to the nines. Their hair was arranged in geometric patterns that would have puzzled the really smart kid in *Good Will Hunting*. Sienna's eye makeup looked like a peacock had gotten hit by a drone.

I pointed the camera at them. "Hey," I said unenthusiastically, "welcome to our party."

Sienna shoved the camera aside. "Get that camera out

of my face," she snarled, her lip curled in a French bob. "What are you doing here, anyway?"

"Abigail and I are throwing this party together. What are you doing here?"

Hayley gave a great sigh. "You know I know you're not popular or anything so it probably doesn't matter, and you probably wore your best thing, but black pants and black top are so Party 101, you know? You could have tried just a little bit harder, I'm just saying."

I didn't bother to answer. I just left the door open and turned around and plunged back into the crowd, taking refuge in the chaos of things while Hayley was busy sucking in enough breath for her next idiotic statement. I wasn't sure if Abigail had invited them or if they'd come on their own, or if sometime over the last several months Abigail had suddenly made friends with her tormentor and her dopey sidekick and I didn't know about it.

It troubled me, this not knowing Abigail, after years of knowing her every move and thought. But I quickly shook off the bad mood Hayley and Sienna had brought into the house. After all, I was cohosting the party by default, and maybe this was my chance to show Abigail I could make friends and hang out with her soccer pals too.

I couldn't believe there were so many people at this party. I worried a bit about the police coming but then I figured that was Abigail's problem. I looked around for her and found her in the kitchen, surrounded by a bunch of the junior varsity soccer players. She was laughing and drinking out of a red cup.

I was not stupid. I knew a Red Cup often was filled with an Alcoholic Drink. And something about her laughter—just slightly manic and high-pitched—concerned me a little. But I decided to play it cool.

"Great party, Abigail, I must admit," I said.

"Told ya," she said. "Keep filming! Everyone, lift up your cups and say 'Avondale!'"

"Avondale!" they screamed, and I got it all on tape.

"You'd make a great journalist," said Samantha, whom everyone called Quinn. I liked Quinn. She was one of the few people who talked to me at the lunch table and was always upbeat and fun to be around. And from attending all the junior varsity soccer games, I knew Quinn was a killer on the field.

"I'm glad you're here, Denver," Quinn added. "Have a drink."

"What are you drinking?" I asked her.

"Punch. Try it."

She handed me the red cup, and I put my recorder down and took a slug of something that tasted like orange juice mixed with grape juice and pulverized embalmed frog. It went down my mouth and burned my throat.

I handed it back. "It tastes like pulverized embalmed frog," I said.

Quinn laughed. "You're so funny. I'll get you a cup."

I looked at Abigail while Quinn was gone. "Be careful, Abigail," I said. "That stuff is strong."

"Hey," she said. "Less talking, more filming."

I was a bit put off by her bossy tone, but I picked up the camera and started filming again. I was starting to wonder if Abigail had just asked me to come over to her party because she knew I had a video camera and liked to make movies. Was this my role at the party? Was Abigail the star, and was I just a member of the crew?

Quinn came back with a cup for me and tried to hand it to me, but I pointed to the counter. "Set it down there," I said, "so I can keep filming."

"Come on," Quinn said. "Have some fun! You don't have to film all night."

"Yes, she does!" said Abigail. "It's her job." She waved at me, not to say hi but to direct me. "Go on," she said. "Circulate a little. Find out what's going on in the other rooms."

"Yes, Master," I said. "I'm glad to serve you."

She took another swig out of her cup. "What bee's got under your saddle?" she asked.

I glared at her through the viewfinder. "Don't worry,"

I said. "I won't even go to the bathroom. I'll just film where I stand and pee down my own legs."

Quinn began to laugh. "You're so funny, Denver," she said.

I picked up the drink and left the kitchen, wandering around the party, drinking, filming. My anger was rising in me. I thought of all the times Abigail had blown me off lately to be with her other friends. She'd texted me on my birthday. Texted me. **Happy Birthday Cowgirl!**

Nice.

I wasn't doing a good job of multitasking. The hand holding the drink was shaking, and the fluid was dropping on the floor and burning through it all the way to China and some illegal house party there. I headed upstairs, padding up that familiar carpeting, and made my way to Abigail's room, where I closed and locked the door behind me and sat down on her bed to drink alone in the darkness.

No one at this stupid party knew her stairs better than me, or her kitchen, or her living room. We'd sat on this very bed so many times, looking out her window into her yard below and the shimmering pool, remarking on the neighbors and the damnable ten-foot fence that had kept her high-strung mother bouncing in and out of sweat lodges. I had come to think of this house as my house too, and Abigail as my sister.

Now it was no longer my house. And she wasn't acting very much like my sister anymore, either.

I took a drink of the vile liquid, and it tasted awful in a way that promised mood enhancement, so I took another swig and another, wrinkling up my face, the music and noise of the party rising through the floor and the bed vibrating against my legs. I kept taking sips of the punch, which didn't taste so horrible anymore. The bitter aftertaste had receded, leaving only a sickening sweetness that my throat continued to swallow despite its best interests.

I was feeling good. Looking good. I was going to go downstairs and show Abigail that this wallflower, this loser, this sad friend she'd been stuck with all these years and was finally learning how to ditch could be the life of the party. I headed back down into the noise and laughter, no longer filming but holding the camera loose at my side. I was not here to lurk behind the scenes, filming everyone else having fun. I was here to be Denver Reynolds, party maniac.

I put on my brightest smile. "Hey!" I'd say as I recognized classmates. "Welcome to our party!"

"Oh," they'd say. "You're helping Abigail throw this party?"

"Yes, I am," I'd say. "I'm kind of like a tall, awkward Martha Stewart." And they'd actually laugh, too.

"Hey, Denver," a girl from math class told me, "you look really different."

"Different . . . how?" I asked. I hadn't had enough alcohol yet to remove my self-consciousness, but it was coming on fast.

"More makeup!" she said. "You look great!"

"Why, thank you."

I kept circulating, staying away from the kitchen and any contact with Abigail. I felt such a strange mix of moods slugging through me. On the one hand, I was doing fine. I wasn't worshipped as a god or anything, but I was making conversation and it was fairly easy. I was fitting into the swirl of the party and not playing the role of the sad wallflower hanging out in some corner covered in pollen. So on that level, I was succeeding. But it wasn't really me. The booze had taken my personality and replaced it with someone more fun to be around.

But maybe Abigail was right. I overthought things too much. I worried too much. And maybe my sleazy, cheating, dirty-dog father was right when he told me not to put all my eggs in one basket. There was a reason people ran around in packs. It was safer that way. One egg in one basket might use its egg powers to disappear one day, leaving you with nothing. Kind of like my father.

I wandered outside, where more people milled around.

Some of them had taken off their shoes and were sitting on the side of the pool, drinking and dangling their legs in the water.

I noticed a row of kids I'd never seen anywhere before. The old Denver would have gone the other way, but the new Denver slunk right up to them, waved around the red cup in greeting, and said a bright "Hello!"

They looked up at me. "Hey!" one said.

"Welcome to our party!" I said.

"Oh," said a pretty girl with olive skin and dark hair, earrings dangling so low they rested on her shoulder, "this is your party?"

"Yeah," I said. "My friend Abigail and I are throwing it. Do I know you guys?"

"No," said a boy sitting on the end closest to me. "We're from Davidson High. We just heard there's a great party going on over here." He had messy blond hair and cool wire-rim glasses, and full lips that were red from the punch. Despite the chill in the air, he was just wearing a pair of board shorts and a T-shirt.

"I'm Drew," the blond guy said.

"I'm Denver."

"Are you gonna film us?" another girl said.

"Nah," I answered. "I'm kind of tired of it, to tell you the truth."

"Want to sit down?" Drew asked.

"Sure."

I took off my shoes and sank down, putting my camera off to the side and let my feet dangle in the water. Drew looked down and laughed. "Hey," he said. "You forgot to roll up your pants."

"Ah," I said as the water went through my pants, making them feel cold and heavy, "I knew I forgot something."

"That's okay," said one of the other girls. "We've been drinking the punch too, and we barely can talk."

"That stuff is lethal," I said.

"Did you make it?" Drew asked.

"No," I said, holding up my cup. "But whoever did is a psychopath."

Drew nodded at my camera. "You getting some good stuff?"

"Yeah, I think so."

"You like to film?"

"Yeah, I mean, it's kind of a hobby of mine, I guess. I don't know what I'd do with it as a career, exactly."

"I'm thinking of majoring in film at UCLA," Drew said.

"That sounds cool," I said, not knowing what else to say.

"This is a soccer party, right?" asked another girl. "Do you play soccer, too?"

"Nah," I said, "I'd trip and fall and die."

"Me too!" the girl admitted with a laugh.

We kept talking like that, the five of us there, just bantering about little forgettable things, and time passed, and I drank a bit more of the punch. At some point the girls started talking among themselves, and it was just Drew and me talking, leaning a bit closer together. I wasn't myself. I was a giggly, prettied-up, shallow party girl. The raw meat of my true self was basting in the punch, turning pleasing colors. The night was chilly; my jeans were wet up to the knees. The pool water was sparkling and blue and calming.

"You must be cold," I told Drew, "in just that T-shirt and shorts."

"You must be cold with those wet pants."

"It's not so bad."

"So what do you do for fun?" he asked.

I shrugged. "This kind of stuff," I lied. "I like parties and . . . music . . . and . . ." I searched for something else. Something that sounded natural and effortless and cool. "Oh! I go to all the soccer games. My friend Abigail is the star forward."

"Yeah," said Drew. "My girlfriend's on the JV soccer team at our high school. She played against you guys last week and got beat."

I put down my cup. He'd lost me back at *girlfriend*.

240

He read my eyes, and his smile faded. "What's the matter?"

"Nothing," I said. "It's just that I didn't know you had a girlfriend."

"Ah," he said. He was quiet.

"Where is she?" I asked.

"We're spending some time apart. We've had some problems. Jealousy. She keeps thinking I'm with other girls and then she'll text the girls and go psycho on them. A lot of drama."

"Sorry," I said.

"Nah, don't be sorry."

"So . . . ," I said. "I'm gonna go inside. Getting cold out here."

"No, wait." Drew took my hand and held it. "Stay here awhile."

"Listen, if you have a girlfriend . . ."

"No, I mean, yes, I guess I do or maybe not. I'm kind of in limbo. Anyway, she's not here."

"Yeah, well . . ." I let go of his hand. "You see, my dad left my mom and moved in with my friend's mom, so I'm kind of careful about whose toes I'm stepping on, you know?"

"Oh," he said. "I'm sorry to hear that." He sounded really sincere. "That must have been so weird."

"Yes, it was. It came out of the blue. I just thought they were friendly, you know?"

"My parents divorced when I was three. My dad lives in Silver Lake and my mom in Brentwood. It sucks, shuffling back and forth between the two of them every weekend."

"Yeah," I said. "Sucks." Then I added, "I don't really shuffle back and forth at all, because my dad and I are not speaking. As a matter of fact . . . he just moved into this very house."

"Really?" he asked. "This house?"

"Yeah."

"That must be really awful for you."

"It is awful," I said, and he gazed into my eyes like he wanted me to confide in him more. He was very cute, he really was. But I didn't like this pesky, psycho, sort-of-broken-up girlfriend situation.

"Well," I said awkwardly, "I better take off."

Drew grabbed my hand again and pulled me toward him, so slowly and effortlessly that it seemed natural to follow along. I'd had enough of the lethal punch to make me flirtatious and giggly. His smile was so beautiful, shy but daring, and his lips came toward me and we kissed. Not a making-out kiss but a friendly and tipsy kiss that was so natural it seemed like I'd been kissing boys all my life as opposed to never.

We were both smiling as we pulled away. I grabbed my video camera and got up, dripping water as I slogged across the grass, forgetting my cup and the warm remnants of the punch. A wind came up and I shivered. My pants were wet up to my knees and my shoes were off somewhere in the dark. The grass was cold to my bare feet. I was weaving a little. This was the greatest party in the world.

I just had to tell Abigail. Even though she had acted so snobby to me, ordering me around like her personal bitch, I had just kissed a boy, and this was big news.

I went to the kitchen and she wasn't there, just another group of drunken kids fighting over the last of the punch and one kid juggling steak knives to show off for the others.

"Hey," I asked a girl I recognized from the soccer team, "where's Abigail?"

"Oh, Abigail!" The girl laughed. "She's in the TV room!"

Something about her tone of voice set off alarm bells. I plowed into the knot of people crowding the opening to the TV room and finally got through.

I couldn't believe my eyes.

Abigail was dancing with another girl in the center of the room. They staggered around, holding each other up, while a crowd of drunken people cheered them on.

Abigail was a hot mess, her hair all crazy and her eyeliner smeared.

"Abigail!" I ran up to her, grabbing her by the shoulder and turning her to me. She looked at me with glassy eyes.

"Denver," she slurred. "Hey, cowgirrrrrl . . ."

"Oh, my God, Abigail, you're wasted!"

Her dancing partner pushed me. "Get out of here," she snarled, just as drunk. "We're dancing."

Abigail closed her eyes. Her head bobbed. "Yeah," she muttered, "we're dancing." She grabbed the girl and started doing some kind of made-up waltz. They lumbered around a couple steps and then fell in a heap together on the floor.

"Abigail," I said, "get up!"

Everyone was laughing and yelling out things, and no one paid me any attention. I knelt down next to Abigail. "I'm gonna take you upstairs to bed," I told her.

"No, you're not," she mumbled drunkenly, her eyes barely open. "Get out of here. I'm fine!"

"You're making a fool of yourself." I took her arm and got up, trying to lift her off the floor, but the other drunken girl held her back.

"Tell her to go away!" she said to Abigail.

"I'm not going anywhere," I replied, defiant.

Sienna and Hayley appeared out of the gloom.

"We need to help Abigail!" I told them.

"Stop being so lame," Sienna said. "You're ruining the party."

"She needs our help, you idiots!" I shouted. I set the video camera on the floor so I could grab Abigail with both hands to try and pull her to her feet. "Come on," I said, "party's over."

"Party's just starting, cowgirl," Abigail mumbled. "You're an old wet horse blanket. Go throw yourself over another party and stop ruining mine."

A great fury came over me at the sound of her scornful tone. I let go of her arms, and she slumped back on the floor, where she suddenly came to life, laughing and rolling around and screaming "Yeehaw! Yeehawwww!" Now I was angry. I grabbed my video camera and started shooting.

"You wanted me to film you, Abigail?" I asked. "I'll film you making a fool of yourself so you can see yourself in the morning."

Abigail cackled drunkenly and gave me the finger, and I filmed that, too.

"Stop," Sienna ordered. "Maybe she doesn't want to be filmed."

"Shut up, Sienna," I said. "This is none of your business."

Abigail managed to sit up and bark at her friends, "Help me up!" They dragged her to her feet and tried to help her regain her balance, but she swayed from side to side. I lowered my camera and tried to steady her arm.

"Go away!" Abigail told me as she wrenched away from me. "You're embarrassing me!"

I stared at Abigail. I couldn't believe it. "You're the one who's embarrassing yourself. You can barely stand up!"

"Get out," she said. "Get out of my house! I knew you wouldn't be any fun."

I had barely any time to react to the bitchiness of that remark when Sienna's face appeared inches from mine.

"You heard her," she snarled. "Get out!"

Suddenly I was being pushed by a tide of drunken people toward the door. I stumbled and recovered and tried to push back, but it was no use. It was like an ocean of drunken, overdressed unfairness had risen up against me, and all I could do was hold on tight to my camera and be swept away by the crowd, protesting and calling Abigail's name until I was forced out into the frigid night air and the door slammed behind me.

The lock turned for emphasis, and I was alone, my bare feet cold, my hairstyle broken and disheveled and ruined, my pants wet to the knees, and my shirt ripped at the seam where the arm meets the shoulder. The party went on and on inside without me, the sound of it pulsating through the doorways and windows. Good times, hardly containable, but none leaking out for me.

I had never felt so betrayed in my life. Here I was trying to save Abigail from making a drunken idiot, slobbery fool of herself. She was on the verge of passing out in the middle of her own illegal party full of underage drinkers, and I was the one punished for it. I felt utterly defeated. Tears stung my eyes. Even Sonny Boy didn't bother taunting me in apparition form, so low had I sunk. I felt humiliated, completely destroyed.

My camera was intact, but my purse, and the cell phone that was supposed to be used only in emergencies, was upstairs in Abigail's room, and I was not going back in that house. There was nothing I could do but sneak around to the backyard and ask the first person I saw to borrow their cell phone so I could call my mom.

"What's the matter?" she asked as soon as she heard my voice, and I burst into tears.

"Just come and get me," I said miserably.

MOM WAS PISSED. At whom? Well, shockingly, at me. The victim in these circumstances. The good friend. The loyal companion.

Me.

"Explain yourself again," she said in a tense voice as she gunned the car down Palisades Highway. "You were supposed to go over to spend the night at Abigail's, just the two of you. And here you are, all dressed up, soaking wet, and drunk?"

"I'm not drunk!" I insisted, hearing my own voice slurring the words and confirming that I was, indeed, a tiny bit off my sobriety. "I was just drinking this punch. . . ."

"So you're saying Abigail planned this party, and you knew nothing about it?"

I sighed. Even in my drunken, angry, humiliated state I could not rat out my best friend. "It was both of us," I admitted.

She braked for the red light at Sunset. "I will never trust you again."

"Well, guess what, Mom? It doesn't matter, because I'm not gonna ever go anywhere again because Abigail has turned into a BITCH and that means, ESHENSUELLY, that I have no friends!"

She handed me a Kleenex and kept driving. "Don't say 'bitch,'" she said. "And I have no idea what the other word you're trying to say is."

"I AM INNOCHENT!" I was making a great effort to control my enunciation.

"You are not innocent. You deliberately took advantage

of my vulnerability and lied to me to get out of the house."

"Eshuenshually," I admitted.

"You are grounded, and I am extremely disappointed in you," she said, her voice close to tears. "I thought I could trust at least one person in the world, but apparently that's not true."

The sound of her weepy voice made me desperate to win her forgiveness, and my rat genes kicked in. And I reversed my earlier loyalty and threw Abigail under the bus. "Look, you should have seen Abigail! All drunk and staggering around and falling on the floor! She was a mess! And I was trying to help her. And they shoved me out of the party. Like physically shoved me!"

I began to cry at the humiliation of it all.

My mother sighed. "That poor girl," she said, directing all her pity at Abigail and ignoring her own daughter's tears. "It's not hard to believe she's gone off the straight and narrow, what with the role model she has." There was considerable bitterness in my mother's voice. The divorce papers had finally come the week before, and she'd been extra-grim all week.

"Poor Abigail?" I echoed. "How about poor me?"

"Sometimes, Denver," my mother said, "you are your own worst enemy."

■ ■ ■

SUNDAY WAS GREAT, just great. I had my first real hangover, Abigail didn't call to apologize, the kiss by the pool was a fading memory, and my mother wasn't talking to me. I had no idea of the aftermath of the party, if the house was wrecked or the police came. All I knew was that the friend I thought I had was proving to be an entirely different person.

That afternoon I got a text from Quinn. I have no idea how she even got my number, but there it was.

> What happened to you at the party? Heard you had a fight with Abigail? True? I was in the back yard, I think. Kind of blotto at that point.

Nursing my hangover, feeling sorry for myself, my indifferent cat by my side, I poured my soul into a mega-text that went on forever.

> Well, hey, Quinn. Got to tell you Abigail was pretty awful to me. She pretty much bossed me around from the start of the party. I thought it was something fun we were going to throw together. Turns out she maybe just wanted me there to videotape. She was really drunk and was dancing with this other girl and fell on the floor and I started filming her, just to show her the next day what an ass she was making of herself, in case she

didn't believe me. Anyway, she ended up telling me to leave and a bunch of girls, led by Sienna Martin, threw me out. Just threw me out of my own party. So anyway, today kind of sucks. Thanks for listening.

I hit Send and then wondered if I'd said too much. After all, Quinn was buddies with Abigail. All I needed was to alienate the only other girl in school who talked to me. But a few minutes later the reply appeared.

OMG! That's terrible, Denver! Are you ok? I can't believe she did that. And after all that filming you did! Let me know if you want to talk.

Thanks, Quinn, I wrote, feeling better.

A few minutes later another text appeared.

Hey. Mind if I see that footage you took of Abigail drunk? Just curious if it's as bad as you say.

I quickly texted back.

Oh, it is! But I probably shouldn't show you. I'm guessing she wouldn't like that.

But Quinn assured me:

Just send me a tiny bit of it. I'll delete it! :)

I went back into my files. There was Abigail, rolling drunk on the floor, caterwauling "Yee-haw!" in her Texas twang. It really was kind of funny, in a super-embarrassing kind of way. I texted back:

Nah! Can't do it. But it is pretty funny!

Immediately her answer appeared.

Come on, Denver, now you've got to show me! What's the harm?

I looked at Sonny Boy. "What's the harm?" I asked him.

As usual, he offered no advice. He neither shook his sleek, pelted head slowly, nor shrieked a warning, nor threw his entitled, ten-pound body over my keyboard to stop me from downloading that video onto my phone.

DIECISÉIS

AT SCHOOL ON MONDAY MORNING, I DECIDED TO KEEP A low profile and let Abigail find me to apologize. I was at my locker after fifth period when Abigail approached me. I saw her familiar gait and kept looking straight into my locker, still deeply hurt but ready to accept her apology and put that terrible night behind me. I had a bruise on my face, no doubt gotten in the struggle to the doorway, and I hoped she'd see it clearly. I felt her drift up next to me.

"You bitch," she whispered.

I turned to her, shocked. Abigail's eyes were hard and glinted with tears. Her face was red.

"What are you talking about?"

"The video! It's all over the web! It's *everywhere*."

I stared at her. "It is?"

"What, do you live *under a rock*?"

More students had come up to join the circle around her.

"Listen, I can explain. I just sent Quinn a little clip because she asked . . ."

"That little clip," Abigail shouted, "is on YouTube right now with two million views!"

I felt the blood drain from my face. I suddenly felt sick to my stomach. "Oh, my God,' I whispered. "I never meant to—"

Abigail tackled me, knocking the breath out of me as we both fell to the floor. Before I could protect myself, she punched me in the face, the blow landing just under my eye. I grabbed on to her kinky hair and pulled as hard as I could. Abigail's face was right in mine, her eyes crazy with rage. The other students clapped and cheered.

Suddenly strong hands were pulling us apart. It was Mr. Godwin, the vice principal, and Mr. Brodeur, the ancient history teacher.

"Girls," said Mr. Brodeur, "this is no way for ladies to act!"

■ ■ ■

I COULD ONLY be a witness as Abigail's life—and mine—crashed and burned. I couldn't sleep that night, obsessed by how fast the numbers grew on YouTube. I Googled "Abigail Kenner Drunk" and twenty thousand items came up. She was internet famous—or infamous, as it were.

"What in the world made you do that to your friend?" my mother asked.

"It wasn't me! I just sent the video to Quinn."

"And she probably sent it to someone, and they probably sent it to someone, and on and on and on. What were you thinking? You know how kids are."

"Is this a good time to tell you I've got detention all week for fighting?"

She sighed. "I don't need this in my life right now, Denver."

I had to be nice to my mom because she had the dreadful task of ringing up my father and making arrangements to get my purse and phone back from Abigail's house. "No, Denver doesn't want to talk to you about it," I heard her say into the phone. "Just drop them off, please." She retreated to Robert Pathway and her own hurt world, where her husband turned out to be a dirty dog and her daughter a drunk liar who couldn't be trusted.

The next day brought more bad news. The junior varsity soccer team had a strict no-drinking policy, and since

Abigail had been caught dead to rights rolling drunk as a skunk on the floor of her house, she had to turn in her uniform. She was no longer a soccer player. No longer a star.

Her dream was dead. And so was our friendship. Abigail never spoke to me again until the night of the Malibu party and the great tsunami.

FOR THE FIRST few months, Abigail laid low. She was the laughingstock of the school, and people stopped talking and stared at her when she passed. Then, strangely, unaccountably, Abigail's internet fame led to social acceptance, and then dominance. She started hanging out with the cool kids like Madison and Hayley, and even Sienna, who seemed to finally accept her and welcome her into her exclusive Bitch Coven. Soon enough she was sitting at the popular kids' table, not just one of them, but their leader.

And me—well, I was the class traitor. The snitch who got the soccer star thrown off the team and the sole person responsible for them losing the championship.

I spent the rest of my sophomore year alone and moody, not talking to my father, barely talking to my mother, and knowing everyone at school was talking behind my back. And whenever traitorous Quinn saw me in the hallway, she went out of her way to avoid me.

By our junior year, Abigail had risen to the party girl of the school. She didn't even try out for soccer again. It was as though she'd just given up on the dream after her countless hours of practice. I have to say, I was disappointed in her, even from afar. I had never thought of Abigail as a quitter of anything. Not soccer, not friendship. I hoped she still at least hated her little brother.

People gradually forgot about Abigail's internet story. A football player got an honor student pregnant, and that news pushed Abigail Kenner, Hot Drunken Mess, and Denver Reynolds, Terrible Friend, right off the front page. I suppose I could have found other friends, maybe joined some clubs or something, but my heart wasn't in it.

I had decided to be a lone wolf. Lone wolves are rarely seen getting hurt or not being invited to parties. They simply keep to themselves and mind their own business, and they keep a dignified air about them, and they eat alone in the cafeteria, fake mashed potatoes flecking their whiskers.

All I wanted to do was get through high school. Until that day when Croix smiled at me just when the tectonic plates were planning their assault on the western shore and the world, as I knew it, prepared for its end.

DIECISIETE

THE NEW SUPPLY OF WATER ALLOWED US TO KEEP GOING, LIV-
ing and breathing and hoping for rescue. We saw several
freighters pass in the distance and signaled frantically, but
they kept chugging along until they disappeared out of sight.

We had stopped talking about the tsunami. It felt like a
phantasm that lived only on land, and land was something
sliding from our consciousness. The dead had already been
counted, I was sure. The missing chalked up as dead. The
twenty-four-hour news cycle talking about poor California would instead be mourning poor Thailand or Japan or
Turkey or whatever country had gotten its attention with
their body count. Maybe by now we were old news.

I know I was not old news to my mother. I imagined her deep in mourning, giving up on life, quitting, walking around in her robe and bursting into sudden tears, grabbing up Sonny Boy's limp, uncaring body to weep into, misinterpreting his desire to sleep all day on my pillow as his young soul grieving, forgetting that what he routinely did in normal times was sleep all day on my pillow. Taking all her Robert Pathway books and throwing them into the fire and lighting a match, all that positivity blackening and curling. My mother's pain hurt me. Though I couldn't see or hear it, I knew she was suffering somewhere.

I wanted my best friend with me in this terrible time. But she was not. She was merely in the same boat. You'd think we would have talked by now, made up finally, forgiven each other. I could tell by the expression on her face that she just wanted to keep pretending I was invisible. It was maddening. It was unfair.

But there were more pressing things I had to worry about. Now that we had slaked our thirst, our hunger was growing ferocious. We had last eaten over a week ago, and I had to do something. No birds ever swooped low enough to catch. And the fish that swarmed in taunting groups around the boat were too fast for me, even though I took off my shirt and tried to use it like a net.

I found the remnants of my bra and fashioned the

remaining underwire into another fishhook and then threaded a few of the twisted rope strands through it as a line. The problem was, we had no bait. I tried using bits of passing seaweed, but it had no affect. I looked around the boat. Sienna and Abigail slept, an increasingly common habit to all of us, and Hayley kept watch, using her signal mirror. She was lost in her own world, no doubt thinking of Trevor, the boy she had loved so briefly and with such secrecy. Her eyes were hollow, her face thin. Her hair a tangled mess. The only artifact left from the days of high school glamour, other than her Fendi purse, was her single dangly earring, still catching the light in dazzling glints.

I stared at it, an idea slowly forming in my head. I approached her.

"Hayley," I said, "I need you to do something for me."

She kept flashing her mirror. "What do you need?" she murmured.

"I need you to let me use that earring."

She finally lowered the mirror and looked at me. "Why?" she asked. Gone was the Hayley who talked in run-on sentences. Now her words were given up reluctantly, as if each one had been sewn into her clothes.

"I have an idea to use it as a lure. Maybe something will strike at it."

She nodded and gazed back at the water.

"Hayley?"

"Yes."

"Can I have your earring?"

"Okay."

She took it off and handed it to me. Without the earring, she seemed naked, somehow. I held the earring carefully.

"You always have such good ideas," she said wistfully.

"We're going to survive this, Hayley."

"But Trevor's not."

"No, he's not."

"I suppose I deserve this."

"No one deserves this," I said. She didn't answer me. I took the sparkly earring and carefully folded the earpiece until it had closed in a tiny circle. I slid the earring onto the hook and lowered the contraption over the side of the boat and into the water, wrapping the extra line around my hand.

I waited, alone with my task, jiggling the lure up and down, imagining it glittering in the ocean depths and hoping it would lure some fish who might not even be hungry but simply curious or just dazzled by the strangeness of it.

"Come on, fish," I breathed. "Come on come on come on."

The minutes passed, but I didn't give up. I couldn't.

This was our last chance. My wrist grew tired and my eyelids heavy. Out of nowhere, I felt a tug, then another, then something angry and struggling in the depths of the sea.

A fish was on the line.

"I got one! I got one!" I screamed. Hayley came over, and Abigail and Sienna woke up.

The battle was on. I gritted my teeth, but I didn't let go of the rope. I was terrified that the line would break any minute, so heavy and powerful did that fish feel, but I kept on moving backward as the rope quivered and jerked.

"Help me!" I commanded, and all four girls pulled together, so little strength left among us. But we pulled and pulled and pulled, and finally a wet fishy head with bold, flat eyes appeared over the rail, and suddenly the beast was flopping around the deck and we pounced on it, holding it down.

There it was, food food food, and Trevor's pocketknife was open and in my hand, and I was stabbing that fish, gutting it, cutting it into pieces, and then we devoured it, tearing into the raw flesh. We couldn't stop ourselves. We were ravenous animals shut out of the cafeteria of life for so many days, and now we had burst through the doors. When at last we were finished, we lay exhausted, fish blood all over us and fish parts scattered all around. We were so exhausted we couldn't speak for a while.

We stared at one another's bloody faces, and I found myself looking at Abigail. She looked away, of course, even though I had given her the gift of food and possibly had saved her life. Over the last few days, she had gone from insulting me to simply ignoring me, which I found suddenly intolerable. Anger welled up in me, and I couldn't help myself but let her have it.

"A bit of trivia," I began.

The other three looked at me.

"Abigail's mother is married to my father. Both of them left their spouses for each other."

Abigail looked startled. "Stop it, Denver."

"Destroyed both families," I continued. "*Boom*."

"Oh, my God," Hayley gasped. "Is that true?"

"Yes, it's true, all right," I said, nodding. "And I suppose my father and her mother are very happy together. Hard to know, because I never hear any news."

"Shut up." Abigail's voice had a hard edge to it.

"You'd think we'd still be best friends," I added. "Being related and all. I mean, she's my stepsister, sort of, isn't she?"

"You know why you're not best friends anymore," Sienna said. "Everyone knows why."

I was ready to talk about this. Newly restored by protein, covered with fish blood, angry and hurt as if it had just happened. The ocean was my forum. And I had the floor. "Okay, right, I'm a traitor and a snitch. I got Abigail thrown off the soccer team, and I ruined her life."

"Exactly," said Abigail.

"No! You know what, Abigail? YOU got yourself thrown off the soccer team."

"Bullshit!" she said as fish-stained and angry as me. "You're the one who filmed me all drunk and sloppy, and you're the one who spread it around the world! I invited you to my party, and that was my thanks!"

"I was trying to PROTECT YOU!" I screamed. "No one else even cared that you were making a fool of yourself! I just took the video to show you how stupid you looked and to keep you from doing it again. It was your pal *Quinn* who said she'd keep it to herself and didn't!"

Hayley looked anxious. "Let's not fight, okay?" she asked. "It was a long time ago and everyone's forgotten all about it and—"

"Nothing would have happened," Abigail snarled, looking at me with hatred in her eyes, "if you hadn't filmed me drunk to start with. And you know why you did it? 'Cause you were jealous. Jealous because I was a soccer star and I was making friends and having parties and you were just a nobody with no goals and no life and you still are."

The boat was silent.

Some surfacing dolphin would have been amazed that girls in such dire circumstances could be arguing about something that had happened over a year ago back on the dry land they might never see again, but neither one of us cared. I got to my feet and so did she and we faced each other, our faces still flecked with blood from our frenzied raw meal. Abigail and I were breathing hard, inches from beating each other with the last of our strength.

"Well, you know what?" I said at last. "I'd rather be a nobody than a drunken, whiny quitter who just blows off the dream she's worked so hard for. You could have tried out for the soccer team again this year, maybe even the varsity soccer team. But you'd rather just trash people's houses and hang around with a bunch of girls you used to hate and pretend you're better than everyone else. You know what? The Abigail I knew would think you were a *total asshole*."

Abigail looked a bit taken aback. But I wasn't done.

"You know what your problem is, Abigail?" I said. "You never take responsibility for anything. Nothing is ever your fault. Well, listen, I may have filmed you and sent a clip to Quinn, and that was a mistake. But you had the party, and you got yourself drunk. You screwed your own dream, not me. You just love playing the victim. Well, wait until we get back to land, and you and your mother can go sit in a sweat lodge in Arizona together and talk about how people fail you with their fences and their texts."

Abigail looked positively murderous now. She raised a bloody fist.

"Go ahead," I told her. "Hit me."

"Hey," Hayley pleaded. Her voice was full of pain. "We're probably going to die out here. Can't we all be friends? Can't we do that?"

"No!" Abigail and I both snarled, and for once we were in agreement.

A FIGHT LIKE that doesn't make for a pleasant castaway experience. We all said very little as we cleaned the blood from the deck and saved the organs of the fish to use as bait. That night, as we were all preparing for troubled sleep, I felt a soft hand on my arm and looked over to see Hayley's face inches from mine.

"I'm sorry. About your dad and about Abigail. I know you probably didn't mean to get her into so much trouble. And if it makes you feel any better, none of the popular kids really know Abigail. She kind of lives in her own

266

little world. She's like one of those Malibu properties with no public beach access."

Hayley was being nice. And had made a successful metaphor.

Death was surely near.

DIECIOCHO

ANOTHER WEEK PASSED. I CAUGHT THREE MORE FISH WITH my homemade hook before it broke and we again were out of options. The water supply was running low, and we continued to drift.

We were like starfish, neither dead nor alive.

I was the only one who wouldn't give up. The others slumped under the crippled sunshade, but I stood watch, scanning the horizon, the sky, moving the mirror back and forth. Hoping for a sign, for anything. I had always thought my passion was for filmmaking. Now I realized my true talent was surviving. I wondered, if by some outside chance we were rescued, how I could turn that into a career in the real world.

Abigail seemed to be worse off than the rest of us. She spent most of her time sleeping, and when she awoke, she thought she saw Mr. Shriek standing on the rail.

"Mr. Shriek," she would mumble. "You did it. You did it. You vamoosed from that terrible cage. I knew you had it in you, cowboy."

Abigail and I weren't friends, or enemies. We just lived side by side, there in that briny-smelling boat, too busy watching our own bodies give up on us to remember why and how we'd given up on each other. The act of dying at sea, I was coming to realize, was a long and tortuous one. It takes quite a while for the body to quit. It's a trooper, and it has unrealistic expectations of survival. The heart keeps on beating and beating, almost to the point that it gets annoying, like Trevor's drumming.

I had a brief, sudden memory of Abigail coming up to my locker one time in eighth grade, her body trembling with excitement, her breath smelling of the strawberry lemonade we'd had in the cafeteria.

"You know how when you go under the covers and after a while it starts feeling hard to breathe, and then you come out and breathe the air in the room and it's so cold and pure? Maybe we could *bottle that feeling!*"

What had happened to that girl? What had happened to me?

I slept a lot. My hand was growing weaker as it held the mirror to the light, and I wondered if its signal, once a shout, had become a pleading whisper.

THE DAY WAS like any other day in our slowly fading world. The sun still high in the sky. A salty sea breeze coming over us. Not a soul in sight. Just an empty sea. But I kept scanning, kept watching, as the other girls slept and my eyelids grew heavy. The rocking of the boat, before I knew it, lulled me to sleep.

I was jarred awake by the sudden thud of the boat striking something. As I rubbed my eyes, I heard seabirds.

We had hit land. Some kind of island with a broad beach, scattered dunes, and a forest of looming palms and other trees I could not identify.

"Hey!" I said. "Hey! Wake up!"

The others slowly roused themselves.

"What?" asked Sienna.

"We've hit land!"

Sienna and Hayley got up shakily and looked over the rail. "So we're saved?" Hayley asked weakly.

"Not exactly. But there might be water on the island. Water and food."

Abigail sat up but remained on the carpet. She wasn't looking so good. I touched her shoulder. "Abigail. We're on land."

She could barely open her eyes. "Mr. Shriek says, 'Who cares?'"

I looked at Sienna and Hayley. "Stay with her while I secure the boat."

The rope was coiled up at the bottom of a hatch. I grabbed it and tied it to a rail, then climbed down the ladder, moving into the water and finding sand about three feet down, the first solid ground I had touched in many days.

I started wading to the shore, but my knees suddenly gave out, and I collapsed in the water. I stood up shakily, fighting for balance. I was so weak, and having been at sea for so long, I wasn't used to my land legs. I struggled to shore and secured the rope around a big rock sitting about ten feet from the shoreline. Sienna and Hayley watched me quietly. There really wasn't much left of them, or Abigail, or me. This island might be our savior, or we might die here.

I signaled to them that I had to rest a minute and

flopped on the warm beach, breathing heavily and hugging my knees. A sand crab crawled toward a dune. Seabirds hunted in the shallows. Palm trees waved. And I couldn't help but marvel at the gifts of dry land. That solid feel where you can be among things that are growing. Things with roots. An island was like a giant anchor in the sea. There had to be water here. There had to be food.

I'd wrestle down and eat one of those seabirds if I had to. I'd eat that crab, the flower I saw blooming on the dune, the bark off the trees. I was that hungry.

When I had recovered enough strength to rise, I staggered back into the water and made my way to the boat.

"Okay," I told Sienna and Hayley, "it's gonna be real hard for you to use your legs. I need you guys to get Abigail to the back of the boat and hand her to me. Then, once we're safely ashore, I'll come back and guide you. We've got to do this slowly and carefully. Okay?"

They nodded. Their eyes were dull. Time was running out for us.

"Okay. Now, Hayley, you take her under the arms and, Sienna, you take her feet. Don't drop her."

They finally got Abigail, who was still mumbling about Mr. Shriek, over the back of the boat and into my arms. Her body was surprisingly light as I lowered it into the water and then tugged my friend to shore.

I got her past the lapping waves and up onto dry sand, where I laid her down and dropped beside her, huffing and puffing.

"You okay, Abigail?"

"Water."

"I know."

With considerable staggering and falling, the other two joined us, and we dragged Abigail to the shade of a giant palm tree near the beach. Her body was limp, her breath coming shallow and fast. All my anger at her was gone. How could I be angry when she looked so ill and defenseless?

"Hold on, Abigail," I said. "You're gonna make it."

We retrieved our supplies from the boat. We were weak and starving and thirsty and moving in slow motion, but we did it. I motioned for Sienna and Hayley to follow me. They obeyed me without any protest. I was thankful, because I had seen an entire Bear Grylls marathon one weekend when everyone else was partying in Cabo, and I was eager to try something. I led them to a place on the beach a few yards up from where the waves lapped. I opened Trevor's pocketknife and gave it to Sienna. "Take those sticks and dig a hole right here," I said. "The water under the sand is a combination of fresh and salt water. If this works, both fresh and salt water will fill the hole. And, since fresh water is less dense than salt water, it will rise to the top, and we can skim it off. In theory, at least."

Hayley looked at me with true awe. "You are the smartest person I know," she said.

"I'm so thirsty," Sienna said.

"Then dig," I said. "I'm gonna go into the jungle before the sun sets and look for water. We've got to help Abigail. She's looking pretty bad."

I took the nearly empty gallon jug and headed into the forest. As I moved through it, the trees blocked out the sky and left the forest dark and cool. I wasn't sure where I was heading, but I knew that some islands contained water sources, and I was determined to find one.

I had to stop every few feet and lean against a tree to catch my breath. The ground became slightly higher, and I reached what looked like a rock cliff that went up about twenty feet. I took off my shirt and fashioned a sling for the jug, put the sling over one shoulder, and slowly began to climb, afraid I was going to lose my grip and fall. But something told me to keep going and so I did, clinging on to the places where the rock had eroded away as I inched my way up.

Just when I felt I was too dizzy to go on, I found the entry to what looked like a cave. It was pitch-black inside. I wondered what kind of beasts it guarded, but I didn't have the time or the strength to worry, so I crawled through the opening, which I judged to be about four feet in diameter, and into the darkness. Clutching the water jug, I inched forward, turning around to see where the light came through the opening to keep myself oriented. I tried to count my paces, remembering each time I moved one hand, then the other, one knee, then the other.

I counted twenty, thirty . . . then froze. I had heard a sound.

Dripping.

Water. Invisible in the darkness, splashing onto the rocks of the cave floor.

I could see nothing, but I held out my hand, moving it in the darkness until the water hit my palm. A steady drizzle. I positioned myself so that it ran into my mouth and gulped greedily.

Beautiful water. Cool and reeking faintly of organic matter and minerals and possibly bat shit. The most astonishing nectar in the world. I knew I wasn't supposed to drink too much at once, but I couldn't help myself. I drank in pitch-darkness, on my knees, as the water splashed on my face and in my hair. It was like a PG-rated rap video for a song called "Shipwreck," and the only thing that tore me away from that miraculous trickle was the thought that Abigail needed it more than I did.

I filled the jug and made my way very carefully down the cliff and put my shirt back on. It took longer to make the return trip because I was lugging a gallon of water. But just my brief, gulping drink had made me feel remarkably restored, as if right now, every organ in my body was shouting to the next: *We're going to live! Pass it on!*

Darkness was falling when I emerged from the forest and found Abigail still slumped under the palm tree, just as I had left her. Hayley and Sienna were hard at work digging in the sand in the near distance, and I motioned them over. As they came limping up, clearly spent by their efforts, I poured some water into an empty Spam tin and held it to Abigail's lips.

"Drink," I said. "Just a little at a time."

"Hey," said Hayley, "your idea is working! The hole is filling up with water!"

"Screw that," I said. "We've got better water now. I found it in a cave."

Abigail had finished drinking, so I poured her a little more and handed the jug to the girls.

"Oh, my God!" Hayley screamed. "Thank you thank you thank you!"

She grabbed the jug and gulped it and then Sienna grabbed it from her and gulped too, and they grabbed and gulped like that jug was the last boy band member in the world.

"Okay, okay, stop," I said. "You'll make yourselves sick." I took back the jug. "I'm gonna make another trip to the cave to get more water. Hayley, I'll need your lighter so I can see in the dark."

Abigail just stared into space. But her eyes seemed a little clearer.

"Denver," Sienna said with a desperate tone in her voice, "I'm so hungry."

She was right. The slaking of my thirst had reawakened a feeling of internal famine so severe I could have eaten a belt or a shoe.

"We're going to eat," I said.

"We are?"

"Yes."

"How?"

"I have plans."

"You always do," said Sienna. She looked at me with something approaching gratitude. "I'm so glad you came to Abigail's party in Malibu. We needed you."

The irony of it made me laugh, but of course it went straight over Sienna's head.

"And who knows . . . ," she continued, "maybe when

we get back home, you can sit at our table with us. Some of the cool kids aren't coming back, and there will be more room." A look of sudden concern crossed her face, and she hastened to add, "Of course, it wouldn't be a permanent thing or anything. Just a one-day honor to show our appreciation."

Hayley gazed at me with hero worship. "I want to sit next to you at the table, because you are a genius, and without you, we'd all be dead."

I flicked the lighter to make sure it still worked.

"I won't be gone long. I need you to stay here with Abigail and keep her company."

"Keep me company," Abigail murmured. I was feeling more encouraged about her. I hadn't heard her mention Mr. Shriek for over an hour. That invisible parrot was becoming her barometer of wellness.

I felt stronger on my second journey to the cave and the water. I had thoughts about spearing fish and building fires and shelter and spelling out *SOS* with the washed-up wood on the beach. And I was proud to be in charge of our iffy prospects of salvation. We had survived for two weeks. And we could keep on surviving until we were back in LA, picking up our lives, embracing our loved ones, and being ignored by our cats.

With much effort, I climbed back up to the cave and

used the lighter to see my way as I crawled toward the water. I hoped the flame wouldn't reveal a pair of bright glowing eyes or I wouldn't hear the breathing of some horrible, awkward-girl-eating beast coming from some dark corner.

But nothing of the sort happened. The water flowed cool and trusty into my container, and I allowed myself to drink some more.

My thoughts now turned to food. I hadn't seen any kind of fruit so far on the island, but I suspected that fish might be lurking in the shallows of the bay, and fish could be caught. Theoretically, at least.

I carried the full gallon jug back to the beach, where I shared more water with my companions. Abigail seemed a bit more alert, but I was still worried about her.

I had Hayley and Sienna help me find driftwood and brush to make a signal fire on the beach. "Tomorrow we'll find a way to get some food," I promised. Later, we dragged fallen palm leaves under the tree for our beds and sat watching the fire we'd built. It was about twenty feet away from us, but we were close enough to feel its warmth, and it was comforting to see it looking so alive, so vital. Perhaps we could all be that way again.

"You guys go to sleep," I said. "I'll keep the fire going."

"Come on," Sienna argued. "You need sleep, too. What

are the chances of a plane or a ship coming by tonight?" I noticed that her lip wasn't as curled as usual. In fact, it was moving normally.

"You never know, Sienna," I said. "And what if someone was out there and didn't know we were here? I'll be fine, don't worry."

I went down the beach and gathered more driftwood for the fire, then stood out at the edge of the waves with the heat at my back, looking out at the sea. The water shimmered. A dolphin jumped in the distance. The wind moved long grasses on the dune and swept a fresh scent through the air. This island was absolutely beautiful, and had we been here by choice, it would have been even more so. But for now I just appreciated the quiet, the sound of the waves, and the warmth behind me to reassure me the fire was still going and we were still visible to anyone who happened to look.

I felt stronger now, somehow. As though with the island had come a new opportunity to test myself with the things I had learned. The others had started to look on me as their savior. I could hear it in their voices, and though I was not so sure myself, that tone with which they spoke to me gave me new determination to get us back home.

A voice in my ear.

"Denver."

I turned around.

There was Hayley, barefoot in the sand, the firelight emphasizing that tentative way she had of approach.

"Hayley, what are you doing up?"

"I couldn't sleep, so I thought I'd come over and see what you're doing."

"Oh, you know, the usual."

She smiled. She seemed to be getting younger as the days passed. It was hard to imagine her at that Malibu party, dressed to the nines and perfectly groomed. I felt sorry for Hayley. She seemed so lost in this new world, and by all rights, she shouldn't be here. She should be in bed in some nice house, asleep under a quilt with flowers on it, and the problems in her head should have been mild and subject to evaporation.

"You are always watching out for us, aren't you?" she asked me.

"Sure I am."

Her face took on a quizzical look. "Can I ask you something?"

"Sure."

"Why are you trying to save us? I mean, after the way Sienna and I treated you. And Abigail hates you. Why do you even care if we live or die?"

I found my answer hard to put into words. Finally I

said, "Because, you see, life is important. It's this magical thing. My life, your life, Sienna's life, Abigail's life. I think I appreciate it now more than I ever did before. Think of all the things you have left to do, Hayley. Think about the songs you'll sing, the mornings you'll get up, the people you'll meet, and the man you'll marry. Maybe even the kids you'll have. Think about everything you could change, just because you stayed alive."

Hayley was quiet for a few moments.

"You know," she said at last, "right after Trevor died, I didn't want to live. But now I do. I want to be a better person."

"You're a good person already," I said.

"No, I'm not. I'm not like Audrey Curtis. I've done things to people I thought were funny at the time but now I realize were just cruel. And Denver, I did something to Abigail once. I did something to you."

I turned and looked at her, puzzled.

"What do you mean, Hayley?"

"Abigail's soccer party. Sienna and I were there, remember?"

"I remember."

"I put something in her drink." Hayley started talking faster, rushing the words. "Sienna told me to do it. She said Abigail was starting to think she was better than everyone else and needed to be put in her place. It was supposed to be harmless, like a prank. She kept pressuring me, so finally I did it. I didn't know she'd get so drunk, or she'd get thrown off the team, or that it would ruin your friendship. I wanted to tell you earlier, but Sienna told me to keep quiet."

I felt a rush of anger. "You have got to be kidding me," I said.

"You must think I'm the worst person in the world," Hayley said.

I wanted to yell at Hayley and ask her if she realized how much trouble she had caused, but she sounded so sorry—on the point of tears—that I forced myself to take a few deep breaths.

"People make mistakes," I managed to say. "People do things that they don't really think will turn out so bad. I wish I could go back and do everything different that night, too."

"Oh!" Hayley cried, looking relieved and grateful. "Me too, me too. I'm so sorry. I'm going to tell Abigail what happened tomorrow. It's my fault you're not friends anymore."

"No, it isn't," I said. "I've been thinking a lot about Abigail and me lately. Our friendship was on pretty thin ice even before that party. My dad moving into her house,

Abigail making the soccer team . . . those things were pulling us apart. I guess it's no one's fault we're not friends anymore. I guess those things kind of happen. Besides, since we're telling the truth here, I filmed Abigail because I was mad at her, and I sent the footage to Quinn for the same reason. I never should have done that. So there's enough blame to go around."

There was nothing left to say. We stood watching the waves crawl in. They were small waves. Trevor wouldn't have been able to surf here. He would be lying on his board right now in the water, his wet hair in his face, drumming on Plexiglas and thinking up songs about calm weather.

Hayley touched my arm. "When we're rescued and we go back home, I'm going to be a better person. You just wait and see."

DIECINUEVE

DAWN ON THE ISLAND.

Abigail was still asleep. I put my hand on her forehead. It felt warm to me.

The others were already awake.

"If you want to help, you can collect some more wood for tonight's fire," I told them. "I'll stay here with Abigail." I sat beside her and watched as Hayley and Sienna ambled down the beach and disappeared out of sight. I'd stayed up all night, and my eyelids were growing heavy. I dug my fingernails into my arms to stay alert, but I was sinking, drifting off. . . .

I awoke with a start. The sun was at its late-morning

position, and Abigail was awake and sipping water.

I sat up and rubbed my eyes.

"How are you doing?"

"Gettin' by," she murmured. But her voice sounded dreamy, and her face was flushed.

"Where are Hayley and Sienna?"

"Don't know. Haven't seen them all morning."

"Wait. It must have been hours ago that I sent them to get wood." I glanced down the beach. It was empty of piled driftwood and girls. "They should have been back by now. I'm going to go find them."

I rose to leave.

"I'll help," Abigail volunteered weakly. She tried to get up but sank back down.

"You stay right here," I said. "I'll be back. Don't start talking to Mr. Shriek again."

I took off down the beach, walking along between the high-tide line and the dunes, calling Hayley's and Sienna's names, over and over until they sounded strange, not like names at all. Were I not so hungry and so worried about the girls, you could almost call that walk pleasant. The sea was a shimmering blue, the waves made a beautiful lapping sound against the shore, and the cries of birds were welcome after so many silent hours at sea. I started losing my breath, probably due to my weakened state. I sat down in the warm sand to rest, watching one wave lap and then another, feeling suddenly so tired. I wanted to lie back and go to sleep, but there was this whole survival thing going on that had become my life's work.

I made myself get up, and I kept walking.

I found them a hundred yards past the first cove, lying side by side in the sand. Their eyes were open and fixed; their lips were stained purple.

I felt a pulse of disbelief run through me. My knees gave out, and I sank to the ground between the bodies.

No. This could not be happening.

I waved a hand over Hayley's face, but she didn't blink. I touched her cheek. It was cold.

"Oh no," I said. "Oh no oh no . . ."

Hayley had something clutched in her fist. I opened her fingers and found a cluster of purple berries. Suddenly furious, I knocked the berries out of her hand.

"Why couldn't you have waited?!" I shouted at them. "I would have gotten you food. I promise I would have!" A wave of grief and loss swept over me as I stared down at their faces, not so peaceful in death but looking scared. Carefully, I closed their eyes with the tips of my fingers. I did not know what to do next. They were dead, and somehow I felt it was my fault. I shouldn't have left them alone. Should have guarded them, because they may have been sophisticated in Malibu, but they were helpless in the wild with no pavement or Starbucks or iPhones.

I broke down, remembering what Hayley had confessed the night before. "Hayley," I said to her, crying, "everyone makes mistakes. You were a good person; can't you see that?"

I found a place a short distance away where the sand was soft and dug their graves with a stick and my hands as tears ran down my face. The sand gave way easily, but it was still hard work to clear a hole three feet deep and six feet long. I dug as quickly as I could, needing to get back to Abigail so I would not have to make a grave for three but knowing Abigail would also want Hayley and Sienna to have a decent burial. The sand turned wet as I dug deeper, and when water began to fill the hole, I stopped. It was barely deep enough, and I didn't like the idea of burying them somewhere wet, but I didn't feel I had much of a choice, and it was better than leaving them in the woods with palm leaves draped over their bodies.

I went back to where they lay and took Hayley under the arms and moved her body across the sand to the new grave, then did the same with Sienna. I arranged them so that they lay together in a spoon position. They looked peaceful now that I had closed their eyes, as though they were dreaming of all the water they could drink and all the food they could eat and all the life they could live, now that they were safe.

I said a few words over their bodies, something about resting in peace and all the typical things I thought were usually said, then I brushed sand over them until the beach was smooth again. If not for a small disruption in the sand, you would never have believed that two girls lay beneath it.

I wasn't sure what I was going to tell Abigail. I didn't want to upset her, but on this tiny island, the truth was hard to avoid. And the truth was that her friends—no, our friends—were dead.

Abigail was asleep when I returned. I knelt down next to her, and she opened her eyes.

"Did you find 'em?"

I helped her sit up.

"Yes."

She looked around. "Well, where are they?"

I swallowed. This was hard.

"Well?"

"I'm sorry but . . . they're gone."

She cocked her head slightly to the side. It was that same quizzical look I had known so well and loved so much in years past, when she was trying to solve a mystery or formulate a plan. Now it broke my heart.

"They ate poison berries, Abigail. They're dead."

She snorted a little through her nose. "Stop horsing around, Denver," she said, but her voice trembled, and her eyes slowly filled with tears. She wiped a streak of watery snot from her nose.

"For real?" she said at last.

"Yeah."

"It's not fair. They made it so far. . . ."

I sat down next to her, and we looked out over the ocean, tears running down our faces for the two girls we had once hated but now mourned. "I didn't mind them so much, in the end. I even kind of liked them," I said. "Hayley more than Sienna, of course."

"I remember when I used to hate Sienna. Seems like so long ago. And Hayley. Always thought she was a blabbermouth. But there was more to that girl." She let out a long breath, as though the two sentences had exhausted her.

I touched her warm hand. "Just so you know, I'd appreciate it very much if you didn't die, Abigail."

She closed her eyes. "I'll give it my best shot."

SURVIVORS CAN'T JUST sit around and mourn the dead. Survivors have to get up and survive. So that is what I did. I found one of the spears I had crafted for Hayley and Sienna, and sharpened it with Trevor's pocketknife. Then

I headed out into the ocean, wading in the shallows, moving down the beach until I found a place where the water was relatively calm and clear.

I waited, my spear poised, my eyes searching the water.

Finally I saw a small group of brightly colored fish languidly swimming toward me. I waited, tensing, the fish coming closer and closer. I picked out the one in the lead and plunged the spear with all my might.

I screamed. The water turned red as the fish scattered. I had speared my own bare foot.

I lifted my foot and saw that the tip of the spear had gone in just behind the toes and emerged between the soft pads of my sole.

Blood was everywhere.

I hopped backward toward the beach, holding on to the spear, the tip of which was still through my foot. When I was clear of the waves, I fell back in the sand and closed my eyes and tugged on the spear with all my might.

That kind of pain is very hard to describe. It felt like my foot was tearing in half, and I wailed in agony; but I tugged on the spear until it was free and cast it to the side and grabbed my foot, desperately trying to stop the bleeding. That would be perfect for me, bleeding to death after spearing myself. Abigail would perhaps find it sadly amusing just before she died, too. And there we'd be, four corpses on the island: two in the sand, one under a tree, and one on the beach clutching her foot.

The blood wasn't slowing down. I needed something to staunch it. I saw some kind of straw-looking material sitting on some nearby dunes, and I dragged myself over to it slowly, leaving a trail of blood in the sand, finally reaching it and realizing . . . it was a nest.

A nest with eggs in it.

Food. Protein. Salvation.

I tore off some of the nest material and pressed it over my wound, waiting until the blood flow finally staunched, refusing to worry about germs and infection.

There were four eggs in that nest. Four perfect, pale-blue eggs. I gathered them in my arms and hobbled back up the beach. The sun was low in the sky now. Abigail was watching me.

"What happened?" she asked, gesturing to my foot. "I heard you holler. I tried to run to you but I couldn't walk."

"It's okay. It's nothing," I said. "I stabbed myself with my own spear. But guess what I found?"

I showed her the eggs.

"And, Abigail, there are more nests up and down the beach. We'll have food. Maybe in one food group, but we won't starve."

"Good," she said, but her voice was weak. We divided

up the eggs and cracked them and let the contents slide down our throats. They tasted exactly as you'd imagine warm beach bird eggs would taste.

"Slightly better than cafeteria food," I announced. "I'm going to go get some more."

"I don't want any more," Abigail said.

"Are you kidding? You haven't eaten in days."

She shook her head. "I'm just not hungry."

"Abigail, you have to eat. You have to."

She didn't answer me.

"Well, great," I said. "Just great. You came this far, and you're just going to give up."

"I'm not giving up, Denver," she murmured. "Maybe my body is giving up for me."

"Well, don't let it." I reached over and felt her forehead. It was hot. "Does your head hurt?"

She nodded.

I made her drink some more water and then I went to get more eggs to bring back to Abigail, ignoring her declaration that she could eat no more of them.

"Come on," I said. "Just one more."

But she shook her head, and nothing I said could convince her, so I ate the eggs myself to give me the strength to build a signal fire. The empty nest made good tinder, and there was plenty of dry wood. I used Hayley's lighter and felt a pang as the flame rose, remembering Hayley's run-on sentences and wondering if she was babbling on right now in heaven to some patient angel.

When the fire got going, I limped back and sat next to Abigail. She seemed a bit more alert than she had the past few days, but I was still very worried about her.

"Signal fire during the day?" she asked.

"Yeah."

"Think anyone's gonna see it?"

"Maybe. And if they don't, I'm going to start building a large *SOS* out of sticks on the beach. It will be so big you can see it from the moon."

I was sitting cross-legged next to her. The fire smelled good from a distance. Made up of dry things that thought their usefulness was over.

"You know what I'd like to see right now?" I asked.

"What?"

"A dog pissing against the side of a building."

"Why?"

"Because it's such a normal thing. And dogs always look so peaceful when they piss."

"Yeah, I guess so."

What I really wanted to see right now was the view of Abigail's pool the way I used to see it, while hanging out on a chaise longue next to hers, as we talked about anything that came to our minds. Her little brother circling out of reach, preparing some kind of verbal or physical attack. Insults or hurled Pop Rocks. Abigail's big red hair drying into kinks and twists. Her freckles multiplying in the sun. Her deranged figures of speech in full swing. Her laughter real. Doing that thing she did with her pointer finger, the way it spiraled in the air when she was trying to explain something difficult. I wanted to be back there, not just because it meant we were saved, but because it meant we were friends.

I sighed.

"What?" she asked.

"Here we are," I said. "Just the two of us. On an island in the middle of nowhere. All our friends are dead. Is this crazy?"

"Pretty loco," she agreed.

I poured some more water into the Spam can for her to drink. She shook her head.

"Come on," I said.

"Ya know what they say 'bout leading a horse to water."

"I don't want you to die," I said. "I don't want to die myself. And I sure don't wanna die without telling you I'm sorry."

Her skin was so burned and freckled. Her eyes so dim.

"Don't worry, Denver. Water under the bridge."

"I am, though, Abigail. Really sorry."

The words seemed to make her tired. "Ahhh, Denver . . ."

"Filming you that night was a terrible idea. I guess I was pissed off because I thought you didn't really want me at the party."

"No, I wanted you there. Guess I was just nervous, trying to impress everyone. Didn't think enough about your feelings. Sorry I got you thrown out. Have no memory of that. I dunno why I got so drunk. I was being careful, honest I was."

"Hayley and Sienna put something in your drink. That's why you were so out of control."

"Huh?" Abigail looked at me, her weak eyes showing confusion.

"Yeah. Hayley told me last night. She was going to tell you herself. She was really sorry about it. She said Sienna thought you were getting too cocky and needed to be taken down a little."

Abigail took a few moments to absorb the information. "Sienna was always a snake," she said at last. "Never trusted her, not even after we started hanging out."

"Anyway," I told her, "I'm not telling you to shift the blame for what happened off me. I just thought you had a right to know."

We were talking just like we used to talk. It felt so natural, even though we were on a deserted island together and that was the most unnatural thing in the world. I thought we might as well keep going, now that we were finally addressing the elephants on the beach.

"And I'm sorry for sending that clip to Quinn," I added. "I honestly didn't think she'd pass it around, but I was dumb, dumb, dumb."

"Well," said Abigail. "The whole thing did give me a certain kind of notoriety, like Jesse James. Of course, it did get me thrown off the soccer team. . . ."

"I'm sorry," I repeated.

"What does it matter now?" She moved her hand over the horizon. "You see any soccer fields out there?"

"I was jealous, Abigail," I admitted. "You had all these new friends, and I only had you."

"Can we stop talking for a minute?" Abigail said. "Got to rest my eyes."

"Of course. Can I get you anything?"

"I'm good, Nurse Denver."

She leaned back against the tree and closed her eyes, and I waited. Minutes passed. The wind blew strands of wild red hair into her face. I fought tears. I didn't want to remember this as the time I apologized to Abigail just before she died.

Finally she opened her eyes. "I'm sorry too," she said. "I've been pretty mean to you. Blaming you for everything. Turning my back on you and taking up with the likes of Sienna. Turning into an asshole who trashed good people's property. Don't know what I thought I was doing."

The long silence that followed wasn't even uncomfortable. A fish jumped out in the calm ocean, not a care in the world, and we watched it together. Then the fish disappeared and the water smoothed over. It was as though some god, half-sentimental, half-monstrous, had planned out this time for us, right here and now.

"Water under the bridge," I said at last.

"Deal, then," said Abigail.

"Our bridge-water deal," I said.

"How's your hoof?" she asked, changing the subject.

"Not too bad, considering a spear went through it." I had cleaned my foot with seawater and fashioned a crude bandage out of palm leaves and strands of rope.

The firelight was still burning high. Abigail looked away from my foot and stared into the flames.

"I missed you, cowgirl," she said.

I couldn't help the tears now. My body had water and was ready to go.

"Me too."

VEINTE

BY NIGHT I KEPT GETTING UP TO KEEP THE SIGNAL FIRE LIT. BY day I brought water back from the cave for Abigail and me and dragged washed-up wood to make a giant *SOS* sign in the sand. And I watched the horizon.

Although I had learned to cook the eggs into a scramble with the Spam can and a stick, Abigail still wouldn't eat them. Out of desperation, I waded into the water with my spear and bad foot and managed to impale my first fish, cleaned it myself and threw the guts to the circling gulls, then roasted the fish on the fire.

"Here," I said, giving the cooked fish to her on a palm leaf, "eat this. It's not eggs."

Abigail stared at it and then sank back into her usual position against her tree. Every day she was slumping down a little farther.

"Come on, eat it," I said.

"Can't," she whispered.

Finally, realizing it was just going to go to waste, I ate it. But it didn't taste like fresh fish. It tasted like dying friend, and I was growing frantic. We could not have reconciled the world's most beautiful relationship on this island only to have her die on me. God, if there was one, couldn't possibly be that cruel.

I stopped sleeping at night, afraid of waking up next to her and finding her dead. I dozed off and on during the day in between my chores, but never for more than a few minutes. I was afraid—terrified—of losing Abigail. I somehow felt that I had been put in charge of our destiny—a task for which I was totally unprepared. Yet I was determined not to fail.

"You just wait, Abigail," I told her. "We'll do all the things we wanted to do, just like we planned. And you can try out for the soccer team again, right? I mean, you'll get a chance before your senior year, won't you?" Abigail's eyes were closed, and I wondered if she was sleeping, but she opened her eyes and managed to whisper, "Sure."

I was thin, and I could feel my own ribs, but at least I

was eating. I was so worried about Abigail. I couldn't stand the thought of being on this island without her. Burying her. Saying good-bye.

"Don't you die on me," I whispered.

She didn't answer. That night I stayed up listening to her breathe.

IT WAS OUR sixth day on the island when I saw it. I was spearfishing in the shallow water and looked up, and there it was. A small boat, bobbing on the waves, chugging slowly by in the distance.

I squinted. It was real.

I jumped up and down, waving my spear like a native, screaming at the top of my lungs.

"Help us! Help us!"

The boat kept moving by.

"No!" I screamed. "No!"

I could not let this happen. Abigail hadn't spoken a word since the night before. This was our last chance.

I had an idea. I ran to where our paltry supplies were piled up near Abigail's palm tree and snatched Hayley's compact mirror.

"Abigail," I said. "There's a boat!"

Abigail lay with her eyes closed. She didn't answer me, but there was no time to waste—the boat was moving past us. I ran down the beach and found the tallest palm tree I could find.

And I began to climb.

My arms and legs felt weak, and the tree was smooth of branches. Nothing, really, to hold on to. My foot was still hurt, but I gritted my teeth and kept going, huffing and puffing, inching up that skinny tree.

I almost lost my balance and fell. My foot slid, and I tightened my grip and hugged the tree. Slowly I began to slide back down despite my frantic efforts to keep my footing.

The healing wound on the bottom of my hurt foot tore open. I felt sticky blood on the trunk as I battled gravity.

My legs were killing me. My foot pain was agonizing. I was running out of energy.

"FUHHHHHH!"

I could not believe my ears.

"FUHHHHH!"

I looked up the tree and there was Mr. Shriek, looking down at me. I blinked. This was clearly an illusion brought on by my desperate circumstance. . . .

"FUHHHH!"

Yet somehow this ghost parrot gave me strength. I recovered my footing and inched up, up, up, until I was thirty feet above the ground. I pulled the compact out of my pocket, opened it, and began signaling with the mirror. Although I didn't know the language of signaling, I knew that the intensity of light just might attract the people on the boat.

I moved the compact back and forth, letting the light from the setting sun hit the glass.

The boat slowed, then stopped.

I wasn't going to wait and see if the people in that boat changed their mind. I slid down the trunk and ran down the beach and dove into the water, swimming hard for me, hard for Abigail, hard for the future that was ours if we could just survive. I kicked my legs so hard and stretched my arms way out to move myself through the sea. As I swam, I went back in time to the Palisades, swimming across pools with Abigail, all those shades of chlorine, the lives around us . . . it was still a mystery, but we were going to live. . . .

I inhaled some water and didn't stop to cough. Kept going, harder, faster, the ocean water turning gray and peaceful around me. I wasn't moving anymore, and try as I might, I was drifting off to sleep. It was peaceful and dark.

I sank.

I woke up sputtering water, flat on my back. I was on

the boat. Four dark-skinned fishermen, three dry and one soaking wet, stared down at me. I sat up, coughing more water.

"You've got to help my friend!" I gasped.

They looked bewildered, speaking to one another in rapid Spanish. I coughed out more water and drew in my breath. I pointed to the beach.

"MI AMIGA ESTA EN LA PLAYA!"

VENTIUNO

AND SO, NEARLY THREE WEEKS AFTER BEING WASHED OUT TO sea, Abigail and I were rescued. We were both taken by helicopter to the UCLA Medical Center: Abigail to the intensive-care unit and myself to a noncritical-care floor for observation and treatment of my wounded foot. The sight of my parents in the doorway is something I'll never forget. They looked so terrified and relieved and drained. They rushed forward to hug me, and I hugged my dad just as hard as I hugged my mom. After all that had happened, I finally realized I not only could forgive my dad, but had already forgiven him. I told him so, much to his gratitude and relief. My mother had read enough Robert Pathway to forgive him too. And in that hospital room, we became not a big happy family again, but a broken, forgiven family, and that was enough for the time being.

After two days I was discharged from the hospital, and my mom drove me home in a car she had bought off Craigslist, since the Subaru I'd driven to the party in Malibu had never been found. I was never so happy to be in my own home again. Everything seemed so calm and clean and stable—no more rocking on the ocean waves.

I climbed the stairs and entered my room, and there was Sonny Boy asleep on my pillow, the afternoon light streaming in on his handsome pelt. I had to say I missed him.

"Sonny Boy," I whispered.

He opened his golden eyes and peered up at me. I thought I detected a glimmer of recognition—fondness, even. I bent down closer to him, nose to nose. He purred softly and licked me between the eyebrows.

"Sonny Boy!" I gasped. "You care!"

He looked at me a moment longer, closed his eyes, and laid his head back down on my pillow.

I ran to the top of the stairs. "Mom!" I shouted. "Sonny Boy licked me!"

She came to the stairway and peered up at me. "Oh,

honey," she said worriedly, "are you sure you're feeling okay?"

"No, Mom, I swear. He showed me affection!" I pointed. "Feel the saliva drying between my eyebrows!"

THREE THOUSAND PEOPLE had been lost in the tsunami— among them fifteen kids from Avondale High—thirteen of the popular kids and two other kids, Evan Drisland and his girlfriend, Rachel Sinclair, who had been driving down the Pacific Coast Highway on their way back from a movie when the wave struck. There were other survivors from that ill-fated party—but none so famous as Abigail and myself, once our story hit the news. Everywhere I went I had to wade past news cameras, not just at the hospital but at my house and at school, where wreaths had been hung on certain lockers and no one got any learning done because all the talk was about the tsunami, and Mrs. Paltos taught the class mourning words: *triste* and *desconsolado* and *la perdída*. News people called my house around the clock, pleading for an interview. Everyone wanted to hear what I had to say. I couldn't even turn on the TV without running into a *Dateline* special about the kids from Avondale High, featuring a clip of Ms. Hanson, our old gym teacher, in front of the camera again at last, going on about how she always knew

Abigail and I were special, even back in seventh grade. It was an acting performance worthy of that world fame she'd always craved. Sadly, James Cameron still didn't call.

Abigail was moved out of the ICU after the third day and spent another week in the hospital recovering.

"I can't believe this," I told her when I visited her. "It's kind of gross. Everyone's going on about us like we're rock stars or something."

Abigail was looking better. Her coloring was better, and she'd been able to eat some food. "Crazy, ain't it?" she agreed. She waved a hand at her room, which was full of balloons and roses and cookies and chocolate-covered strawberries. "Look at all this crap. Even my brother is being nice to me. But what the hell did we do besides getting washed out to sea and then drying out?"

"We survived."

"Yeah, well, big whoop."

"That makes us newsworthy."

Abigail looked somber. "I don't feel all that damn newsworthy. After all, it was my shindig that got so many Avondale kids wiped out."

"No one thinks that."

"Sure they do." Abigail shook her head. "I feel so guilty."

"You don't have anything to be guilty over. But I know

a way we can maybe give something back."

"Oh yeah?" she raised an eyebrow. "And what would that be?"

"Neither one of us has said a word to the press," I said. "Just like we agreed."

She nodded. "None of their business."

"But if we gave an exclusive interview about what we learned? Since people are so interested in what we have to say, maybe we can make the world a little better."

"I kind of like it," she said. "Now, what did we learn again?"

"Come on, you know. 'Sometimes it takes losing it all to learn what's really important.'"

"Sounds like you already thought that up and practiced it."

"Yeah, kind of."

"I agree, though. And we sure lost it all."

"And when are we ever going to have everyone's attention again? I mean, maybe we're just teenagers, but we have something to say! We lived through more in three weeks than most people live in a lifetime."

"Hmmm," Abigail said, "I'm not really the type to get all teary-eyed on national TV. But if you think we got something to say, I guess we can try."

■ ■ ■

WE HAD THE press conference set up in Abigail's hospital room. A reporter from NBC, blond and tall and efficient, talked to us from a chair they'd crammed into the room. We were miked up, Abigail was propped into a sitting position by pillows on her cot while I perched on a stool next to her.

The reporter spoke into the camera. "I'm here with Abigail Kenner and Denver Reynolds, the only survivors from what is being called the Lifeboat Clique, a group of Avondale High School students washed out to sea after the devastating tsunami that hit the coast of California last month."

She looked at us. "Well, you girls have certainly been through a lot, to say the least."

I nodded.

Abigail said: "That's for sure."

"How did you survive such incredible odds?" the reporter asked.

"We didn't have any other choice," I said. "We had to find out a way to live. It's not that we were anything special. The others on that boat were special, too. And we think about them every day."

"Denver and I were best buddies for a long time," Abigail added. "Then we had a falling out. Pretty much hated each other. It took a disaster for us to be friends again. She needed me and I needed her if we were gonna make it. But honestly, she saved my life. I would have been a goner if it wasn't for her."

"And do you have a message for all the people out there listening?" asked the reporter.

Abigail and I exchanged glances. We'd rehearsed this, and since I had the best use of grammar, Abigail had told me I should speak.

"The tsunami was a terrible thing to happen," I began. "Our high school suffered a huge loss of life. But as awful as the tsunami was, good things actually came of it. We learned that out there on the ocean, there's no such thing as popular kids and unpopular kids. We were all equal and all valuable."

I paused. Deep down, I still thought Sienna and Hayley had been fairly useless from a survival perspective. But I was here to make a point about humanity, and I kept that particular point under my hat. "When you don't know whether you're going to live or die, you figure out what's important. Generosity, friendship, forgiveness, hope, and faith." My eyes were watering a little by now. "Let's all use this tragedy to be better people. Let's all be equal. And all be friends."

"Right," said Abigail. "Nothing like a big-ass wave to teach you how to cut the bullshit."

The reporter looked at Abigail severely. "We can't use that," she said.

WE WERE PRETTY proud of ourselves after that interview aired. We envisioned a post-tsunami LA where people let each other into traffic and didn't quarrel about ten-foot fences; and everyone forgave everyone; and band geeks were just as important as cheerleaders; and overweight, studious girls walked hand-in-hand with small-waisted skanks down the hallway. Our message went all over the web, and people made memes out of some of the quotes and passed them around, and we thought we'd done some good in the world.

Another bit of news also made us happy: the day after the tsunami, a distracted custodian had accidentally left the window open while cleaning the cage of Mr. Shriek and his mate. The two parrots had flown out into the sky and were never heard from again.

"Ah," said Abigail when I told her about it, "good for them."

"You know," I said, "Mr. Shriek would have actually been a better name for Trevor's Man Part."

A HUGE MEMORIAL service for all the lost kids of Avon-dale High was held on a Sunday evening at a church in downtown Los Angeles. Before the service, Abigail and I met with the parents of the kids from that fateful party and told them what we knew of their last hours. The whole thing was pretty awkward, but I suppose it gave them closure. Trevor's dad had on a Hawaiian shirt and wore an earring. He had the same habit of drumming on things. The entire story of Trevor's time at sea and his heroic sacrifice was scored by the tapping of his father's fingers, and I told my mind not to go to Ranger Todd Senior, which of course it did.

Special seats had been reserved near the front of the church for Abigail and me and our families. Just before the service began, Abigail elbowed me in the ribs. "You notice something?" she asked.

"What?"

"Look behind you."

I looked and saw what she meant. "Oh, my God," I said. The popular kids were all in the first rows, and then the next popular kids, and then the next popular kids, all the way to the back. It was like a version of our cafeteria.

"How did they manage that?" I whispered.

"What a bunch of idiots," Abigail whispered back in disgust.

A senior kid—Chris Something—from the drama department walked across the stage. He was wearing a suit and tennis shoes. His long hair was back in a ponytail. He was kind of known for publishing weird poems in the school paper. Now he proceeded to read another one:

> *"When the water rushes in*
> *We will stay strong*
> *And the earth will have a new dawn*
> *And we will meet in the corridor*
> *And sing together*
> *Yes, together we will sing*
> *For we are birds whose beaks were left in drawers . . ."*

"What the hell is he talking about?" Abigail whispered to me.

"I don't know. Something about water."

He went on and on. Finally he stopped in what seemed like midsentence and bowed his head dramatically. People didn't really know what to do. Someone clapped, but it didn't catch on. Finally the school principal came out and kind of tapped him on the arm, and he came to life and slunk away.

"Students of Avondale, friends and parents," the principal began. "Blah blah blah blah blah . . ."

Or at least that's how it sounded to me. I was afraid I'd get too emotional at this service and cry in front of everyone. But this was just a canned speech that sounded more political than sad.

"This is actually boring," I whispered to Abigail.

"An embarrassment," she whispered back.

The principal finally finished his dumb speech, the lights lowered, and the memorial video began. It was a slickly produced homage to all the kids who had lost their lives, done up to the soundtrack of "In the Arms of the Angel" by Sarah McLachlan, with tons of shots of Sienna zooming down the soccer field and Matthew scoring touchdowns, of Audrey singing in the church choir and Croix acting lead in *Oklahoma!* and Madison and Trevor and all the other cool kids. An editor had been hard at work on different effects: slow motion and close-ups and fades.

"Holy cow," Abigail muttered. "This is so Hollywood."

The popular kids in the audience clapped and whooped and cheered at the sight of their favorites. When the video came to Rachel and Evan, the two non-popular kids who died on the Pacific Coast Highway, it just showed their yearbook photos to brief and scattered applause.

My heart sank. This was terrible. I thought this was going to be a celebration of life. Little did I know that some lives were still apparently more important than others. Nothing we imagined for post-tsunami LA was coming true. Everything was exactly the same.

"Let's go," I said, and Abigail and I got up from our seats and crept out through the dark church, into the hard light of LA. Our parents and Maxwell came trailing after us.

"What's wrong? Why did you run out?" asked Abigail's mother, who was dolled up for the event in a black mini dress and smoky eye shadow.

"It's disgusting, Ma," Abigail said. "A popularity contest, even in death."

My mother put her arm around me. She had on her best dress and was holding a new clutch purse. "Maybe you weren't ready for a public event so soon."

"Let's go home," I said miserably.

Abigail was going to spend the night with us, so she rode with my mother and me back to our house, her bag already packed for the night. We hardly spoke on the way home, although my mother helpfully put on a radio station with some kind of elevator music that was meant to soothe and inspire but instead made me gently claw my face.

When we arrived at our house, Abigail and I looked at each other, exchanging a glance that said everything.

"Can we borrow the car, Mom?" I said.

"For what?" she asked.

"We just need to drive."

I took the wheel, and Abigail rode shotgun, in the car Mom had bought off Craigslist. The elevator music was still on the radio, and I clicked it off, leaving us in silence. At first I drove aimlessly, up and down the streets. The elementary schools had let out for the day, and kids were walking through the crosswalks with backpacks. We watched them silently, the outgoing kids laughing and talking, and the shy ones walking alone. Ready to be sifted and sorted for another high school, somewhere in the LA future.

We didn't speak. There was nothing to say. The wheel felt good in my hands, the car heavy and steady underneath us. I drove down the 10 Freeway and then up the Pacific Coast Highway, past the familiar landmarks of Santa Monica, the mountains on one side, the ocean on the other. I'd traveled this very same route over a month before, to go to an exclusive party on a Malibu bluff given by my ex-best friend who was now my friend again, skinnier and quieter, who sat with her chin resting on her hand, looking out at the sea that had swallowed us and then spat us back with a message no one wanted to hear.

I had seen photos on the internet taken right after the tsunami hit: houses flattened into piles of wood, cars dumped upside down, uprooted palm trees and broken furniture washed up in the middle of the road. It was amazing how much could be restored in just a few weeks. The road had been cleared, and construction crews were out in full force. Scaffolding was shoring up the mountain, and some of the few restaurants still standing had signs that said We're Open! The kayak rental place on the border of Malibu was even operational, the kayaks sitting loaded on a flatbed truck and a young shirtless guy in board shorts waving a sign that said Kayak Specials! $15/hr!

Most of the houses that lined the beach were gone. And without those houses there, we had a clear view of the Pacific Ocean, so calm that it seemed like a different ocean must have been the one that clobbered us, a bully ocean whose little brother was there now to apologize.

We didn't speak, but we both knew where we were going. Back to the beginning, or the end, or the beginning that started the end as we knew it. That house on the bluff. Traffic was light, but we had to slow down for lanes blocked off for work crews restoring the road or trying to put the mountain back in place with backhoes and shovels. The lights weren't working, just blinking red. And cops were everywhere, motioning, warning, pointing.

I turned right; we climbed up a steep road. We parked on the side of the road and got out of the car. Neither of us spoke. There it was on the bluff: the site of the house party that had started it all. There was nothing left of the house but the foundation and the driveway. No work crews were around it. No reporters, no people. It sat alone and forgotten. Just a few wreaths sitting on what used to be an exclusive Malibu property.

"Wow," Abigail said at last.

"Yeah," I said.

We walked up the driveway and onto the foundation.

"Are you sure we're supposed to be standing here?" I asked. "Is this like a grave or something?"

"Anyone's guess," Abigail said. "Wanna go?"

"No. Weird as it sounds, it kind of feels peaceful here."

Abigail sat down, and I sat next to her, the cement cool under our legs. A breeze came up that smelled of sea air. Clumps of palm leaves were still scattered here and there. We looked out at the ocean across the Pacific Coast Highway.

"Some party," Abigail said. "Just a whole bunch of us hanging out in a place where we didn't belong, trying to be cool, thinking we're better, somehow. And then it's all gone in the blink of an eye. Hell of a lesson to learn."

"It's too much education at once, if you ask me." I said. "I would rather have it spread out over a few decades and given to me as internet links."

"Yeah," she said.

"Can I ask you something?" I said.

"Yeah."

"Soccer." I didn't even ask the question, just said the word.

She nodded. "Dream is still there. Never went away. Even when I went away from it, drinking and partying, it was waiting for me."

"Are you gonna try out again next fall?"

"Maybe."

"You should, Abigail," I said. "You have a real talent."

"Well, so do you."

"Talent for what?"

"For anything you want to do. You proved that out there on the ocean. You can do anything."

"But what if I don't know what that is yet?"

"That's fine. Lots of people don't know when they're our age."

I leaned back on my elbows. The sun came out from behind the clouds, and the sky reminded me of that day so long ago when Abigail had sprung us both out of gym class, at my expense, and we had lounged on a table outside and tried to figure out if we liked each other.

"No one learned anything, did they, Abigail?" I asked. "I mean, from our news conference."

"Guess not."

"Everyone just went right back to being the way they were before. Nothing we went through mattered. It didn't change anyone."

"Whoa, now. Just hold your horses. We changed. We got better. And you forgave your daddy, and I forgave my mom, and so our families got better. So that's a start, right?"

"That's a start," I admitted.

"And your cat licked you," she said.

"He sure did." I pointed between my eyes. "Right here."

"And who says that's got to be the finish? We can keep going, just being the best people we can be, and if people want to come along with us, that's good. And if they don't, we'll keep on doing what's good for us."

Abigail leaned back on her elbows next to me.

We both stared out into the Pacific. The waves so orderly and small.

"Whoever thought a tsunami would be our best teacher," she said. "Half a dozen more, and maybe I wouldn't hate my brother."

"Nah," I said. "No amount of water can wash away that hatred. Maybe a good tornado."

Then there was nothing but silence and the wind and, in the distance, tiny waves crawling up to the shore and LA healing around us. Knitting itself back together, getting to its bony knees and then to its French-pedicured feet. LA would survive, and so would we.

The ocean was back in its place, plotting its next move or simply just existing, the waves out there perfect, not the ones you surf on, not the ones that take everything away from you, just the ones you watch until it's time to go home.

ACKNOWLEDGMENTS

THIS BOOK WOULD NOT HAVE BEEN POSSIBLE WITHOUT THE passion, guidance, and badassery of Mollie Glick at Foundry Literary + Media. Then Claudia Gabel, my amazing editor, came along and cut it like a gemstone. I thank these great women.

Thank you to Katherine Tegen and everyone at Katherine Tegen Books/HarperCollins: Melissa Miller, Rosanne Romanello, Lauren Flower, Alana Whitman, Carmen Alvarez, Kelsey Horton, and Rebecca Schwarz.

Heather Daugherty and Marla Moore made the best cover ever.

My mother, Polly Hepinstall, served as my first copy

editor, as always. And Paige Robertson gave me great soccer pointers. Thanks also to Dallas Jones, Dawn Dekeyser, Becky Hepinstall Hilliker, Jessica Hepinstall, Glenn Stewart, Linda Birkenstock, Jason Kreher, Carrie Talick, Cam Giblin, Greg Wells, Arla Wood, Kaeleight James, and Riley Alger.

Go on a different sort of adventure
in Kathy Parks's next book

NOTES FROM
MY CAPTIVITY

one

My mother puts a lot of stock in dreams. She says she dreamed of me before I was born, knew the color of my eyes and hair. She named me Adrienne in her sleep, and that's the name she gave me when I came along, blond haired and blue eyed just as she'd predicted. The night I lost my father, she dreamed a heart-monitor line went flat. But I'm not a superstitious person, or one inclined to believe in the magical or the supernatural. So I'm not alarmed, just annoyed, when, the morning my stepfather and I are leaving on our trip, Mom wakes from a nightmare about what will happen to us in Siberia.

She's talking about it, totally agitated, when I wander in for breakfast. She's flipping pancakes as she speaks. The pancakes are falling apart. Dan, my stepfather, watches her. He is on the tall side, thin, and his teeth are a tiny bit too big for his mouth, giving people the perception he is smiling.

But he's not smiling right at the moment. The look on his face says, *Oh shit, we were almost home free and now this stupid dream.*

Jason, the stepbrother who was foisted on me seven years ago, lounges at the breakfast table in an old T-shirt and board shorts, looking amused. He's just jealous because he wanted to go on this trip—if only to meet some Russian girls on the way to Siberia—and I'm going instead. Or, I think I'm still going.

"It was terrible!" Mom exclaims.

I glance at Dan. "Let me guess. Mom had a dream."

"Just a dream," Dan says quickly, directing that at Mom more than at me, his tone reassuring and just a little dismissive. "Dreams mean nothing. They're just chemical reactions in the cerebral cortex that occur during REM sleep. . . ."

Great, Dan. Calm her right down with geekspeak.

My real father was a quiet district attorney, a man of few words, with body language that never gave away his game. Dan is a frenetic anthropologist with jazz hands. His hands are busy right now, in the air, helping form his nonsense about REM sleep.

"Nothing's going to happen to me, Mom." I go to her and touch her shoulder, feel the tension there. She flips another pancake. It tears in half. I'll be having scrambled pancakes for breakfast, with a side of nightmare.

She shakes her head. "You and Dan were sleeping in tents, and then they came through the woods with knives and sliced your tent open."

They. She's talking about the Osinovs, the family of mysterious Siberian hermits Dan has been studying for years. He's an anthropologist at the University of Denver, and a very well respected one—at least he was . . . until last month.

"Then what?" Jason asks. My stepbrother seems eager to hear about horrible things done to me even in my mom's subconscious. He's thoughtful that way.

"I woke myself up screaming."

"Sorry, Jason," I say. "She didn't get to the beheading part."

"Stop it," Mom orders, shooting me a fierce look. "This isn't a joke."

I roll my eyes. Some girls are stricken with Resting Bitch Face. I've got Argument Bitch Face, in which my mild features turn into an unconscious embodiment of Teenage Attitude when I'm about to state my case. And my voice. I can't keep the sarcasm out of my voice at such times. It's like trying to take the calories out of a cupcake. What I want to say out loud but cannot is that the crazy, possibly murderous Osinov family won't sneak up on me with knives because there is no family. They're just another legend like bigfoot and the Loch Ness monster. But I can't say that out loud because Dan has based his entire academic career on them. Dan's article "The Vanished: The Story of the Osinovs" was published three years ago in the *New York Times* and made him a star. That is until Sydney Declay, badass journalist and my own personal hero, wrote the now-famous article in the *Washington Post* last month debunking the whole thing.

"It's perfectly safe," Dan assures her, rising on his toes like he always does when he's excited, which is often, jazz hands going, words pouring out. "Remember I've done it twice, and Adrienne is a smart, responsible girl, and she'll be with me at all times, *please*, honey, this is a trip of a lifetime. . . ." He lowers his heels to the ground, raises them again, as though performing an exercise to strengthen his calves.

"A trip of a deathtime," Jason chimes in.

I glare at him. "Shut up, Jason."

He laughs evilly. Dan pauses for breath. Mom shakes a dollop of butter onto my sad pancake, sloppy as an unmade bed. Her eyes are troubled. I've been begging to go for months, have finally gotten permission, inoculations, a ticket, everything, and now it's all going to hell.

It's rare that Dan and I find ourselves on the same side. Sure, he usually wants to be on my side. He's still trying to fill that void where my father used to be. It's weird to be allies with him. But I find myself drifting over next to him as though our argument will be more powerful if we are standing closer together.

"Adrienne wants to be a reporter," Dan says. "She needs to see the world." A wave of guilt rushes through me at his words. I wish I believed in his Russian family. But it's like belief in anything. I need proof, and wouldn't he have found it by now if it existed? Besides, Sydney did an amazing job of discrediting him with her article.

"I wouldn't bring her if I didn't think it was safe," he adds.

I join in the argument. "I'll be going with a whole crew." *Two people at least.* "And a guide."

"Dan, she's a seventeen-year-old girl!" Mom protests.

"Eighteen in three months," I say.

Jason's already halfway through his pancake. "I'm nineteen. And I'm a *guy*."

"What's that supposed to mean?" I ask. "Like, a girl can't make it in the woods? Besides, why do you want to go? You're not interested in Russia. You've never been out in the woods, and you're not a reporter."

"*You're* not a reporter," Jason sneers. "Editor in chief of the Rosedale High student paper means absolutely nothing."

"My article on fracking ran in the *Denver Times*, douchebag," I shoot back.

"Jason," Dan said severely, "stop making fun of your sister. At least she has goals. She didn't flunk out of community college for missing half her classes."

Jason winces. I stifle a snicker.

"Whatever," he says. "Siberia sucks, anyway."

"It's freezing there," Mom says. She stares down at the new pancake, wanting to guard it till it grows up perfect.

Dan's getting annoyed now. It's two hours before we leave for the plane, and I can see the exasperation on his face. "We've been over this again and again. Siberia warms up in June." His hands rise in the air. Is he trying to communicate heat rising off the earth? Who knows.

"Unless there's a freak snowstorm," Jason pipes in. "You've mentioned that possibility, Dad."

"God, Jason." I'm exasperated now. "Don't you have anything better to do than ruin my trip? Go fail at something."

Mom's pancake is now burning, and she hasn't noticed. Dan reaches over and moves her pan off the burner.

"Are you packed, Adrienne?" he asks pointedly. "You need to double-check your supplies."

Mom gives him a look. She has a pretty mild appearance. Hair down to her shoulders, a heart-shaped face. But her eyebrows are monsters. They can take an argument and bend it like a pretzel. And now her eyebrows are slowly contorting.

"*The dream*," she says again, as though those two words are all she needs to keep me in Boulder all summer.

I let out my breath. "You can die anywhere. At any time. Out of the blue. Just minding your own business."

Mom gives me a look. I see the grief that never goes away. I shouldn't have said this.

"I'm sorry."

She shrugs. We're great communicators.

I quickly change the subject. "Imagine how this will look on my college applications. And you know I have to get a scholarship to go to Emerson. You know we can't afford it."

I realize that in trying to divert Mom's attention, I've accidentally slammed Dan and his habit of draining our money away on his fruitless wild-goose chases.

"You know what I mean," I add lamely.

"The university is providing a Thuraya satellite phone," Dan says, ignoring my remark. "That's the best there is. We'll be in constant contact with the outside world." He seems weary, dejected. His hands aren't waving anymore. They're hiding in his pockets. Maybe I've made him sad with the budget talk.

"Bears." My mother quickly moves on to other arguments. "Wolves."

"Osinovs," Jason pipes up.

"The guide will have a gun, and we'll all carry bear spray," Dan insists. One hand struggles free of his pocket, points a finger for emphasis. "This is not some crazy stunt."

"And this family?" she asks. "This group of hermits or lunatics or whatever they are supposed to be? What if Adrienne runs into them?"

"Based on all my research," Dan retorts, using the kind of professorial sentence structure that usually annoys me but now might bolster my case, "the Osinovs were a harmless yet eccentric couple when they disappeared thirty years ago. I don't believe these crazy tales of their being dangerous." He doesn't mention his source, Yuri Androv, and his tale of being captured and menaced by the legendary family before he managed to escape.

"Your source says the family kidnapped him," Mom reminds Dan.

"And if you read the article—" Dan retorts.

"I've *read the article*, Dan." Mom's getting pissed.

"If you read the article," he insists, "you'd know that I don't believe he was ever in any danger. Yuri exaggerates. But I do believe he was at their campsite. Too many details ring true. The Osinovs wouldn't have hurt him."

The Osinovs. He must have said that name ten thousand times. And I'm really sick of hearing it.

Mom flips the burned pancake onto a plate. I know she will eat it herself because she hates waste and because she's the mom. She tries one more time. "Okay, Dan, but something you've never explained is why *now*? What's the hurry?"

I study Dan's face to see the reaction. He looks flustered. He doesn't say anything at first.

I know a secret. I know why now. I know what's the hurry.

There's a very fine line between being a reporter and a snoop, and I crossed it last month, a few days after Sydney Declay's article came out. I got the mail that day and noticed a letter for Dan from the chairman of the anthropology department. That night, I watched Dan's face as he read it. Something was up. Something urgent and serious. That night, after everyone was asleep, I went into his office, found the letter, and took a photo of it with my iPhone. It began: "Dear Dr. Westin . . ." A sure sign that Dan was in trouble because he and the chairman had been friends for thirty years. Why such an icy greeting? As I read on, I found out why: Sydney Declay's article had not only humiliated Dan, it had embarrassed the entire university, and if Dan didn't find proof of the Osinovs, they were going to pull his grant.

He'd already taken out a second mortgage on the house. I had learned that from another midnight raid. So that's why now. I watch Dan's face go dark.

"Because," he says at last. "Next year it will be too late."

"Too late for what?" Mom asks.

Dan doesn't answer.

The look on his face makes me wince. But whenever I start feeling too bad for him, I think of all the things he's ruined. Like my life. Like our well-built, well-balanced family that liked to hike in the woods and believed in very little except one another. Then my dad died and Dan swept into the house, bringing his dumb son and his belief in the Osinovs. It reminded me of a particularly fervent brand of Christianity, except the Osinovs weren't coming back; they were supposedly here already. Dan has the glassy-eyed stare of the true believer. He never misses a chance to tell me about some new detail he's found through his research—all word-of-mouth, legend, rumor. Things my father would have dismissed from any trial. The tool that Yuri Androv, his main source, claimed the eldest son used to cut firewood. The mystical powers of the father. The fishermen downstream who claim to get a glimpse of two brothers fishing from a crude boat. The shoe sole—Grigor Osinov's size—found at the remains of an old campsite, along with a charred biography of the life of Carl Linnaeus, the botanist with whom Osinov was obsessed. The letters Osinov wrote his cousin detailing his escape plan. Every tiny item in the proof of their existence has been discussed at the dinner table.

And I'm tired of that life.

Tired of Dan's religion.

Yes, I want to write the article and get into journalism school. But I also want to be free. Free of the Osinovs forever.

Jason doesn't go to the airport with us. He's got a very important *Call of Duty: Zombies* battle to fight in the rec room downstairs. Mom, of course, has to go with us to make me feel guilty every mile to the airport. Soon as we pull out of the neighborhood, she starts in again. Am I sure I'm going to go? Why don't I stay home with her this summer? In return, she'll take me to Montana. Haven't I always wanted to go to Montana? It will be just the two of us. . . .

From the back seat, I watch Dan's hands tighten on the wheel. I know they are dying to join the argument. "Martha, stop trying to bribe her with a trip to Montana. She wants to go with me!"

He and Mom start at it again, and I decide it's a good time to tune them out. I take out the Dictaphone I bought online—the same one Sydney Declay uses—and speak softly into it.

It's a bright, clear summer day outside as we set off for Denver International Airport, full of those plans and dreams and expectations that always happen before a trip, but this trip is bigger, deeper, darker, and more vast than any I've taken in my life. I wonder, What is the day like in Siberia? Will the landscape represent the one whose—

Dan gasps. The tires screech as the car brakes hard, out of nowhere, jerking me out of my reporting. I can hear Mom shriek as I'm jerked forward and back again. The Dictaphone flies out of my hand. The car is still. A brief silence and then Mom whips her head around.

"Adrienne! Are you okay?"

"I'm okay, Mom," I manage shakily. I'm confused and

disoriented and rattled. It's like Siberia reached out a paw from across the world and disrupted a simple thing like a car moving down pavement.

Dan peers into the road ahead.

"Dan!" Mom has a hand on her chest, breathing hard. "Why did you slam on the brakes? Are you trying to get us killed?"

He turns to her, eyes wide. "Did you see the little girl?"

"Little girl?" Mom echoes. "What little girl?"

My heart steadies. I look around us. We're alone.

Dan shakes his head. "I'm telling you, there was a little girl standing in the middle of the road."

DON'T MISS
THESE DARKLY HUMOROUS
SURVIVAL STORIES FROM
KATHY PARKS

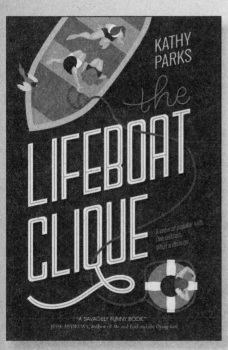